The Gossamer Crown

The Gossamer Crown

Book One
The Gossamer Sphere

By Melissa Conway

Copyright © 2011 Melissa Conway
3rd Edition published by Winged Pig Press 2020
www.melissa-conway.com

Paperback ISBN: 978-1-954352-08-7
Digital ISBN: 978-1-954352-09-4

This is a work of fiction. Names, characters, businesses, organizations,
places, events and incidents are the product of the author's imagination
or are used fictitiously. Any resemblance to actual persons, living or
dead, is coincidental.

Chapter One

The North Sea

Some people were cut out for life at sea, and some weren't. Kevin Guzman's feet were firmly planted in the "weren't" camp. In fact, after two months of suffering through the flow and ebb of low-grade seasickness, he longed to plant his feet deep into solid ground far from the nearest ocean.

At the outset of the expedition, when they'd left the harbor and plowed through a rough North Sea, he'd regretted his last meal of authentic British fish and chips. Luckily, it only took the greater part of that first day to reach the drill site, and since then the ship's special stabilizers had kept the rocking and rolling to a minimum.

Still, he often had to abandon his duties as Dr. Weinstein's student intern and all-around gofer in order to stand on deck and fill his lungs with fresh sea air.

Today the normally peaceful deck of the old scientific drilling vessel had been invaded by men and women too excited to stay below in the shipboard labs. Kevin hovered between two chattering groups of scientists, pretending to stare out at the calm blue water while eavesdropping on their conversations. An entire summer in their company and not one of his shipmates had gotten to know him enough to realize he was fluent in multiple languages. He didn't really blame them for not wanting to hang out with a seasick intern, and besides, he enjoyed his solitude.

To his left, Mr. Yamata with the big teeth spoke to his fellows in Japanese, "Mr. Masters wants us to believe it's some kind of alloy. It's iridium, but we can't identify the other components. We should compare the sample to the iridium in the clay layer of the K-T Boundary."

To his right, Astrid, an attractive blonde researcher, said in Swedish, "The amount of iridium in the core sample was astounding. At that concentration, the impactor must have been *composed* of iridium."

Back at the first conversation, the Japanese men began a rapid dialog about the implications of discovering what could potentially be a new element for the periodic table, while the Swedes focused on the issue of mining. Never mind that the precious metal was located under forty meters of water and three hundred meters of sediment.

All of the core samples retrieved until today had been sedimentary, as the drill worked its way through millions of years of seafloor buildup. The multinational conglomerate of scientists on board had dutifully examined the chemical and biological makeup of the initial samples, finding nothing out of the ordinary. Now that the drill had finally penetrated to the outer layer of the actual impact crater, however, the earlier core samples were quickly abandoned in their refrigerated compartments.

Kevin took a deep, steadying breath and focused on the horizon, willing this latest bout of nausea to pass.

From the moment Dr. Weinstein first described the internship to his Marine Geology students, Kevin knew he had to get the job: a summer at sea drilling into the unusual sub-sea structure of concentric rings that formed Silverpit Crater. He'd been slacking in class up to that point, since his interests were more for the geology of terra firma, but the crater in its watery grave drew him. The age of the crater, the date that the object impacted earth, was debated in scientific circles. Some thought it was part of the same asteroid family that hit in the Yucatán, wiping dinosaurs from the planet. Kevin didn't know how old it was, but he suspected, sensed really, that it was beyond ancient.

"There you are."

He turned as Dr. Weinstein reached his side, wispy grey hair on end. Kevin, who cursed the unknown ancestor he'd inherited his lack of stature from, still managed to tower over the diminutive professor.

"Masters says the drill is jammed," Dr. Weinstein said, referring to Bill Masters, the head of the project.

"What?" Astrid stepped closer.

"How long will it take to fix?" One of the Japanese scientists asked in English.

"They don't know. He said it must have hit something pretty damned hard, though."

2

Astrid whipped her head around to her companions and said, "A solid mass of iridium! I told you."

"That's very unlikely," Mr. Yamata said.

"Besides, iridium is hard, but brittle. It would shatter at that temperature," Dr. Weinstein said.

Kevin eased backward towards the rail as the discussion gained contributors and volume. Something felt wrong. He listened, thinking that Masters must have shut down one of the engines, but that wasn't it. He reached out and grasped the rail. It was the ship. Even with the stabilizers, he'd always felt the movement of the sea.

Everything had gone eerily still. The water shimmered like glass. A thrill of excitement washed over him.

His whole life had been one unexplained thing after another. He'd long since stopped fearing these flashes of insight, the bursts of comprehension that had no basis in fact. He knew with certainty that whatever lay at the center of that crater didn't want them there.

A rumble began below the ship, all around them, in the air, in the water. No one but Kevin noticed until he shouted, "Hang on!"

Nothing dire seemed to be happening, so the others gaped at him in astonishment.

Suddenly, the deck beneath his feet lurched and it felt – impossibly – as if the ship lifted up in the air ten or fifteen meters. Then his stomach dropped as the ship came back down. A muffled, metallic, grinding protest rent the air. Displaced water rushed in from all sides and slapped the hull, rolling on deck and toppling those not holding on. Kevin scrambled to help a soaked Astrid regain her feet, realizing as he did that the sound he'd heard was that of the deep-sea drill buckling under the weight of the vessel as the water level lowered abruptly.

"Earthquake," Dr. Weinstein gasped. "There'll be a tsunami."

"What? Where?" Astrid looked all around.

"We're on top of it," Dr. Weinstein said. "It's heading out in all directions away from us."

The ship's alarm sounded. The captain came on the loudspeaker and advised everyone to stay calm, but to don life vests and report to their safety coordinator. Everyone began to run at once.

Kevin stood frozen at the rail. This was why he'd come.

Chapter Two

Fairbanks, Alaska

Stupid Katrina.

Lizbeth Moreau sat on her grandmother's weather-worn wooden porch, her booted feet crossed at the ankle, heels resting on the second step. The air already had that fall feel to it, crisp and woodsy, and leaves had begun to turn yellow.

Not that there were a lot of trees around here that didn't have pine needles.

She closed her eyes and imagined what she'd be doing if she were still back home in New Orleans, if home hadn't washed away so thoroughly there wasn't even a pile of rubble left to sift through.

Stupid, stupid Katrina.

She would have graduated among friends instead of a bunch of strangers who'd never really accepted her. Lizbeth wasn't the only dark-skinned kid in school, but the color scale was heavy on the light end and chintzy on anything browner. Being so far north meant hardly anyone even got tanned in the pathetic excuse for a summer.

Her one good friend, Stephanie, claimed to be envious of Lizbeth's permanent light-brown tan. That was because Steph didn't see the sideways looks Lizbeth got from a certain factor at school. Steph didn't believe bigotry existed in this day and age, but Lizbeth knew it was there, not rampant necessarily, but there.

Stupid Katrina.

"Lizbee!" Her grandmother called. Lizbeth hated that nickname, it sounded too much like "Lezbie." Thank God no one from school had ever heard Granma say it, or it would have stuck like pine pitch.

Inside the cabin, Lizbeth wrinkled her nose at the sulfur of a struck match and saw that Granma had lit a row of candles on the rustic stone

4

fireplace mantle. *Oh, no.* She better not be having one of her embarrassing voodoo ceremonies again.

In the kitchen, Granma was seated at the table with a cup of tea, dressed in jeans and a flannel shirt. *Good.* If the cabin was about to be invaded by a horde of believers, Granma would be attired in her robes.

"Do you feel it?" Granma asked.

Lizbeth did feel it, something in the air, but she wasn't about to admit it. With two sharp tugs, she yanked open the decrepit refrigerator and peered inside.

"On the news today, they said the North Pole moved," Granma said.

Lizbeth snorted. "That's impossible."

"No. It isn't. If you'd paid more attention in school, you'd know that."

"Are we talking about the geographic North Pole or the magnetic one? Because the magnetic pole is constantly on the move, that's nothing new. Last I heard, it was drifting on its way to Siberia," Lizbeth said.

"Well it's drifted back our way, according to Channel Eleven, and very rapidly at that. And, smarty-pants, it's not impossible for the geographic pole to move. It wobbles all the time."

Lizbeth stuck her head further inside the refrigerator to hide a smile. Her mom worked long hours at the fish market, leaving Granma with the responsibility of seeing to Lizbeth's education. Since Granma hadn't made it past the ninth grade, she picked up facts here and there and threw them at Lizbeth, with the end result being that Lizbeth learned from her grandmother a little about a lot of things, but not much about anything in particular.

Voodoo, for instance, was a subject Lizbeth knew well, not that she'd ever brought it up in casual conversation in the cafeteria. That's why her grandmother had moved here in the first place many years ago, to escape the competition in New Orleans and find a fresh clientele. She'd done surprisingly well.

It was almost supper time, but Lizbeth pulled out a half-eaten chocolate cake and cut herself a slice. Granma raised her eyebrows, although not in chastisement for the inappropriate meal. Lizbeth cut another slice and handed the plate to her grandmother.

"Ah. There it is again," Granma said.

There it was indeed. Lizbeth felt it as a tingle all down her spine, like an electric current. She abandoned her cake and went back outside on the porch.

5

The early evening sky was ablaze.

Lizbeth had seen the Aurora Borealis once or twice, but this display, this she doubted anyone anywhere had ever seen before.

Every color of the rainbow undulated in iridescent ecstasy from one end of the horizon to the other. The phenomenon was not diaphanous at all, but thick and heavy as if an enormous cosmic prism had exploded in the sky.

"Am I on acid?" Granma asked, not an unreasonable question for a voodoo priestess.

"Not that I know of," Lizbeth replied.

Their nearest neighbors, the Cunninghams across the road, ran out en masse, all thirteen of them. Mr. Cunningham wielded his video camera while Mrs. Cunningham snapped photographs. Lizbeth heard their excited voices on the cold evening air.

In a daze, she resumed her earlier seat on the porch, head tilted upward. Her grandmother joined her.

"Now we know why we're here," Granma said.

"Where?

"Alaska, silly."

"We do?"

"Well, we don't know *why*. We don't know what it means, but it does mean something, mark my words. And it's yours."

"My what?" Lizbeth asked, distracted by the mesmerizing show.

"Your duty, child. Whatever needs to be done, needs to be done by you."

Lizbeth didn't ask what she meant. Ever since she was a child, her grandmother had been grooming her for some indefinable task, some fate not within her control.

As much as she wanted to watch the fireworks, she was even less inclined to enable her grandmother's delusions. Lizbeth stood and brushed her hands across the back of her jeans. Without acknowledging the celestial burden Granma would like to place on her shoulders, she went back inside the cabin to her bedroom.

She could ignore her grandmother and her supposed destiny but the crawling, tingling sensation that had spread from her spine to every nerve in her body was another thing altogether.

Stupid Katrina.

Chapter Three

San Francisco, California

On a secluded patch of grass in an exclusive neighborhood park, fourteen people ranging in age from maybe twelve to eighty slid into various versions of the Tai Chi pose "snake creeps down." They followed the slow, controlled movements of their instructor, a muscular black man whose sweaty bald head reflected the morning sun.

Zach Wong sat on a park bench, studiously ignoring the class. If he watched, he'd have to actively suppress the urge to wander through the group offering advice and correcting stance, posture, everything. Even for the instructor – especially the instructor – who kept entreating his class to keep their "joints soft" while his own technique was stiff and his movements jerky.

Zach focused on his laptop, which had a tenuous link with the Internet half a block away from home. He'd rather sit out here and watch poorly executed Tai Chi and deal with a spotty connection than listen to his parents argue. Although they called it a "discussion," as if his mom and stepdad screaming at each other in Chinese was *that* civilized.

His email service provider took forever to load. While he waited for his cursor to stop spinning, he read the news headlines, "Massive Aurora Blankets Alaskan Sky," "Interview: North Sea Tsunami Survivors," and "Electromagnetic Pulses Predict Earthquakes." He clicked on the last one and waited for the story to come up. A glance at the fumbling Tai Chi class and he couldn't help but laugh. The instructor, who should have been in a meditative state of mind, gave him a dirty look. Zach shook his head and looked back at the earthquake story. Some scientists were claiming that a series of strange electromagnetic signals had been detected in and around the city. Apparently, similar signals had appeared just prior to earthquakes in the past, and they were anxiously watching the sensors along the San Andreas Fault, hoping to link the occurrences.

Electromagnetic pulses? This morning he'd been awakened by a strange sensation, like all the hair on his body was made of metal and some unseen hand had passed a huge magnet over his bed. He'd burst from under the quilt, ready to fight, but tripped over his sheets and landed in the kind of undignified heap he didn't often find himself in. It had affected him that strongly.

The story didn't say anything about people being able to feel the pulses, so Zach shrugged it off and read his email. Then he pulled his tablet out of his backpack and opened a graphic file he'd been working on.

Within minutes he was completely engrossed in the drawing. It wasn't for school – although technically he could submit it for his portfolio class – but for a girl he knew online. She'd written a story and wanted a picture of her main character, a warrior princess. For trade, she was writing an essay for him for his English class. It annoyed him no end that to get his degree he had to take boring courses like English that took time and energy away from his precious art.

He'd sketched, scanned, outlined and colored the drawing. Now he was working on the details of the character's costume, an elaborate strappy leather thing with buckles and about a dozen sheaths with ornate knife handles sticking out every which way. The "princess" bristled with armament, but his challenge was to make her appear feminine. He did this through the exaggerated curves of her body and the flowing waves of her long red hair. On her head, he placed a silvery crown. It was this that had his concentration, as his virtual pen stroked back and forth with feathery lightness to get the complex pattern on the crown just right.

As absorbed as he was, he still knew when the Tai Chi class ended, and the instructor approached him. Zach looked up, mind still on the drawing.

"You find something funny about me and my class, boy?" The instructor spoke in a southern accent.

"No."

"Because folks who exercise instead of spending all day playing video games do a helluva lot better in life, hear?"

Zach clicked on the save button and set his laptop on the bench. He stood and faced the instructor. They were about the same height, six foot, but Zach was much leaner.

The man opened his mouth wide and let out an uproarious laugh. "You want to take me on, grasshopper?"

Zach bowed. "I have no wish to fight, Sensei." It wasn't true. Zach was itching to get into it with this joker, but he would do nothing to instigate it.

The instructor wiped a finger under his eye and shook off an imaginary tear of amusement. "Well, I have no wish to swat a fly, but if it irritates me enough, I'll roll up my newspaper."

Zach held himself still. Six of the instructor's students were still around, two in Zach's line of sight, two in a car parked at the curb ten yards behind him at 7 o'clock and two walking south on the sidewalk. The grass was damp with dew and would be slippery. The sun was shining in the instructor's eyes, and his skin would be slick from the sweat of his exertion. Earlier Zach had noticed that the older man favored his left leg at the knee.

"You think you picked up enough Kung Fu moves from watching cartoons and playing your little Xbox?" The instructor asked. "I'm a third-degree black belt, son. My hands are registered as lethal weapons."

Where Zach came from, they didn't use the belt-ranking system. He'd used the Japanese word "Sensei" because after a few minutes observing the instructor, it was obvious he'd trained in the U.S. under the highly westernized martial arts. Zach wanted to shut the guy up and then shut him down, but he bided his time.

"You know," The instructor said, raising an arm. "I think I'm going to give you a free lesson. Something to help you out when the bullies come calling."

"Do not touch me," Zach said.

The instructor looked from left to right, checking, Zach knew, to see if anyone was around to witness his next move. Then the moron shifted position so slowly a kindergartener could anticipate the strike. Zach easily avoided the simple karate punch aimed at his shoulder, but otherwise didn't react. He was beginning to feel guilty for stringing this guy along, playing him.

He just had time to register the surprised look on the instructor's face, when Zach's body suddenly stiffened involuntarily. From his scalp to his toes, he felt as if waves of electric energy were passing through him, like being struck by lightning once, twice and then a final time. The last shock left him gasping, but he still saw the instructor's next punch before it reached him.

Zach caught the man's arm and with a quick twist threw him to the grass. Two steps and he closed his laptop and shoved it and the tablet into his backpack. He left the instructor babbling on the ground like an idiot. Zach didn't think he'd done permanent damage, but that wasn't important now.

Right now, he had to warn San Francisco that the big one was coming.

Chapter Four

London

Every chair was occupied, forcing the remaining travelers to stand or wander about or sit on the carpet in the newly refurbished terminal. Hours ago, Kevin had given his seat to an elderly woman who seemed content to sit next to Dr. Weinstein and chat him up. Kevin was worried about the professor. The excitement of the last few days had put bruised-looking circles under the old man's eyes, and the tremor in his hands had increased.

Their flight to Houston was postponed, as were all flights in or out of Heathrow, due to a series of violent electrical storms coming out of the North Sea. After recent events, instead of irritation, the general mood among the stranded travelers was somber.

As thrilling as it had been for Kevin to witness the birth of a tsunami at its origin, the aftermath had been sobering. The countries bordering the North Sea, including Sweden, France and the United Kingdom, had been forewarned just in time to evacuate before waves up to fifteen meters in height swept the coasts. To the panicked confusion of scientists worldwide, seismic sensors hadn't been able to pinpoint an epicenter. Speculation placed the instigating event at Dogger Bank, a vast undersea accumulation of glacial debris, kilometers from Silverpit Crater. Most of the scientists aboard the drill ship felt otherwise, but they had no proof. The ship had been briefly disabled until the crew disengaged from the broken drill, then they'd raced to the English coast to assist the crew of an overturned fishing vessel.

Kevin wanted to stay with the ship, which was now anchored offshore while rescue efforts continued and cleanup of the harbors began. Dr. Weinstein's health, however, required that he accompany the professor back home. He didn't know how he was supposed to focus on his studies, go back to life as usual in the quiet Texas university town. Call it the spirit of adventure, the call to action – whatever – but his desire to brave the elements and his seasickness and zoom back out to the crater got stronger the farther away he got. Leaving the site had been one of the most painful things he'd ever been forced to do.

"Me cousins are off on 'oliday," said the old woman sitting with Dr. Weinstein. "You know where? Sumatra. Isn't that a strange coincidence? We haven't 'eard, but their cottage is right on the beach down at Scarborough. I 'ope it's still standin'.'"

Kevin shifted from one buttock to the other on the cold carpet and leaned back against their stacked luggage. He looked at the old woman. She'd said her name was Caitlin, said it was old Irish for "pure," but then she'd winked. Sitting on the chair, her feet hardly touched the ground she was that petite, just the right size for Dr. Weinstein, who seemed oblivious to how attractive she was. Caitlin was beautiful. Her burnished copper hair floated in loose ringlets over narrow, alabaster shoulders. Large, heavy-lidded eyes, and skin so smooth and clear Kevin swore he saw her spirit shining through, a delicate, effervescent halo. She rose from the chair and walked towards him with such dainty grace she seemed to float. All the time holding his gaze with her mesmerizing deep blue eyes, deep as the North Sea.

"Kevin?"

He blinked at Dr. Weinstein's voice, and Caitlin became an old woman again, seated demurely, beady blue eyes looking at him with mild curiosity.

Must have been... dreaming or something. Kevin shook his head to clear the cobwebs.

"I'm going to stretch my legs," Dr. Weinstein said. He stood and shuffled towards the men's room.

The old woman patted Dr. Weinstein's seat and said, "You'd best sit in it, or it'll be taken by one of those circlin' sharks," she gestured to a few people who did look like they were eyeing the abandoned chair. Kevin got stiffly up off the floor and parked himself on the still-warm vinyl.

"So yer a student of geology, then?" Caitlin asked.

"Yes."

Through the wall of windows overlooking the tarmac, a thick, jagged bolt of lightning lit the night sky. A collective exclamation went up from the crowded terminal, immediately drowned out by the crash of thunder.

12

After the echo faded away, Caitlin said, "That's some display."

Kevin nodded, staring out with the after burn of the lightning on his retinas.

"A man of few words, are you?"

He smiled and glanced at her, then did a double take. She was beautiful again. Young.

Kevin rubbed his eyes and peeked out from between his fingers. Still young. The fingers went back to rubbing. He knew he was tired, but not so tired he'd be hallucinating like this. He felt her hand on his arm and jerked away, not from surprise but from fear. Her touch sent a shock through him, a zing. He jumped out of the chair and faced her.

"Who are you?"

"A friend."

He looked to his left and to his right. Had anyone else seen it? Seen the old woman drop fifty years? A few people nearby *were* looking – at him, as he stood over Caitlin with his fists clenched.

"Sit down," she said.

He straightened and took a breath. "Are you for real?"

"Depends on your definition of real. Sit."

It was an order, and he sat. Dr. Weinstein was nowhere in sight.

"The storm is going to let up soon, so we don't have much time," Caitlin said.

"What's happening to me?" he asked. *Why do I feel like I know things that don't make sense? Why do I have all these strange electric sensations?*

"Nothing's happening to you. Something's happening to the earth, and we have to stop it."

Chapter Five

Fairbanks, Alaska

There was no sky, just low, grey clouds. No rain, just the misty kind of drizzle that made an umbrella useless. It hissed softly against the windshield every time the driver got the old bus over thirty miles per hour.

Two children who'd gotten on at the last stop with their mother had turned around in their seats and were staring at Lizbeth. Even her long puffy coat couldn't disguise the neon purple and orange harlequin patterned Clowntastic Pizza uniform. The children, a boy with a buzz cut that showed off the bumps in his skull and a girl whose mousey brown hair was so messy it looked like she was working on some dreads, seemed to be waiting for Lizbeth to do something. She wanted to inform the children that it would be a colder day than today before she'd willingly serenade them with the Clownee Birthday Song. Nothing could induce her to sing the smarmy song, with the exception of her pathetic paycheck.

The children had looked miserable, though, when they'd gotten on the bus in their second-hand coats and dollar-store plastic galoshes. Their mother had dragged them up the steps and down the aisle and ordered them to sit quietly, which they'd done admirably.

Lizbeth pulled her hands from her warm pockets and showed the children a quarter pinched between the thumb and forefinger. She palmed it, pretended to put it in her other hand and "found" it behind the boy's ear.

"How'd you do that?"

"Prestidigitation," Lizbeth said, waggling her eyebrows at them.

They demanded she do it again, so she did, over and over. They giggled throughout but became almost hysterical with laughter as Lizbeth began finding coins all around the back of their mother's head. When the woman figured out she'd been the butt of a joke that her children were

14

really enjoying, instead of going along with it, she glared at Lizbeth and forcibly made her kids sit facing front.

What a crab.

Lizbeth caught sight of their sad faces reflected in the window and she wanted to box their mother's ears. Instead, she leaned her head against the cold glass and began singing under her breath.

At her stop, she waved and smiled to the children, who waved back.

It was a half mile to Granma's cabin, a cold, wet half mile. Normally, she enjoyed walking past the Hunt Family pasture, but the friendly horses usually looking for a nose rub were all in the warm barn tonight. She wished she'd brought her MP3 player, because she sure could use a distraction from her thoughts. She had her cell phone tucked away in an inside pocket, but she'd been ignoring Steph's texts. All Steph did was rave about college, how much fun she was having, how many cute guys she'd met – not topics Lizbeth was feeling charitable about at the moment. Especially when her hair and skin stank of greasy, inedible pizza.

She opened the cabin door to see Granma sitting on the armchair across from the couch. A woman sat facing her, a thin, black, strangely familiar woman. As soon as Granma turned to look at her, Lizbeth knew with a strong sense of dread that something had happened.

"Is it Mom?" she asked.

"No, baby. Your mother's fine. Everything's fine," Granma said. She hadn't called Lizbeth "baby" since Lizbeth had *been* a baby. No lit candles meant this woman was not a client. Besides, she didn't have that wide-eyed look about her that screamed, "Believer."

"Caitlin, this is my granddaughter Lizbeth."

Lizbeth moved forward and shook the older woman's hand, murmuring an apology about her own cold hand. She looked at her grandmother for permission to leave the room, go hide in her bedroom and sulk some more about not being able to afford college, but Granma said, "Have a cup of tea, dear. Sit with us for a few minutes, please."

Her earlier dread resurfaced, but she sat on the couch next to her grandmother's guest. Granma handed her a cup of tea in the antique china that was only used for special occasions. Lizbeth's face had begun to thaw in the heat of the room, but the cold outside must have affected her vision. When she looked directly at this Caitlin woman, everything was fine, but every time she sipped the tea, her peripheral vision wavered, giving Caitlin a strange glow.

15

"Caitlin worked with your father," Granma said.

"Really?" Lizbeth's interest went from zero to sixty.

"You look very much like him," Caitlin said.

"I would if I were a little whiter."

"Lizbeth!" Granma said.

Lizbeth shrugged. "It's true."

"Trust me when I say that you are more like him than you know," Caitlin said.

Oh-kay. Lizbeth reevaluated Caitlin. Formal speech, formal manner. Definitely a believer.

"I'll have to trust you, since you knew him and I didn't."

She looked on as Caitlin exchanged a look with Granma, both of their faces impassive.

Granma said, "How was work today, Lizbee?"

"Horrible. Sucky. Same as ever, why?"

"I'm here to offer you a job," Caitlin said.

"How much does it pay?" Lizbeth asked.

"If we're successful, the reward will be great."

Lizbeth absorbed the statement without scoffing, but it was difficult.

"Successful at what?"

"Preventing the destruction of earth," Caitlin said.

Lizbeth laughed. She stood and said, "I'd love to save the world, but I need to change out of my uniform and get a shower, so I'll take a rain check on that 'job' of yours. Good luck."

She started out of the room, but Caitlin spoke again, and it wasn't what she said, "Luck has nothing to do with it," but how she said it. The words had been spoken calmly, quietly, but Lizbeth felt them reverberating in her skull as if she were in a cavernous, echoing chamber instead of the tiny cabin. She put her hands to her head and turned to Caitlin, *who'd completely changed appearance.* Black hair pulled back in a bun had been replaced with red curls; milk chocolate skin was now plain milk.

Lizbeth looked around the room. The performer in her knew the trick was possible, but the realist wondered why Caitlin and this new woman, probably her assistant, would go to so much trouble.

"What are you trying to pull?" she asked.

"I told you she was a tough nut," Granma said to the assistant.

"I'm a shapeshifter, Lizbeth," the assistant said in Caitlin's voice. "Like your father."

Lizbeth rolled her eyes. "My father was a magician. I've read every article and seen every bit of footage on him. He never once changed shape. They call it a magic *trick* because the trick is what's real. I don't know why you're messing with me, but I don't appreciate it."

Caitlin's assistant stood and walked over, placing her hands on Lizbeth's shoulders. She was shorter by several inches. Lizbeth found it difficult to maintain eye contact – there was something very weird about the woman's blue eyes, like looking into some kind of bizarre swirling galaxy. A shaft of fear went through her. She tried to think of it as irrational but wasn't quite convinced.

"Is it real, this incarnation?" The woman asked.

Lizbeth sucked in a breath. She'd heard that phrase a hundred times, watching her father's clips. It was his greatest magic trick, the one where he changed a person from the audience into a white jaguar. The woman, it *was* Caitlin, wavered right before Lizbeth's eyes. Her nose flattened out and the transformation spread quickly down her cheeks, to her mouth, forehead, ears. It wasn't like a computer morph on television. The change was fast, but Lizbeth saw each hair sprout, whiskers grow, teeth become thin and pointy. The eyes, though, they didn't change at all. The white jaguar gripped Lizbeth's shoulders with her claws, blue swirly eyes staring out of a sleek, spotted face.

In her mind, Lizbeth heard the rest of her father's incantation, "*Or is it prestidigitation?*"

Chapter Six

San Francisco, California

Zach had done all he could, which wasn't much. It wasn't just that people were disinclined to listen to an eighteen-year-old kid. It wasn't even that his scientific credentials were nonexistent. The problem was the message. No matter how he worded it, "The Big One is coming" sounded like something a lunatic would say.

For someone as accomplished in martial arts as he was, Zach didn't exactly have a reputation for being levelheaded. Through his art, fantastical creatures came to life. His designs were brilliant fractals and complicated mathematical patterns. His imagination was legend among family and friends, many of whom didn't quite "get" him.

So when he'd requested that his mother pack up and leave for a while, she looked at him like he'd grown a second head. He tried telling his friends about the electromagnetic pulses and they'd fondly accused him of messing with them. He called every scientific institution that seemed relevant in the Bay Area and got nowhere. He finally took the ultimate and admittedly harebrained step of filming an appeal to the masses and posting it on YouTube. For dramatic effect, he made two big signs and strapped them together to wear over his shoulders. In retrospect, he probably shouldn't have written "The End is Near" on the front and "Goodbye San Francisco" on the back. It was supposed to be a satirical attention-getter, and it worked, but not like he'd intended. He received thousands of hits on his YouTube page over the course of the next two days, but comment after comment entreated him not to take his own life. Early Monday morning a mild earthquake shook the region, not The Big One by any stretch of the imagination, not even Zach's.

He still believed something was wrong, but realized the problem was much more likely to be health related. Even after the little earthquake

18

he kept getting those electric shock sensations. In fact, they were getting more frequent and more severe. He reluctantly asked his mother to make an appointment for a checkup.

At school, he walked into the student lounge and overheard some kids talking about his idiotic meltdown. He had no idea how she knew, but the cute new cashier at the snack bar came right out and asked him if he was "Doomsday Guy." It was his second week of college, and he'd gone from nondescript freshman to infamous loon in one weekend. If the doctor didn't find anything wrong, he suspected his next appointment would be with a shrink.

He sat down at an unoccupied table and hunched over his laptop, trying to become invisible. He had an hour until his first class, so he opened the graphic file he'd been working on for his friend. Just a few finishing touches to the intricate silver crown nestled in the warrior princess's mass of red hair and he'd be done.

He sipped his coffee and grimaced. She might be cute, but Cashier Girl couldn't brew a decent cup.

"Hey."

Zach looked up. *Think of the devil.*

"I'm sorry if I embarrassed you," Cashier Girl said. Her nametag read "Alice."

"You don't look like an Alice," he blurted.

She smiled. "It's not my apron. I'm filling in today. Can I sit here?"

"Yeah, sure."

She pulled out a chair and sat. "So why'd you make it, anyway? The video."

Zach gave a short laugh and said, "Too much electrical stimulation to the frontal lobe, I guess."

She raised her eyebrows.

Damn she's pretty. He couldn't see her hair. It was tucked under an old-fashioned frilly cap with the snack bar logo on it. Her complexion was unblemished, a genetic coup for one so young. She had blue eyes and straight white teeth in a delicate mouth that all of a sudden looked familiar. Where had he seen her before?

She was waiting for him to explain, so he said, "Look, I've already made a complete fool out of myself. You wouldn't believe me if I told you why."

Her head drifted to the side as she regarded him. "Try me."

Zach took a deep breath and let it out in a sigh. "Electromagnetic pulses have been known to appear in some places prior to an earthquake. I can feel them. At least, I've deluded myself into thinking I can."

"What does it feel like?"

He couldn't figure out why she was still talking to him after his crazy revelation. In order to avoid her intense blue eyes, he looked down at the drawing on his laptop screen and said, "I don't know, like dropping a radio in the bathtub or getting struck by lightning. I have nothing to compare it to since I've never felt that way before. Anyway, I'm sure I'm either insane or I've got some incurable disease."

"Perhaps not."

Something in her voice made him study her face again. Then it hit him – the reason she seemed so familiar. He looked at the digital image he'd created on the screen and back to the young woman seated across from him.

"I don't believe this," he said.

"What?"

Zach half-stood and reached out to tweak the hat from her head. Lush red curls tumbled out. She didn't protest, just looked at him with those eyes and repeated, "What?"

He turned his laptop around so she could see the screen. She'd been so composed throughout the whole strange conversation that Zach was almost gratified when she gasped. She didn't comment on the striking resemblance between herself and the warrior princess, however. Instead, she demanded, "Where did you see that crown?"

Confused, Zach said, "I didn't. I designed it."

She collected herself so quickly he wondered if he'd imagined the outburst. "It's lovely. You're very talented."

"You don't find it odd that this," he gestured to the screen, "looks exactly like you?"

"Odd? No. It actually gives me a better idea of your…abilities."

Zach paused to consider that enigmatic statement, but then he stiffened as he felt the hair on the back of his neck rise; prelude to an electromagnetic shock. "Not again," he muttered.

"Give me your hands," she said.

He frowned and shook his head, but she reached out and took them. A split second later, he went rigid as the pulse hit, but instead of being immobilized by an excruciating jolt, the charge flowed through his body and exited from his hands to hers. He tried to pull away before she got hurt, but she clasped his hands tightly. Four, five, six pulses and her face remained expressionless throughout. When it was over, Zach's legs gave out and he sat, staring stupefied at the mysterious woman across from him.

"What did you do?" he asked.

"I grounded you."

"Grounded?"

"I'll explain later." She stood, untied Alice's apron and dropped it on the table. "Get your things. You're coming with me."

"I have class in a few minutes."

She set her jaw and said, "Let's go," and Zach found himself following her out the door with his pack slung over his shoulder.

The sun had broken through the morning mist and the trees lining the parking lot waved their branches in the brisk breeze. Everything looked normal, certainly not like a major disaster was about to happen. Zach inhaled the spicy scent of eucalyptus and tried to calm his mind as he followed her to her car. She got in and cleared the passenger seat for him, tossing a packet of paper into the back seat. He saw "Enterprise Rent-a-car" on the packet and asked, "Is this a rental?"

She snapped her seatbelt and said, "Yes. Buckle up."

"Where are we going?" *Why am I going with you? Am I losing my mind?*

"You're not losing your mind, and we're getting out of San Francisco."

He ignored the fact that she seemed to have *read* his mind, and asked, "There really is going to be an earthquake, isn't there?"

"Yes."

"Are you a scientist?"

"Yes, but that's not how I know the earthquake is going to happen."

"Who are you?"

"My name is Caitlin. I need your help."

He looked out the window. Caitlin had gotten onto the freeway and was headed toward Sacramento.

"Take me home. I need to get my mom – kidnap her if I have to."

"It's too late for that."

He knew it was true. Besides, he'd already tried to warn his family, spent all weekend at it in fact, and they were likely to respond to any further attempts by slapping him in a special white jacket. At least he'd stocked the house with bottled water and batteries.

"Why do you need my help?" he asked.

21

"Have you always felt earthquakes before they happened?"

"No, it just started."

"That's because this isn't your average earthquake."

He believed her, believed everything she said, but had no logical reason to do so.

"What's different about it?" he asked.

"Ever heard of ley lines?"

Of course he had. To demonstrate his knowledge, he said, "Mythical lines of power stretching between ancient monuments?"

He noticed she drove in the fast lane, well over the speed limit, aggressively tailgating anyone slower until they moved out of her way.

"Most myths have a grain of truth to them," she said. "About fifty years ago researchers were looking into variations in the Earth's magnetic field. They found magnetic stripes at regular intervals crossing the ocean floor, which they attributed to seafloor spreading."

Zach looked at her profile. "But that's not what it was?"

She shook her head. "The earth consists of layers. The core, outer core and mantle."

He said, "Like a jawbreaker," and then suffered through her sideways look of disapproval. "Sorry. I make jokes under pressure."

"On top is the crust, and below that is a thin layer no one knows about, a grid of metal that circles the planet," she said.

"So the metal is the ley lines?"

"Not exactly. The metal is an iridium alloy, a biometal. It's not magnetic itself. The stripes the researchers detected were normal planetary magnetism. Where the magnetism was *absent* indicates where the iridium grid is."

"*Bio*metal?"

"Yes. The iridium is the reason you can feel the electromagnetic pulses, at least these specific pulses, which are not a byproduct of normal movement of the crust. The grid is causing the pulses, creating circumstances along the fault line that will lead to an earthquake."

Zach looked out the window at a hillside covered with identical houses. He tried to ignore the fact that he was in a car with a stranger speeding away from his home, listening to a fantastical tale that she'd like him to believe was truth.

"I get what you're saying, not that it makes sense. How come nobody ever dug up this underground metal grid?"

"It's too far down in the lithosphere. And unfortunately, someone did hit it. Recently. That's one of the reasons it's...upset."

He looked at her in disbelief for a moment before responding with a burst of laughter. "Okay, lady, you finally lost me. I've had some weird things happen to me lately, which is probably why I've swallowed everything you've said, but that's too much. A biometal that controls the earth? I don't think so. You can turn around at the next exit and drop me off anywhere."

He expected her to protest, but she stepped on the brake and pulled to the shoulder. He was about to request that she at least take him off the freeway, when the car began to shake violently.

"Hang on," she said.

Chapter Seven

Sacramento, California

After the airport shuttle dropped Kevin off at the hotel entrance, he checked in and left his luggage in the room to go for a walk along the Sacramento River. He needed to clear his head after the flight, and maybe walk off the resurgence of the nagging feeling that something bad was going to happen.

It was a windy day, and the mature palm trees lining the sidewalk moved rhythmically against a bleak overcast sky. The river water flowed drab and murky brown in comparison to the crisp blue-grey of the North Sea.

Caitlin wasn't due to arrive for another hour or so. She'd told him she was picking someone up in San Francisco. He'd like to say she told him more, but she'd gotten his cooperation with a surprisingly minimal amount of information.

He did know there were to be four of them altogether, counting Caitlin. Four people to save the earth, one of whom at least was completely clueless as to how they were supposed to accomplish the task. That wasn't the only thing that baffled Kevin. As real as the events of the past week had seemed, he'd had plenty of time on the trip to Texas and now the trip here, to question not only his judgment, but his sanity.

His deep certainty vied with deep doubt, back and forth. Just when he convinced himself that Caitlin was some kind of grifter pulling off the con of the century, he remembered how she'd changed, *shapeshifted*, from old woman to young. That would be some trick if it weren't real, and why would she bother to fool a nobody like him? He had no money and wasn't related to anyone with money – that he knew of. He'd been adopted, and he thought it ironic now that his mother used to call him her little changeling. Caitlin hadn't said as much, but Kevin suspected that she'd picked him because he was like her, whatever she was.

He noticed as he walked that there weren't very many people willing to brave the stiff breeze along the river. One woman, bundled up in a fur-lined parka as if it were minus zero, was walking her poodle, two men were jogging and talking at the same time, and a young woman was skipping stones on the shore. Kevin stopped and leaned against a rail to watch the young woman. She took her time selecting the perfect flat rock, but with an apparently careless flick of her wrist sent it skimming far out along the surface of the water. He counted ten hops before it sank in the middle of the river.

As if sensing she was being watched, she turned and looked up at him. Her black hair was pulled back into a ponytail, revealing high cheekbones and a delicately pointed chin in a smooth, light brown complexion. She was squinting up at him, just far enough away that he couldn't see the color of her eyes.

"That's pretty impressive," he said.

"Nothing else to do around here." Her tone told him more than her words. She was young and bored and discontent. And apparently not looking for conversation. She turned and walked away towards a thick dirt bank jutting over the water.

"Be that way," he muttered.

The rail underneath his hands began to vibrate, and he glanced behind him along the path, expecting to see a heavy truck coming his way. The only thing on the path was the woman and her dog, although she, too, seemed to be trying to identify the source of the shaking. The vibration got stronger and he looked all around to find the cause. He noticed the trees seemed to be moving to and fro more emphatically and wondered if the breeze had picked up enough to make the ground shake.

Someone screamed, "Earthquake!" and he swung around to see the young black woman balanced precariously over the river.

Kevin saw that her scream wasn't just histrionics; the dirt under her feet had shifted, and he saw a huge dark gouge sliced from the bank, moving in a slow slide towards the water. She tried jumping, but the ground beneath her crumbled and water rushed in to fill the void. It instantly turned the dirt to mud, and she slipped and fell forward. Without thinking, Kevin hurdled the rail, jumped onto the shore and ran pounding across the dirt. By the time he reached her, she was thigh deep in mud and water, flailing her arms and screaming for help.

25

He didn't have time to assess the situation. The earth was still quaking and the mass of dirt, with its patches of tall reeds swaying, slid inexorably forward. He leaped onto an area that was moving but seemed stable enough to hold his weight, and then stepped quickly to the nearest patch of reeds. Throwing his body onto the growth to bend it down, he yelled, "Grab on!" The young woman grasped the reeds and pulled herself hand over hand, knees churning through the muck like a marine recruit. She kept pulling until she extricated herself from the sucking mud and lay panting face to face with Kevin.

The ground stopped shaking and the dirt bank shuddered and stopped sliding. Everything was still and quiet for the moment.

"You okay?" he asked.

"I guess so."

"Let's get out of here." He sat up carefully, aware that the ground may have stopped moving, but it was unlikely to be safe. They scrambled along the disrupted soil until finally making it to the pavement.

The woman in the parka gripped her poodle in her arms and asked, "Are you guys alright? Wow, that was a big one!"

If Kevin thought his daring rescue was going to get him the girl, she proved him wrong by sprinting away in the direction of the hotel like a pack of wolves was at her heels.

His addled brain had just formed the thought that she hadn't even thanked him, when she slowed and ran backwards along the path long enough to shout, "Thank you!" He watched her lithe body wink out of sight behind some bushes. He shrugged and brushed his hands down his mud-coated jeans. Hopefully, the pipes hadn't burst in the quake, because he'd just made a date with the hotel shower stall.

Chapter Eight

Sacramento, California

Warm water cascaded down her body, bringing thousands of goosebumps to exquisite life. Lizbeth enjoyed a series of luxurious shivers as she rotated under the spray to warm her chilled flesh. Her muddy clothes lay in a bundle on the floor of the bathroom. She'd have to hurry if she was going to get them washed and dried in the hotel laundry room before Caitlin arrived.

Caitlin.

Lizbeth wasn't sure if she hated her or just disliked her intensely. She wouldn't admit to being intimidated by her, that's for sure. Bad enough the strange woman showed up and immediately won the trust of her grandmother, but then Lizbeth's own mother told Granma to hand her over like she was some kind of slave to be bartered.

"Oh, sure, take my underaged daughter. Go save the world," Lizbeth said as she lathered her hair with the almond-scented hotel shampoo. "It's not like she has anything better to do."

Since her mother had been working, Lizbeth hadn't even had a chance to talk to her or say goodbye.

Once she was clean for the second time that day, she dressed in one of her rapidly dwindling outfits and rushed out into the hall to put yesterday's traveling clothes and this morning's mud-crusted jeans, t-shirt, jacket, socks and tennis shoes into the washer. After she chose "heavy load," she lined the coins up in the slot and pushed it in.

She decided she'd best get some breakfast, or rather, brunch, since it was getting closer to noon than she'd like. She reached for the door, but it opened, and a young man entered. He was not tall, maybe her height or slightly shorter, but solidly built. His brown hair was wet and slicked back with a spicy-smelling gel.

"Oh, sorry," he said. He leaned against the door to hold it for her. In his arms was a bundle of muddy clothes.

There was no way he wouldn't recognize her, so she waited for him to say something. When he didn't, she looked at his face. He stared at the ceiling with a carelessly aloof expression stamped on his features, the kind of look she herself might have cultivated had she been blown off.

She sighed. He did rescue her, and although saying he saved her life seemed a bit dramatic, for all she knew, the mud might have buried her alive. The least she could do was thank him properly.

She backed away from the door and waved him in, saying, "The washer on the end is free."

"Thanks."

She waited silently for him to get his laundry started while he ignored her. Just when she thought he was going to leave without further acknowledgement, he shut the lid and said over the sound of the shushing water, "My name's Kevin. You want to get something to eat?"

"Lizbeth. Sure."

When they walked into the hotel lobby, they encountered a crowd of excited people clamoring for attention at the curving marble counter. One family rushed past them, wheeled luggage clattering along the floor tile, the flapping arm of a shirt sticking out of the zipper. A large flat-screen television mounted on the wall next to the front desk had a blaring news report about the earthquake. When she'd gotten back from the river, Lizbeth had come in a side door. A few things in her room had tipped over, but the walls and ceiling were intact. She hadn't thought the earthquake had caused much damage.

"Oh, my God," Kevin said. He was staring at the television screen. "Look at San Francisco!"

Lizbeth watched as horrific footage shot from a helicopter news crew filming down on the city flashed on the screen. Through plumes of black smoke, the camera caught glimpses of crumbled buildings, a collapsed overpass, deep chasms in streets and highways with chunks of asphalt thrusting upward. Fires everywhere spewed flames into the sky.

Her stomach clenched in fear when the announcer came on and said that preliminary sensor readings put the quake at 7.8 on the Richter scale. Strong aftershocks were rocking the region, causing further damage. It was too soon for an accurate death toll, but hospital emergency rooms throughout the county were overflowing with casualties.

"Caitlin," she whispered.

"What did you say?" Kevin asked.

Lizbeth shook her head. "I'm worried about a – a friend who's in San Francisco. Well, maybe not. Maybe she made it out. She was supposed to be on her way here."

"Caitlin?" he asked.

She tore her eyes from the devastation and looked at him. The way he said Caitlin's name made her ask, "Do you know her?"

"Petite redhead, blue eyes, possibly not human?"

Lizbeth felt her mouth drop open and stay that way.

"Are you here to save the earth, too?" It burst out, and she felt monumentally stupid as soon as she asked it.

Kevin laughed and spread his arms wide. "Yep. Am I not what you expected?"

To her embarrassment, tears of relief flooded her eyes. He was one of the four. He would understand her, maybe answer a few questions about this whole crazy scenario.

"You're perfect," she said, and then felt herself blush. "I mean, you already saved me, what's the big deal about saving the rest of the world?"

His smile faded as his eyes drifted back to the television. "We sure as hell didn't save San Francisco."

Chapter Nine

Vallejo, California

During the earthquake, Zach gripped the sides of his seat and stared out the windshield at the long, straight stretch of highway ahead. He could see the movement of the earth in great waves along the road. Rigid cement and asphalt might as well have been fluid as water. It fascinated and horrified him, but also served to distract him from the fear.

As soon as the shaking subsided, Caitlin shifted the car into four-wheel drive and muttered, "We didn't get far enough."

"What are you doing?" Zach asked.

"Getting out of San Francisco."

"The road's not safe."

"Call your mother," she replied.

"What?"

"The cell towers that haven't gone out of commission will get overloaded fast. Call her now."

Caitlin didn't sound worried in the slightest. Not about the earthquake, not about the huge cracks in the road they were slowly traversing, and especially not about his mother. He suspected she wanted him to call home so he would be reassured and thus easier to manage.

He flipped open his cell, pressed speed dial and held it to his ear.

"It's not ringing," he said.

She didn't respond. Instead, she put the car in park and opened the door, standing on the frame to look out along the highway. There were plenty of cars parked haphazardly, and many of the drivers had gotten stuck or given up and begun walking. All of the people Zach saw were heading towards the city of Vallejo that he and Caitlin had passed before the quake hit.

"Come on, get out," she said.

He sighed and grabbed his backpack, not bothering to question her this time. They abandoned the car and walked north along the I-80. Zach felt like a salmon swimming upstream with all the people going south. All around them plumes of smoke began rising into the sky. Sirens blared. After about ten minutes of jumping over foot-long cracks in the highway, Caitlin stopped at a black Hummer. She didn't even look to see if anyone noticed, just opened the door and got in. Zach went around to the other side and followed suit.

"Good, there's a full tank," she said.

"Yeah, but no key."

She put her hand on the steering column near the ignition and the big vehicle started with a roar. Zach wasn't surprised, he was simply happy that she'd allowed him to see a demonstration of her – he didn't know what else to call it but "power." The doubts that had begun to surface again quieted down. He still didn't have all the answers, but he'd follow her, for now at least.

The Hummer got them almost to their destination before they had to stop for gas. Twice they'd had to circumnavigate collapsed overpasses, and once they stopped to help an injured woman until an ambulance, already carrying three wounded people, reluctantly added her to their human cargo. The further from San Francisco they got, the less destruction they encountered. They listened to the radio for the first hour and then Caitlin shut it off, with no complaints from Zach.

As Caitlin pumped gas, he went inside the convenience store and impulsively stocked up on energy bars, chips and a six-pack of cola.

"How bad was the quake here?" he asked the clerk over the blaring television behind the counter.

"Man, it was rough. We just now got done cleaning up from stuff coming off the shelves. I wanna get home and check on my fish tank, but the boss is paying me double to stay."

On the television, a news anchor announced the latest death toll at fifty-six people, with untold numbers still unaccounted for.

Zach paid for his purchase and said, "I hope your fish are okay."

"Yeah, thanks, man."

He tried for the tenth time to call home and it rang, but no one picked up. He tried everyone on his speed dial, all his friends and family members and finally got an answer out of his uncle Tommy – sort of. It was his voice mail, but he'd updated it.

"Hello everyone, this is Tom, post-earthquake. My house is still standing, and I am well. Bai lost the oak tree in front of her house, but it fell into the street. Zach is missing, but there were no casualties at his college, so we are assuming he is trying to get home. His house is fine, Vernon and June are fine. The Ling's have major damage to their foundation, but they are unhurt. We have not heard from Jesse or Huang, but the phones are spotty at best. If this is Zach, Jesse, Huang or anyone else not mentioned here, please leave a message so we may stop worrying."

Caitlin was waiting behind the wheel, but Zach stayed outside to leave his response, "Hey Uncle Tommy, it's me, Zach. I'm good, but not in the city at the moment. Let Mom know I'll be back in a few days and she can call on my cell. Glad to hear everyone's okay. Talk to you later."

He climbed into the borrowed Hummer. His mom was going to have a fit when Tommy gave her that message. Zach might be officially an adult, but his mother wasn't planning to cut the apron strings any time soon.

For the rest of the drive the highway was undamaged, and when they entered Sacramento, he experienced a flash of disorientation at the normalcy all around him. Caitlin pulled into the parking lot of a hotel and placed her hand on the steering column. The big engine stopped growling.

"What are we doing here?" he asked.

She sat back in the seat and with her profile to him, said, "We'll be leaving in the morning."

"We're staying in the hotel?" He felt his face go hot as he struggled briefly with the idea of sharing a room with Caitlin.

"There are two others. You'll be bunking with the dwar- a young man named Kevin."

Zach's ears perked up at the word she'd almost said, "dwar." Even someone who hadn't seen the Lord of the Rings trilogy a dozen times would have added the logical "f" sound at the end. He couldn't wait to meet his roomy.

Chapter Ten

Sacramento, California

Kevin sat at the foot of the bed since Lizbeth had taken both pillows, propped them up against the headboard and promptly fell asleep. He found the television remote and flipped channels on mute so he wouldn't wake her. All of the major stations had footage of the earthquake, but he shied away from seeing any more destruction, especially after the gruesome scenes of a gas explosion at a pet hospital.

He and Lizbeth had exchanged information and he'd learned little that he hadn't already guessed about Caitlin, but a lot about Lizbeth. She'd been almost desperate to talk and wasn't shy about expressing her opinions, from the mortification of having a voodoo priestess for a grandmother to the disappointment of missing out on a scholarship. They'd spent considerable time over lunch trying to figure out a.) what was going on, and b.) how on earth they were supposed to help.

A knock on the door and Lizbeth jackknifed instantly off the bed. She had the door open before he even finished standing. Caitlin came in, followed by a tall Asian-looking guy. The four of them stood there, and Kevin wondered if he was supposed to feel like this first meeting was momentous or something. He couldn't tell if the others felt that way or if they were all just waiting for Caitlin to say something. He was surprised Lizbeth hadn't hammered Caitlin with questions the second she entered.

Caitlin gestured to the table in the corner. "Sit."

Kevin held a chair for Lizbeth, but she took the one opposite him. He let go of the chair for the Asian guy to occupy.

Caitlin pointed around the table and said, "Lizbeth. Zach. Kevin. Now we're introduced. Zach, set up your laptop."

Zach pulled it out of his backpack, opened and turned it on. While it booted up, no one spoke. Lizbeth looked groggy from her nap. Kevin shifted his gaze and caught Zach looking at him. He tried to smile at him, but Zach ducked his head and tapped on the keyboard.

"Pull up the drawing," Caitlin said.

A few more keystrokes and Zach turned the laptop around for them all to see.

The picture on the screen was vibrant with depth and color, almost photographic in its precision. It reminded Kevin of an old Frank Frazetta poster his nerdy dorm roommate had hung over his bed. The woman in the drawing was Caitlin, but sensuous and bold, not the fully clothed and untouchable woman sitting across from him. There were also a few glaring enhancements. He tried but couldn't suppress an abashed grin.

"This is the Gossamer Crown," Caitlin said. "Zach, can you zoom in on it?"

As Zach did as she asked, Kevin wondered if Caitlin knew the word, "please."

Then she said it. "Please."

Zach turned the laptop around again and they all examined the detailed silver crown.

"The Gossamer Crown was created centuries ago," Caitlin said. "I was its keeper. It was my duty to guard it; keep it from falling into the wrong hands. I failed. It was stolen from Dublin Castle in 1907, along with the Irish Crown Jewels."

Kevin did a quick calculation. Assuming Caitlin had been twenty in 1907, she'd have to be over 120 years old now. He thought back to the old woman who'd been sitting next to Dr. Weinstein. He'd seen photos of centenarians, and Old Lady Caitlin had looked much younger, maybe about sixty. He wondered what she really looked like, and then it irked him that instead of being incredulous at what she'd just said, he was more curious about her true appearance.

"I request that each of you suspend disbelief, for I have a lot of information to impart," Caitlin said. "First let me say that none of what you've witnessed thus far has been the result of magic. Although I was brought up to believe magic existed, I have long since educated myself against that superstition. I am very old. In my lifetime I have obtained degrees in nearly every major scientific field, especially those that pertain

34

to the function and origin of what we are about to discuss. I begin my studies anew periodically to stay abreast of scientific advances."

Sitting there in the anonymous hotel room surrounded by strangers, it occurred to Kevin that under normal circumstances he'd be feeling disassociated. Instead, Caitlin's every word held him enthralled. Her delicate features were highlighted by the yellow glow of the lamp hanging over the table. He searched her face for signs that she was as unbalanced as the words coming out of her mouth but saw nothing but calm conviction.

"The crown is made from the material of an object that struck earth 65 million years ago. Scientists have attributed that extinction event to an impact that formed the crater at Chicxulub in Mexico. However, the asteroid that produced the Chicxulub crater was not alone in causing the event, nor was it the instigating factor. The object I speak of, called the gossamer sphere, was really to blame. My calculations suggest that the sphere entered our solar system and passed through the asteroid belt between Jupiter and Mars. It disrupted the gravitation of the belt and pulled dozens of common asteroids along behind it. The sphere consisted of a metal almost identical to iridium. It is a biometal, alive in a very rudimentary way. Iridium is rare on earth, but common in meteorites found on earth, and its paramagnetic properties cause it to be highly attracted to magnetic fields. I believe the sphere was intended for a lifeless planet such as Mars, but somehow, maybe because it was deflected by the asteroid belt, it collided instead with earth. Earth's magnetic field strength waxes and wanes, and if you can imagine it, on that long-ago date at the end of the Cretaceous period, field strength must have been particularly powerful and thus suitable for the sphere's needs. I like to think that earth's magnetic currents, its gossamers, reached far into space, beckoning to the sphere."

"Little did earth know what it was asking for," Zach muttered.

"Indeed," Caitlin said. "The speed of the sphere's oblique entry into earth's atmosphere would have violently compressed the air on its leading edge, heating it to over 3000 degrees Fahrenheit. Any accumulated ice, dust and rock particles would have ignited in a massive trailing fireball. Despite the heat, the core of the sphere would have remained frozen from the deep cold of space. It slammed into a shallow sea with a tremendous shockwave, penetrating several kilometers into the thin oceanic crust and expelling debris high into the sky. Over the course of the next few weeks, several members of the asteroid family created by the passing of the sphere would have followed suit, smashing elsewhere into the planet at sites like Chicxulub, and initiating massive worldwide destruction."

"Bye-bye dinosaurs," Zach said.

"Yes. The resulting increase in volcanic activity, acid rain, poisonous gasses and global cooling from dust clouds blocking the sun would have wreaked instantaneous as well as gradual havoc on the ecosystems. 300,000 years later, the majority of marine and terrestrial life on earth was extinct. The planet continued to spin on its axis, the iron dynamo at the center, with its white-hot cushion of liquid metal, unaffected. The impact would have shattered the brittle frozen sphere, which I estimate to have been less than 200 meters in diameter. Gravitational forces exerted a steady influence on the material of the planet as always, pulling dense substances like the iridium in towards the mantle. It sank into the relatively rigid lithosphere, where it slowly transformed into a grid that circled the planet."

She'd asked them to suspend their disbelief. Kevin was trying, but he interrupted to insert what he hoped was a logical question. "Does a 200-meter-diameter sphere contain enough metal to go all the way around the earth?"

Caitlin cocked her head to the side as she looked at him. "It wouldn't seem so, and yet my studies bear out that the grid is indeed there. It is not symmetrical that I can tell, but seems to have formed some pattern, very likely a deliberate design. Iridium is the rarest element in earth's crust. Normal planetary iridium is a siderophile element, which means it's attracted to iron, and like iron, it is assumed that most iridium was pulled inward by gravity to earth's core. I surmise that the extra-terrestrial iridium recruited the existing iridium in earth's crust to fill itself out so it would stretch across the planet, thus causing the shortage of iridium in the crust. The biometal isn't normal iridium, however, and although it did sink inward toward the core, it stopped at a point somewhere at the bottom of earth's lithosphere, as I said, between the deeper, more flexible mantle layers and the rigid crust, which is broken into the eight major tectonic plates."

"Does anyone else know about this grid?" Lizbeth asked.

"I've found obscure references throughout history proposing that such a structure exists, but the concept always drew ridicule from the establishment."

"Didn't anyone see the crater, though?"

"The sphere hit in what is now the North Sea. Eons of ocean sediment served to disguise the impact site. It has remained undisturbed until recently." She looked at Kevin.

"The drill ship," he said.

She nodded. "Silverpit is the impact crater."

"I was on a scientific drilling vessel," Kevin explained to the others. "We'd just penetrated almost down to the impactor – the meteorite. Immediately afterwards, something happened right beneath us to create that tsunami in the North Sea."

He turned to Caitlin. "Bill Masters, the head of the project, said that the ship was delaying the next assignment to go back out to Silverpit."

"Our number one priority is to find the crown," Caitlin said. "But first, we have to stop that ship."

Kevin opened his mouth to inquire how they were supposed to do that, when Zach asked, "How could I have drawn the crown if I've never seen it?"

Caitlin's gaze touched upon each of their faces.

"When the sphere struck the planet, dust and ash that was microscopically permeated with the iridium biometal settled all over the world."

Kevin remembered what the Japanese scientist said. "The K-T Boundary."

"Yes. Whatever life on earth that wasn't destroyed by the event, evolved. When medical technology advanced enough to enable me to get my degrees in molecular biology and biochemistry, I focused my research on my own DNA. I discovered that the cells in my body—in all life, plant and animal—have a certain DNA mutation I attribute to the event, a code for shapeshifting characteristics. Without the crown, my experiments were limited, but I believe the newly evolved lower life forms lacked the conscious thought necessary to activate the mutated genes. Of course, I could be wrong, and life at the time could have been shapeshifting in response to fight or flight stimulus, thus contributing to the amazing biodiversity on earth, but I digress."

Kevin saw Zach's chin go down and a crease appear between his brows. He seemed about to say something, but Caitlin went on.

"Once the biometal sank into the lithosphere," she said, "and all but disappeared from the environment, the genes became dormant and remained so throughout evolution. It appears exposure to the biometal alters the three-dimensional structure of DNA-binding proteins, which

37

control gene expression. Thus, the dormant genes responsible for shapeshifting can be 'unlocked.'

"You asked how you could know what the crown looks like, Zach. It is because it is literally in your blood. When the crown was created, those exposed to the biometal were tainted by it as I've described. Most got sick and died. Those who survived passed on certain traits to their progeny, who were then more likely to survive when exposed to the biometal themselves."

"So we're, like, the progeny?" Lizbeth asked.

Kevin sat there, stunned. His parents hadn't hidden the fact that he'd been adopted, and upon reaching the age of majority, he'd tried to locate his birth parents. Turns out there wasn't even a trail to follow; he'd been left in the emergency room of a Dallas, Texas hospital. Authorities had never discovered who'd abandoned him. He'd convinced himself that his mother had been a teen who'd concealed her pregnancy, a happier thought than the more realistic notion that she'd been a prostitute or a drug addict, or both. Now his mind's eye conjured a twisted, nebulous creature, wisping in and out of the hospital, leaving a wailing infant behind.

"All of you descend from the ancient lines, but your blood is dilute. I am the last pure Shapeshifter," Caitlin said.

Kevin detected no pride in the statement, or sadness. Not that Caitlin ever seemed to show much emotion. He wondered if she were capable.

"I don't—I don't get it. You want us to believe you're a Shapeshifter now?" Zach asked.

"She is. I've seen it," Lizbeth said.

"Me, too," Kevin said.

Zach clearly hadn't, but he seemed to take Lizbeth and Kevin at their word.

"Isn't Shapeshifter another word for fairy?" Zach asked.

"There have been many names given to our kind, and many attributes, some false, some true," Caitlin said.

Lizbeth shifted forward to put her elbows on the table and rest her chin in her hands. She didn't look tired anymore. "So me and Kevin and," she looked at Zach, who obliged her with, "Zach."

"Yeah, Zach. We can't shapeshift or anything?"

Caitlin shook her head. "No."

Kevin was almost afraid to ask, but he croaked out, "What does the sphere do?"

38

"It was sent to harness the magnetic field. Earth is an enormous communication satellite."

Kevin's voice was even weaker when he asked, "For whom?"

Caitlin shook her head slowly. "That, I do not know."

Chapter Eleven

En route to London, England

The charter jet had ten luxurious leather seats, only three of which were occupied. Lizbeth wondered at the expense. Caitlin sat in the co-pilot's chair, so Lizbeth hadn't seen her at all throughout the flight to New York, where they refueled before taking off again for London.

Kevin snoozed in his seat and Zach had his head buried in his laptop, leaving Lizbeth to her thoughts. They were as turbulent as the jet stream propelling them across the Atlantic.

She'd waited in the hotel room last night for Caitlin, who told them she had to arrange for their flight and would be back later. As Lizbeth lay in bed under the soft yellow light of one small lamp, she stared at Caitlin's luggage, a nondescript black nylon bag placed in the middle of the unoccupied bed. It had a tag that read, "Caitlin O'Connor," with an address in Ireland. Both zippered compartments were secured with tiny silver padlocks. The bag was normal, not at all intriguing, unless you considered who it belonged to. For Lizbeth, it might as well have been Pandora's Box.

She'd finally given up on sleep while the temptation of Caitlin's bag sat so invitingly close at hand. Lizbeth could be in and out in less than a minute, with no one, not even the all-powerful Caitlin, the wiser.

She peeled back the heavy polyester bedspread and slid off the stiff mattress. She walked to the door and peered out the peephole, then for good measure, opened the door and looked up and down the hall. After closing the door, she flipped the security lock that would keep Caitlin out even if she used her key card. The bag sat there like a present on Christmas morning.

She opened her own suitcase and took out her makeup case. Underneath her eyelash curler were three metal tools she hoped could be passed off as dental picks. She'd only brought three in case her luggage was searched and she had to explain why she was in possession of a professional lock-picking set. The smallest pick was in her hand when she heard the quiet beep of the key card in the door. She was surprised and yet not surprised when Caitlin entered as if the extra security lock had never been fastened.

Lizbeth didn't say a word, just replaced the pick and put her makeup case back in her suitcase. Caitlin lifted her bag off the bed and took it into the bathroom. Lizbeth got back into bed and tried to reconcile the ordinary sounds of sleep preparation, water running, teeth brushing, toilet flushing, with the extraordinary person making them. When Caitlin returned to the room, Lizbeth pretended to be asleep, knowing it was futile, but not caring.

Now, on the plane, she wondered if Caitlin had known she would try to break into the bag. Caitlin had been a friend of her father's, a cohort even, since she'd participated in his magic act. She'd be aware of his legendary skills and might logically conclude that Lizbeth had inherited them. Although Lizbeth wouldn't exactly say she'd been born with her talents. She'd worked long and hard to develop the expertise of a lock picker and the nimble fingers of a pickpocket. Not that she ever stole anything, really. Not much and not often, and never from anyone who couldn't afford the loss.

Lizbeth concluded grudgingly that there had probably been nothing in Caitlin's bag worth seeing. The woman was the mystery, not anything she might have on her.

Kevin stirred in his seat across the aisle from her, letting out a noise that sounded like he either snorted or ripped one. Lizbeth plugged her nose just in case and saw from Zach's profile that he was suppressing a smile. He looked back at her and waved his hand in the air. Lizbeth grinned.

"I snore sometimes, and it always wakes me up," Kevin said, rubbing his nose and stretching his short legs out in front of him. "You people ought to grow up."

Lizbeth heard Zach say quietly, "Do we have a choice?" before he turned back to his laptop.

"What are you doing?" she asked. The screen was split into two windows. In one, he'd isolated the gossamer crown from the rest of the picture he'd drawn. In the other window, it looked like he'd accessed a search engine.

"Trying to find the crown. It's our primary mission, isn't it?" Zach answered with the mild sarcastic tone she was beginning to associate with nearly everything he said.

"Caitlin said the crown was in your blood," Kevin said.

"It's in your blood, too, dude. You want a knife so you can look inside?"

Kevin said something Lizbeth didn't understand, a short phrase in another language. Zach placed his laptop in the seat next to him and stood in the aisle. He responded back in the same language.

With a flash of alarm, she realized they were about to get into some kind of ridiculous altercation. "Hey! We're supposed to be a team. Don't be jerks, okay?"

After a tense moment with the young men staring each other down, Kevin finally looked away. "Yeah, whatever."

Thinking fast, Lizbeth said, "Maybe we should pool our resources. You know, try and figure out what Caitlin thinks we're capable of. I mean – I can do stuff."

Zach didn't relax his stance one bit, but he said, "So can I."

"Like what?" Kevin asked. Lizbeth was relieved that it didn't sound like a challenge. Zach was tall, but Kevin was solidly built. She didn't know which one would win in a fight and didn't want to find out at cruising altitude above the Atlantic Ocean.

"I could tie you into a pretzel," Zach said matter-of-factly.

Kevin raised his eyebrows. "I believe you. But you can bet I'd get in a few punches first." He held up a fist, and to Lizbeth, it looked as big as a ham.

"You got short man complex or something? Must be the dwarf in you," Zach said.

That did it. Kevin lunged for him at the same time that Lizbeth shouted for Caitlin and threw herself into the aisle between them. Lizbeth and Kevin scuffled briefly, as Zach stepped back to let her body slow Kevin down. She felt Kevin's hands on her shoulders and prepared herself to get tossed aside, but Caitlin poked her head out of the cockpit.

"You're going to want to sit down," she told them.

Lizbeth felt strange all of a sudden, just like she'd felt during the massive aurora. She subsided into her seat.

"What is that?" Zach asked. "Is there going to be another earthquake?"

Caitlin shook her head. "A message is coming in. It's what scientists call a substorm in space."

Lizbeth had a hard time thinking of the earth as a huge communication satellite, but this made sense. "That's what causes the aurora effect. A message."

"Yes. The sphere harnesses the earth's magnetic field lines, which stretch far out into space. They are the gossamers that capture an incoming message. The problem is: the sphere is having trouble receiving the messages, so it's tuning itself."

"You mean, like trying to find better reception on the radio?" Zach asked.

"Exactly. The sphere is going to keep switching channels until it's working properly again," Caitlin said. "It will adjust everything it can, including plate tectonics."

The implication that more devastation was coming struck Lizbeth hard. Her mother and grandmother lived in one of the most earthquake-prone regions in the world.

Caitlin looked out the nearest window. "You need to brace yourselves. Now."

Lizbeth fastened her seatbelt. Kevin and Zach sat as Caitlin disappeared back into the cockpit.

Moments later, the lights in the cabin dimmed and the plane dipped. Lizbeth's stomach lurched just like on a plunging roller coaster. She saw Zach's laptop screen go black. The plane dipped again, and she gripped the arms of her seat. Then a wave of vertigo hit. She felt sick and dizzy, like being trapped in a whirlpool, but the plane wasn't spinning, just falling. They were falling at a steep angle now and she couldn't seem to catch her breath. An oxygen mask popped out of the overhead and dangled in front of her. She couldn't let go of the armrests. Across from her, she was vaguely aware of the sound of retching.

Then it was over. The vertigo disappeared, the lights blinked back on and the plane leveled out. She saw Zach sit up from a slump and tap some keys on his laptop. Kevin looked sheepish as he mopped something up with a handful of tissues. He mumbled an apology about the smell. Caitlin appeared in the cabin.

"What happened?" Lizbeth asked.

"It's as I feared. The gossamer sphere has caused a magnetic reversal."

"What does that mean?" Zach asked.

43

Lizbeth knew. A magnetic reversal hadn't happened in 800,000 years and scientists surmised that the process was thousands of years in the making, not instantaneous.

"The north and south poles have switched," she said.

Chapter Twelve

East of England

Zach expected another hotel room, but Caitlin directed the cab driver out of London proper to a cottage on several acres of ungroomed land. The cottage looked to Zach like it'd been built in Victorian times. Patches of siding that weren't overrun by ivy appeared to have once been white. On the far side of a thick, green pasture, a fenced paddock leaned into what looked like a barn or stables. As Caitlin recovered a key from under a web-encrusted flowerpot, he heard a plaintive neigh on the cool morning air.

Before she could use the key, the door opened and a large man with grizzled stubble on his slab of a chin frowned down at them. He was so wide and tall, even Zach had to crane his neck to see his face. While Kevin hadn't turned out to be an actual dwarf, this man was clearly a giant. The man made a noise that sounded like, "Yup," and disappeared into the dark interior, leaving the door open. Caitlin entered and Zach and the others followed.

"Friendly," Lizbeth said.

Past the gloom of the entranceway, Zach saw into a room lit by a lantern. The orange light cast dark shadows from a grim dozen or so mounted hunting trophies. Caitlin led them the opposite way, up a dark, narrow wooden staircase to the second floor. The floorboards creaked every step of the way, and Zach thought a person wouldn't be able to sneak around much in a place like this. An ordinary person, that is.

Upstairs, Caitlin must have felt her way to a doorknob in the blackness, because she opened a door and muted light flooded the cramped landing space. She pointed to another door and said, "Kevin, Zach." Zach looked at Kevin, who shrugged and went first.

The room was spare, with no light source other than that filtering in through the one small, shuttered window. Brown wool blankets covered metal-framed twin beds about a foot apart from each other. A bureau with four drawers was the only other furniture. Kevin dropped his duffle bag on one of the beds, and Zach watched as he rooted around inside and pulled out a clean shirt. Zach's precipitous leave from school meant he had no clothing besides the jeans and shirt he'd been wearing since yesterday.

"I'm going to find a bathroom," Kevin said. "I hope they have an indoor toilet."

"Don't fall in."

After Kevin left, Zach tried in vain to find a light switch or a lamp. In a sudden burst of panic, he dropped to the floor in a desperate search for an outlet. When he didn't find one, he went to the window and looked out across the pasture to the lonely country road, trying to remember how far it was to someplace with a power source for his laptop. He'd used it on the plane until the battery went low. Then he'd tried to get some sleep in his seat, but Kevin proved to not *always*, as he'd claimed, wake himself with snoring.

The blanket looked soft as sandpaper and the bed as inviting as a church pew, but Zach eyed it anyway. He was so tired and overwhelmed by the events of the last twenty-four hours that he felt his control slipping. Anger, his constant companion for as long as he could remember, boiled beneath a tightly sealed barrier of what he liked to think of as psychic energy. He knew it wasn't fair to take his frustration out on Kevin, but the guy just grated on his nerves. He was so affable, so weak, couldn't even handle a little nose-dive without spewing barf all over the plane.

Not that Zach would admit it, but he'd been scared, too, especially after finding out how many airplanes had gone down after communications had been crippled. All over the world, the powerful substorm and unexpected magnetic reversal had disrupted essential systems, many of which hadn't recovered in time to avoid disaster. There hadn't been any lasting problems at Heathrow, though, and they'd landed without incident.

Zach sat on the bed, not surprised when the thin mattress sank beneath him on squeaky springs. Sleep would be impossible. Unlike his roommate, Zach was a light sleeper. Besides, Caitlin might drag them off at any time, since they were supposed to find a way to stop the drilling vessel from going back out to Silverpit.

His eyes had adjusted to the darkness now and he noticed something on the wall across the room, an irregular bump in the faded wallpaper. The bed squealed as he bounced up and strode across the room.

"There you are," he said to the outlet. He hadn't seen it before because it was located halfway up the wall next to the bureau, and the plate was covered in the same brown-on-burgundy flower pattern as the walls.

He had his laptop out and ready to plug until he realized the outlet was shaped differently. He thought about how nice it would be to put his fist through that horribly papered wall.

Someone was coming up the stairwell. From the sound of the heavy steps, Zach figured it was the huge man who'd let them in. Moments later, the man appeared in the doorway. He had to duck considerably to get under the doorframe and Zach noted the top of his balding head was only inches from the ceiling.

"Thought you might need these," he said in a rumbling baritone.

He handed over a desk lamp and what Zach hoped was a plug adapter.

"Thanks."

The huge man nodded and turned to leave.

"What's your name?" Zach asked.

Brown eyes under an exaggerated brow met Zach's. "Simon."

"Are you a giant?"

The corners of Simon's thick lips dipped in a frown. "My pituitary gland produces too much growth hormone. The politically correct term for it is 'horizontally challenged.'"

It took Zach a couple of heartbeats to get the joke.

"Oh," he said with a little laugh. "So what is this place? Some kind of hostel for travelers on their way to save the world?"

Something flickered in Simon's eyes. "It's called a farm."

"No offense, man, but this place doesn't look very prosperous."

"It's secluded and serves my needs." Simon ducked under the doorframe and turned. "You may want to consider carefully who you talk to about your plans. Not everyone wants the crown to be found."

He disappeared into the gloom of the landing before Zach could question him further.

"Great," Zach said to the empty room. Now he had to keep an eye out for enemies. He wasn't intimidated, far from it, but for some reason he thought of Lizbeth. Of the four of them, she seemed the most vulnerable.

Kevin came back into the room and asked, "Heard anything about what the plan is?"

"No." Zach attached the adapter and plugged in his laptop, gratified when it booted right up and even more pleased when he discovered Simon had wireless Internet. The network was unsecured, but out here in the boonies there probably weren't a lot of hackers lurking about, and he didn't hesitate to connect to it. Behind him, he heard Kevin sit on his bed.

Zach pulled up a search engine and typed in "shapeshifter." The results ranged from products to games to personal websites. He clicked on a Wikipedia article and read it. Nowhere did the article suggest the phenomenon was anything other than make-believe. After following almost every link included in the references used to write the article, he checked out the external links section. Most were sites showcasing stories about shapeshifters, but there were a few that claimed shapeshifters were real. The first one Zach visited made him shake his head at the loonies on the net. The site's forum was populated with people claiming they had proof, usually via badly doctored digital photos or video, that shapeshifters were among us. He scoffed inwardly until it occurred to him that he'd flown halfway around the world in the company of one such. But Caitlin said she was the last one. So unless these idiots had managed to get *her* on film, they were just as deluded as they sounded.

The second site he clicked on didn't even appear to be about shapeshifters at first. The site graphics—interlacing lines and knot work from traditional Celtic art—framed the topics. The banner at the top proclaimed, "Home of Seamus the Bard." Below it was a subheading that read, "Before the Celtic people had a written language, they had a rich oral tradition. In the employ of kings and nobles, druidic bards recited generations of family histories and sang of long-ago heroic deeds." A column to the right had a blog with titles such as, "Bards—the First Rappers?" and "Neo-druidism: These Blokes are Just Making this Dreck Up."

On the left was the site map. Zach clicked on "About Me." Under a photograph of a blue-eyed man with his hair pulled back, he read the first paragraph.

"In the first century AD, Agricola, the governor of Roman-occupied Britain, was instructed by the emperor to find a way to conquer the intractable peoples of Ireland. To that end, he gave asylum to Eithne, the exiled queen of a deposed Irish High King, and her son Túathal. Agricola offered the loan of a legion of Roman soldiers for an invasion on Túathal's behalf, but Eithne discovered his true plan was to arrest Túathal after the victory. In secrecy, she summoned her loyal bard, the Druid Seamus, whose name means "one who supplants." On her orders, Seamus killed Agricola, disposed of the body, and took his shape. From that day forward, Governor Agricola became a respected administrator and commander. Ireland was safe from Roman rule."

Zach thought this Seamus guy, at least, had an imagination. He closed the link and went back to the research he'd been working on before his battery conked out. He'd forgotten all about Kevin until his voice startled him.

"So what are you doing?"

"Research."

"On what?"

Zach pulled up one of the web pages he'd been reading on the plane. "Caitlin said the gossamer crown was stolen along with the Irish Crown Jewels, but there's no mention of it in any of the articles on the theft. She also said that just about everyone who touched the crown would get sick and die, so I traced each person reported or suspected to have come in contact with the jewels."

He heard the bedsprings squeak again as Kevin came up behind him. "Find anything?"

"Actually, yeah. The guy everyone figured stole the jewels was named Shackleton. He was the brother of the famous explorer. One of his acquaintances, who was considered a possible accomplice, was a passenger on the Titanic in 1912. He went down with the ship."

"I don't see the connection," Kevin said.

"That's because I haven't gotten to it." Zach tried not to sound as irritated as he felt. "So, there were a lot of court cases in the eighties and nineties about who has salvage rights to Titanic, right? I guess under international maritime law, you have to recover something from a wreck in order to have a claim to it. One of the salvage companies that originally filed a claim had to drop out because everyone involved died. The owner, his wife, the captain of the ship and about half the crew. All died of some mystery illness."

"What artifacts did they recover from the Titanic?"

"I don't know, but the name of the salvage ship was *The Gossamer*."

Chapter Thirteen

East of England

Caitlin gathered them all together with no apologies about skipping breakfast and herded them into the barn. Two Clydesdales watched placidly from their stalls as she headed for a late model SUV parked next to a stack of moldy-smelling hay bales.

"I call shotgun!" Lizbeth leaped over a pile of muck for the passenger door.

Kevin got into the back seat next to Zach, who filled Caitlin and Lizbeth in on what he'd discovered about Titanic and *The Gossamer* as they drove.

When he finished, Caitlin said, "Griffey."

"Yeah, that was his name. Brian Griffey. The guy who died on the Titanic," Zach said.

Caitlin's head dipped in acknowledgement. "He was a friend."

Kevin searched her profile for any hint of emotion, but it seemed carved out of ice. Whoever Griffey was, he'd been dead for nearly a century. If Caitlin had cared for him, time would have blunted the pain even if she were inclined to share it.

The quaint English countryside flew by as they headed for the coast. After about twenty minutes, Kevin saw the steel blue water of the North Sea slicing across the horizon. His stomach gave a little gurgle and he wasn't sure if it was from hunger or from the memory of his queasy summer at sea. As they got closer, buildings cropped up and got thicker, as did traffic. Caitlin seemed familiar with the route. She turned down one street after another until they reached a dockyard.

All around was evidence of the tsunami. Kevin didn't know what business-as-usual looked like in this district, but he doubted it involved so many boats dry-docked for repair or salvage.

Caitlin pulled up alongside a brick warehouse and shut off the engine. It didn't look to Kevin like an official parking place, but he doubted something like illegal parking would deter her. He and the others got out and followed as Caitlin wove her way through workers pushing loaded dollies, past helmeted welders, and around slowly moving forklifts. The air smelled of the sea and diesel exhaust with an undertone of fish.

Kevin spotted the drill vessel anchored out on the bay and wondered how they were going to get to it. Then he saw an ambulance halfway down the dock, pulled up next to a boat he recognized.

He pointed. "That's the outboard from the drill ship."

Two paramedics and another man, all with surgical masks over the lower half of their faces, carefully traversed a gangplank with someone strapped to a stretcher. As they got closer, he saw the mussed blonde hair of the Swedish researcher, Astrid. Her head tossed back and forth, and her cheeks were puffy and bright pink.

Caitlin stopped, her delicate features frozen – all but her eyes – which darted from the drill ship to the ambulance to Astrid. Her head turned and he followed her gaze, where just beyond the ambulance, a tall, dark-haired man in work pants and a plaid shirt stood on the dock talking with two men in business suits.

"That's Bill Masters," Kevin said. From Bill's angry face and quick gestures, the discussion with the official-looking men wasn't pleasant. Kevin started forward, but Caitlin stopped him.

He expected her to make him wait there as she barged over to introduce herself, but she said, "Find out how many are sick. Tell him to isolate the iridium."

Kevin didn't think Masters would listen to a student intern, but he nodded and started over. The nearest paramedic bent to lift the stretcher into the ambulance, and Kevin got a good look at Astrid. The whites of her eyes were blood-red. She suddenly surged up against her restraints. Her body twisted frantically, and she ignored the paramedic's entreaties to lie still, until she'd worked one arm free. Eyes wide, face cast in a terrible grimace, she pointed and made desperate, garbled sounds in her throat. Kevin thought for a moment that she was pointing at him, but he stepped aside to see that Caitlin was the target. Caitlin's chin lifted and she shook her head slowly. Astrid sank back onto the stretcher as if exhausted. Just before she was loaded into the ambulance, Kevin caught sight of the glisten of tears on her flushed cheeks.

Disturbed, he walked on, but when he approached the three men, they ignored him.

"It's not a bloody epidemic," Masters was saying. "It's just a flu bug."

"If it's flu, it's clearly virulent," said one of the other men. "She's the fourth one this week, and the first is on life support. Until we determine what this 'flu bug' is exactly, consider the ship quarantined."

The man slapped a handful of papers against Masters' chest. Kevin stood his ground as the men brushed past him. Masters glanced at the sheaf of papers in his hand and looked disgusted. The ambulance driver began backing up, and probably to encourage people to get out of the way, he turned on the siren. The sound was different, more plaintive than a siren in the states.

"What are you doing here, Guzman?" Masters asked. "Are you sick, too?"

"No," Kevin said. "How many *are* sick?"

"Is Weinstein with you?"

"No. You need to isolate the last core sample. Make sure no one touches it with their bare hands."

"You were there," Bill said, looking at Kevin strangely. "You know it was strict protocol to glove up around the core samples."

"How many are sick?" Kevin asked again.

"What do you care? And what are you doing here, kid? You flew back to Texas with Weinstein, didn't you?"

Masters just wasn't listening. He seemed to be almost deliberately avoiding Kevin's questions. Kevin turned to shrug in Caitlin's direction and found that she'd walked over.

She stopped a few feet from Masters and said, "William."

He looked mildly surprised, but only said, "Caitlin."

Chapter Fourteen

East of England, Suffolk County Coast

Lizbeth thought Bill Masters was the best-looking man she'd ever seen. His nose was a little too large and would have been patrician if not for a bump that sent it ever-so-slightly to the left. His lips were thin with a deep Cupid's bow and his eyes were plain brown under a wide forehead. Separately imperfect, his features came together in a fascinating whole.

It wasn't the way Caitlin and Bill looked at each other that hinted at more than a casual acquaintance. Caitlin had no discernable expression on her face, and Bill only had a faint wrinkle of consternation between his brows. It was the length of the stare, as if they'd each forgotten what the other looked like and got caught up in refamiliarizing themselves.

"They're a little young, aren't they?" he asked.

"Youth has advantages."

He glanced at Kevin and shook his head. "He was there the whole time."

"I warned you, and now look what you've set in motion."

"We got a sample, though. A little deeper and we could have gotten enough to make you a new crown."

"You must not aggravate the sphere any further."

Bill's eyebrows went up and he waved a handful of papers in Caitlin's face. "Don't have much choice. Idiotic authorities have quarantined the ship."

"Brilliant." Caitlin spun on her heel and walked away. Zach and Kevin moved to flank her, and Lizbeth scrambled to catch up. She took one last look over her shoulder at Bill Masters and caught his eye. He wasn't nearly as handsome with that calculating look on his face.

53

Caitlin might be small, but she walked fast. Zach, with his long legs, had no trouble keeping up, but Lizbeth and Kevin were almost forced to break into a trot.

They reached the SUV and Caitlin beeped the locks. After they got in, Kevin cleared his throat. "Is Bill…like us?"

Caitlin started the engine and shifted into reverse. "He'd like to be," she muttered.

"How do you know him?" Kevin asked.

She didn't respond right away, ostensibly in order to navigate a narrow section of road, but Lizbeth suspected she needed a moment to think.

"The information Zach found out about Titanic was correct," she finally said. "Brian Griffey recovered the crown from Shackleton. In fact, he was on his way to return it to me in America when Titanic sank. Unfortunately, many decades passed before technology advanced enough to plumb the depths to reach Titanic. When I first approached William, he was in charge of a deep-sea salvage vessel. I convinced him to take on the project."

Nothing in Caitlin's voice indicated the manner in which she'd convinced him but given the way they'd looked at each other on the dock, Lizbeth suspected she'd used the age-old enticement of feminine wiles.

"But you didn't find the crown," Lizbeth said.

"No. The litigation began and we received an order from the courts to desist. Even that wouldn't have stopped me, but I learned about *The Gossamer* when the news reported the deaths of the crew. It was obvious what killed those people, obvious the crown had been found. I investigated, but the trail was cold. By then Bill had knowledge of the crown's existence and became very – interested – in the properties of the biometal."

"He's acting like those scientists on his ship have the flu, but he knows they're going to die, doesn't he?" Lizbeth heard contempt in Kevin's voice. "That's what he meant when he said I was there the whole time. If he knew I was descended from a shapeshifter, he could have had me handle the iridium the drill ship recovered without anyone getting sick."

"There is no guarantee you would survive," Caitlin responded severely. "And do not judge him too harshly. If I thought his method would have succeeded, I, too, would have risked my life and that of those scientists to stop the sphere. Many more will die before this is done."

Lizbeth looked askance at Caitlin's profile, thinking about Bill Masters' motivation. Caitlin was beautiful and intelligent, powerful, and virtually immortal. Lizbeth doubted there were many men who wouldn't want a woman like that, or many who wouldn't want to have that power and immortality for themselves.

"Why didn't you just change into a dolphin, swim down to Titanic and get the crown yourself?" Zach asked.

"Dolphins can only dive to 300 meters. Titanic is much deeper."

"So, change into a deep-water fish or something," Zach said.

"We are oxygen breathers and are thus limited to the forms we can take. We may not change size, and we cannot become inanimate objects."

Lizbeth looked out the window where the sun had broken through the clouds. Three perfect rays beamed down on the rocky coastline. She thought about what Caitlin had said to Bill Masters, "Look what you've set in motion." The tsunami was the first disaster to have occurred, and it hit right after they drilled.

"Is everything that's happened because of Bill?" she asked.

"Drilling into the crater was certainly the catalyst, but the sphere has been struggling to receive messages for some time now. Climate changes caused by greenhouse gasses, space cluttered with orbiting satellites and junk, all have interfered." Caitlin paused. "It was inevitable."

Chapter Fifteen

East of England

When they arrived back at the farm, Caitlin pulled up in front of the house and dropped Zach and the others off, saying, "I'll be back later."

Simon appeared in the doorway. "Breakfast is almost ready."

"Thank you," Caitlin said, looking up at him.

"Where are you going?" Lizbeth asked.

"To dig deeper into the origins of the salvage ship that found the crown, *The Gossamer*. There must be something I missed. Maybe the crew members who survived can help, if I can locate any of them. Stay here and keep an eye out for each other."

As she walked back to the SUV, Zach looked around at the isolated plot of land and wondered where they would go, but then he got a whiff of bacon on the air and his mind shifted to the growling of his stomach.

He followed Lizbeth and Kevin inside. Simon went through a door off the murky living room, and Zach saw him pick up the receiver of an old-fashioned telephone before shutting the door.

The kitchen consisted of a long, narrow room with a windowed alcove that had a built-in bench and table. A dark-haired woman tended to the sizzling pans on the stove. She was short and very heavy, wearing a floral-print cotton dress, with furry mukluks on her feet that came up almost to her knees. She gave them a gap-toothed smile over her shoulder and bobbed her head up and down.

Kevin said something in another language and the woman's smile increased. She responded back, in what sounded to Zach like Russian or Polish, and gestured for them to sit at the table. Kevin took a stack of plates and a handful of silverware from her and set the table.

Everyone turned at the burst of music coming from Zach's pants pocket. He fished his cell phone out and saw the number – home. He went back into the living area and answered.

"Zach Wong! Where are you?"

"I'm fine, Mom. How is everyone?"

"Where? *Where* are you? We've been so worried."

Zach struggled briefly with the idea of lying. He didn't relish the thought of trying to explain why he'd abandoned his life to go on this crazy quest. He decided to go with a strictly limited version of the truth.

"I'm staying at a house in the country."

"Which country?" his mother asked. Zach had forgotten her uncanny ability to zero in on the facts.

"England," he said reluctantly.

After a silence in which he imagined his volatile mother's face going red with anger, she astonished him by saying, "I consulted the I Ching."

His mother was a woman of culture who avoided any discussion of her humble beginnings in a rural Chinese village. Confessing that she'd resorted to divination – frowned upon in educated circles as a practice of the peasantry – told him more than words how worried she'd been.

"Mom-"

"There is danger in whatever you are doing, my son. Do not trust anyone."

He thought again about Simon telling him that not everyone wanted the crown to be found.

"I'll be careful," he said.

"I've transferred some money into your account."

"Thanks."

"I want you to call me every day, do you hear me?"

"Alright."

"I love you. Be safe," she said. Before she rang off, she added, "The hexagrams were very clear. You have da zhuang - use it wisely."

Zach closed his cell just as Lizbeth called, "Eats on the table!"

He went back into the kitchen to see a table crowded with food. He sat and served himself a slice of toast, two soft-boiled eggs and four pieces of bacon.

"What's this?" he asked, pointing to an unfamiliar dish.

Kevin said, "Twaróg, Polish cheese, and that's Kielbasa, Polish sausage."

"So I take it our cook is Polish?"

"Her name is Werka. She's Simon's wife."

Zach's mouth was already full of egg and toast, so he smiled at Werka, who gave him a jaunty little wave from behind the refrigerator door. She brought a pitcher of milk to the table and said something to Kevin.

"Oh," he said. "Fresh from the cows this morning."

Zach looked askance at the milk and said, "I'm lactose intolerant."

Lizbeth called him a chicken and poured herself a glass. She took a swig and set the glass down with a satisfied, "Ahhh." A foamy white moustache coated her upper lip.

Zach took another bite of egg and toast, noticing that her lips were full, but not overly so. He thought she was very pretty. Her features and skin color suggested a mixed heritage. She looked up from her breakfast and caught him staring. He covered himself by saying, "You got a little something," and pointing to his own upper lip.

She grinned and didn't wipe it off. "Who was on the phone?"

"My mom."

"I take it from your tone you don't get along with her?"

He took another bite to avoid the question, but Lizbeth looked at him with her big brown eyes, obviously waiting for an answer. He finished chewing and said, "She's – a character."

"Really." It wasn't a question. "I doubt she's worse than my granma."

"Why's that?"

Lizbeth reached into her shirt and pulled out a leather cord tied to a small cloth bag with a peacock feather sticking out of the top.

"Granma made this for me. It's a voodoo wanga, a magical fetish. For protection."

Zach laughed. "Voodoo, huh? That's strange."

"You have no idea."

"Yeah, well, my mom's into the Chinese occult. Apparently, I have da zhuang."

"What's that mean?" Lizbeth asked.

Zach looked at Kevin, who obliged by answering, "Great power."

Chapter Sixteen

East of England

Kevin cleared the table and offered to help Werka wash dishes.

"Thank you, but no," she said in Polish. "The kitchen is barely big enough for me. Why don't you and your friends go for a walk? There used to be a church on the other side of the woods, you can still see bits of the foundation. Simon's grandfather told him it burnt down in the seventeenth century."

"Really? Okay, thanks." Although his major was geology, Kevin was also fascinated by archaeology and paleontology and—anything really—to do with the earth.

He told the others about the church. They agreed to go, but Zach said, "Nothing better to do until Caitlin gets back."

Werka let them out the back door and pointed beyond her well-tended garden and another green meadow to a stand of huge oak trees, whose leaves were just beginning to turn yellow in the cooler autumn weather. Zach, with his long legs, walked ahead, leaving Kevin content to keep Lizbeth company.

An unseen bird warbled plaintively, and as they got closer to the oaks, a fat grey squirrel shot down a tree trunk on the edge of the wood and scooted up another. Lizbeth took a deep breath of the fresh country air and said, "It's beautiful out here."

In the shade under the thick canopy of leaves, the ankle-length grass thinned out and was replaced by packed dirt crisscrossed by the thick, gnarly roots of the old trees. Kevin's eyes quickly adjusted to the darkness. The air was cooler here and the atmosphere quite gloomy, in stark contrast to the golden day they'd left behind in the meadow. Kevin saw Zach up ahead springing from root to root in long, graceful leaps. When Zach reached the far side of the stand of oaks he turned, his black hair gleaming in the sunshine, and called, "Here it is!"

"Careful through here." Kevin grasped Lizbeth's elbow to help her over a section of roots with black voids underneath, like the extensive warren of some family of wild animals. Once they were back in the light of day, he saw her cast a strange look behind her.

"It got spooky in there, huh?" he asked.

She nodded.

There wasn't much left of the foundation of the old church, just a flat stretch of ground overgrown with weeds and four weather-worn stones, none higher than Kevin's knee, marking the structure's corners.

"There's a stream down there," Zach said, pointing to what would have been the south side of the churchyard. "Hear the frogs?"

Once again Zach walked ahead, followed by Lizbeth. Kevin dawdled behind, eyeing the closest cornerstone. There was nothing remarkable about the stone, but there was something about this place that made him uneasy. He had that feeling he always got when something was about to happen.

Reluctantly, he left the foundation of the old church. Up ahead, Zach squatted on the shore of a rocky, fast-flowing stream. Lizbeth stood halfway between the church and the water, staring intently at the ground beneath her feet. Kevin stopped next to her and asked, "What's up?"

She met his eyes and shook her head, but he didn't need to hear the words. He *felt* it, something in the ground, something buried here.

"Zach!" he called. Zach looked up from whatever he'd been doing by the stream. Kevin waved him over.

"Stupid frog," Zach said when he reached them. He brushed fastidiously at a line of moisture on his jeans. "This is my only pair of pants and he peed all over them."

Kevin ignored him. He knelt down and ran his hands over the grass. "There's a mound here." He grasped a handful of sod and tugged until the roots let go of the sandy soil. "Help me."

Zach found a heavy stick and began digging at the dirt in the areas Kevin uncovered. Lizbeth stepped back and watched, arms crossed. The layer of soil covering the object was only a few inches deep. After several minutes of excavating, Kevin brushed the remaining dirt away and they all stared.

A flat slab of stone lay flush with the ground. He touched the dark slate and ran his fingers across an ornate inscription.

"Can you read it?" Lizbeth asked.

Kevin nodded. "It says, 'Here lies Mr. Richard Allen, who died the year 1656.'"

Lizbeth frowned and looked all around her. "This is a graveyard?"

"Cool," Zach said.

From his vantage point kneeling by the gravestone, Kevin picked out several more slight mounds in the grass nearby. In fact, it looked as if they'd trod over quite a few on the way to the creek without even noticing.

"Don't you feel it?" he asked Zach.

"Feel what?"

Kevin stood up and gestured to the gravestone. "Stand on it."

Zach's eyebrows went up, but he stepped on Mr. Richard Allen's last resting place and looked at the cracked stone between his feet. After a moment, he raised his head and said, "Feels like Caitlin."

"That's it!" Lizbeth said. "That's the exact feeling I get around Caitlin. Sort of a hair-sticking-up-on-the-back-of-my-neck sensation."

Kevin straightened and brushed the dirt from his pants. "I think you're right. But if we all have the 'ancient blood,' why don't we feel it when we're around each other?"

"Probably because like Caitlin said – it's diluted in us." Zach shrugged.

"So what does that make Richard Allen?" Kevin asked.

Lizbeth looked down at the dark stone. "He must have been a shapeshifter, too. Like Caitlin."

Chapter Seventeen

East of England

Looking down at the final resting place of someone who could very well have been one of her ancestors, Lizbeth fought against an unexpected rush of tears. She wasn't sad for poor Mr. Richard Allen, who'd been gone for centuries and was probably nothing more than dust and bones. It was Caitlin she thought of. Caitlin, who was at least one hundred-years-old. In the ground before them was evidence of a shapeshifter's mortality. How long had Mr. Richard Allen been alive, and what eventually killed him? Up until now, Caitlin had seemed invincible. Distressed, Lizbeth took a few steps away from Zach and Kevin so they wouldn't see her blubbering about a woman she didn't even like. Luckily, they were busy placing the clumps of sod back on the grave so it wouldn't seem as if they'd desecrated it.

She looked through the trees towards the house and saw Simon approaching on horseback, his chestnut Clydesdale lifting its large white hooves high in an animated trot. The big beast didn't seem to be laboring under Simon's bulk, but the horse-to-rider ratio resembled that of a normal-sized man riding a Mexican burro. The way Simon was waving his arm seemed urgent, so she said, "Hey," and was pleased when her voice didn't give away her melancholy. "I think we should go back."

They met Simon at the edge of the oaks. He began tossing their luggage from the back of the Clydesdale. Zach intercepted his backpack with the laptop inside before it left Simon's hand.

"You must leave, and quickly," Simon said. "Caitlin has been taken and it won't be long before they come here. I have no vehicle for you, and everything on my farm has to appear normal, so I won't risk sending you on horseback. Don't draw attention to yourselves-"

"What are you talking about?" Zach interrupted.

"Go back the way you came," Simon continued as if Zach hadn't spoken. "Follow the creek upstream for two kilometers. You'll see a road. Stay off it! Just keep it in sight and walk downhill into town. The very first building you find will be a tavern. Tell the owner I sent you, but don't stay long. You're safest in London where you can hide in plain sight."

He turned the Clydesdale back towards the house. Over his shoulder, he called, "Don't use credit cards. Don't call home. *Go!*"

Lizbeth watched as he urged his horse into a trot and left them standing there, shell-shocked and open-mouthed.

"Are you freaking kidding me?" Zach said. "Is this some kind of joke?"

Kevin hefted his knapsack onto his back and picked up one of Lizbeth's bags. "You heard the big man, let's go."

Lizbeth thanked Kevin. She had the most luggage of any of them and felt bad about it, but if they were to disappear, she couldn't leave anything behind.

She and Kevin entered the stand of oaks again, leaving Zach spluttering behind them. "What did he mean, Caitlin's been taken?"

Lizbeth said, "Stuff it, Zach. Come on. We'll ask the tavern owner." She spoke matter-of-factly, but only to hide her fear.

After walking for a few minutes, Kevin said, "I was just thinking about her when Simon showed up."

"Me, too."

"Um, you guys," Zach said from behind them. They'd just reached the part of the woods where the roots were difficult to navigate. Lizbeth didn't want to take her eyes off the treacherous ground, but she heard the distinct sound of a bird's wings flapping. She glanced around.

A raven had perched on Zach's head. "Little help here?" he said.

Lizbeth couldn't help it; he looked so comical she laughed. Kevin started back to help him, and Zach said, "Yeah, laugh it up. This is the only shirt I've got and if my feathered friend here decides to crap on me..."

"Won't hit your shirt," Kevin said. "He's aiming for the part in your hair."

Lizbeth pressed her lips together to banish her smile. She cleared her throat and said seriously, "Knock it off. The bird, that is, off his head. We have to get moving."

Kevin set the bags down, jumped up and down and waved his hands in front of Zach's face, yelling, "Augh!"

The sleek black bird tilted its head and regarded Kevin with one eye.

"Are its claws tangled in your hair?" he asked.

"No! I tried to get it off as soon as it landed on me, but it just kept coming back."

"Its eyes are blue," Lizbeth said. "Is that normal for a raven?"

"How should I know?" Zach bent forward at the waist and shook his head. The bird flapped its wings but lifted up only a couple of inches and settled on Zach's bent back.

She stepped closer. "Go away," she whispered. The bird looked at her. Then, for no reason she could name, Lizbeth asked, "Did Caitlin send you?"

She didn't really expect the bird to respond and wasn't disappointed when it didn't.

"That's it," Zach said. "I didn't want to hurt you, bird-brain, but – no more Mr. Nice."

He spun around so fast that, to Lizbeth, his body seemed to blur. His hand connected with a dull thwap, and the bird let out an outraged "Caw!" and flew awkwardly to a nearby branch. Zach straightened up and said, "And don't come back."

Chapter Eighteen

East of England

They'd followed Simon's directions and found the one-lane road but hiking through the thick scrub alongside it slowed them considerably. Zach's laptop seemed to get heavier the further they went, and he'd taken the bag Lizbeth had been carrying as well. The back of his shirt was soaked with sweat and the deodorant he'd borrowed from Kevin that morning had been unable to combat two days with no shower. He took the rear of the procession so the others wouldn't get a whiff. The raven with a crush on him had followed them the whole way, cawing from the trees, but at least it hadn't tried to land on him again.

"No one's driven by for the last fifteen minutes," he said. "Let's walk on the road."

Lizbeth turned to him, her brown curls stuck to her forehead in the heat of the day. "Simon said not to."

"Oh, and you always do what Simon says," he muttered.

"Look!" Kevin pointed up ahead. "There's a building."

The small one-story structure set back from the road had a pink neon sign in its front window that read, "Beer, Wine & Spirits." A lone car was parked in the gravel out front.

When Zach walked into the dark establishment and saw the scowl on the face of the man behind the bar, he halfway expected to get challenged for his I.D.

The scowl wasn't for them, however. The man was watching a small television on the bar and shaking his head. "Bleedin' volcanoes going off all along the ring of fire in the Pacific. Brutal."

"Are you the proprietor?" Lizbeth asked.

The man nodded. He switched off the television and reached behind him into a glass-fronted refrigerator. It was hard to tell from the other side of the bar, but it looked to Zach like he was even shorter than Kevin. He had greasy white hair pulled into a ponytail and a long, pointed grey beard. His green flannel shirt was covered by a scarred leather apron. If Santa were a diminutive biker, he might look a little like this guy. "Name's Len," he said in an Irish brogue. "Yer late."

Zach gratefully took the bottle of soda Len held out to him, noting how small his wizened little hands were. "We had some trouble with a raven, of all things."

Len chuckled and then he surprised Zach by stepping down off something behind the bar and disappearing entirely from view. When he walked out from the far end, Zach saw that he was not just shorter than Kevin, who was maybe 5'4" or so, he was a little person.

"We're off, now, to London-town," Len said, with a bit of singsong. He went to the front window and flipped a switch. The neon sign flickered and went out. He opened the front door, they all trooped out obediently, and he locked it behind them.

As soon as he stepped into the sunshine, a black streak left the roof of the building and settled on his shoulder. Len pulled half a bagel from his pocket and gave it to the bird, which immediately flew off with it.

"This I sat engaged in guessing, but no syllable expressing," Len recited. "To the fowl whose fiery eyes now burned into my bosom's core; Quoth the raven, 'Nevermore.'"

"Edgar Allen Poe," Kevin said.

Len nodded. "Caw would'a left you alone if you'd just given him a bit o' somethin' to eat."

"We'll remember that next time," Zach said.

"In you go." Len gestured to the parked car, a red Mini Cooper. "Put your things in the boot."

The "boot" turned out to be a narrow trunk area at the back of the little car, too small to hold more than Lizbeth's things. Kevin and Lizbeth got into the back, Kevin with his duffle bag in his lap. Zach bent nearly double and squeezed into the passenger seat, trying not to make a fuss about the fit so he wouldn't insult Len. Although he couldn't very well hide the fact that the backpack resting on his knees was only inches from his chin.

The car was specially fitted with a booster seat, extensions on the gas pedal, brake, gearshift and clutch. Len hopped in and said, "Now you know how they get so many clowns in those little circus cars."

Once they'd travelled through the quiet little town and gotten onto the highway, Lizbeth said, "Mr. Len, sir? May I ask you some questions?"

"For certain, you can. Caitlin's not much of a talker, is she? Simon's no better."

"That's an understatement," Zach said.

"And you've got a bit of a smart mouth on ya," Len said. "I like it. But you also smell to high heaven, which I don't like. Roll down yer window."

Embarrassed, Zach did as he was told.

"Now go on with ya, Miss," Len said.

"First of all, who's got Caitlin?" Lizbeth asked.

"Well, the police, who else?" Len said. "And don't you believe none of those trumped-up charges, either. Caitlin's many things, but she's no international terrorist."

Chapter Nineteen

London

By the time they reached the outskirts of the city, Kevin was convinced that Len was the most talkative person he'd ever met. He now had working knowledge of how to raise a raven from an egg, how to mix a really "sound" alcoholic drink and how to pick the right dog in a greyhound race.

What he didn't know was what they were supposed to do once they got to London.

"Where exactly are we going?" he asked.

"London," Len said, like he was talking to a half-wit.

"Right, but to a hotel, or where?"

Len straightened his shoulders, and Kevin got another glimpse of the tattoo on the back of his neck. The stylistic curlicues coming out from under Len's ponytail looked a bit like wings.

"Fact is," Len said, "I don't want to know where you end up. It's best if I can't answer, were the police to ask."

"Where's the jail?" Lizbeth asked.

Len produced a raspy laugh. "Don't go there. Caitlin won't be detained long, you can be sure of that. Find yourselves a safe hideaway and wait for her. She'll find you."

Ten minutes later, he dropped them off on the corner of a busy street.

"Stay off the radar," he said. "You'll be fine."

"Thank you," Lizbeth said. They waved as he drove off.

For a moment, they all stood there, looking around at the shops, the people and the noisy vehicles driving by. It was business as usual here, as if the recent disasters both close to home and far away had never happened.

68

Zach broke the silence. "Who's got money? We need to eat and find a place to sleep."

Kevin pulled the change from his pocket. "I've got about three American dollars in coins."

Lizbeth shook her head. "I'm broke. Granma told me I wouldn't need any money."

Zach displayed a debit card. "My mom said she was transferring some to my account, but Simon told us not to use it."

"I'm not sleeping on the street," Lizbeth said with a little wobble in her voice. "My mom and I spent weeks in a shelter after Katrina, and I'd rather sleep with the skunks at the zoo."

"If I don't get a shower soon, you'll get your wish," Zach said, with a smile. Kevin thought he noticed something unsaid pass between Zach and Lizbeth, and he felt a twinge of what? Jealousy? Sure, Lizbeth was cute, but now wasn't the time to think about romance. He tried to shake the feeling off.

"Alright, people," he said. "Ideas?"

Zach's face was blank, but Lizbeth's went through a quick gamut of emotions; first worry, then upset, then determination.

"I'll take care of it," she said. A moment later, she slipped into the crowd.

"Um…is she coming back or are we supposed to follow her?" Zach asked.

Kevin watched Lizbeth's slim form weave through and around people. Normally graceful, she seemed to bump into just about every other person she passed, flashing her bright smile in apology.

"Hang on. Remember on the plane she said she could do stuff? I think she's doing it right now."

Zach frowned. "You think she's robbing people?"

A woman pushing a baby carriage looked up. Kevin elbowed Zach in the ribs and hissed, "Shut up. You want the world to know?"

Zach lowered his voice. "Is that what she's doing? Because getting arrested isn't a very good way to lie low."

Kevin spotted Lizbeth on her way back up the street. She looked calm and unconcerned, and didn't bump a soul. "I don't think she's going to get caught."

When she joined them, her first words were, "Get moving." Kevin and Zach turned and walked alongside her. After three blocks, she led them to a small park in between two skyscrapers and they sat on a bench. She pulled three men's wallets from her pocket and quickly removed the bills.

"Anyone know how much this is?"

Kevin took the cash and counted it. "It's enough to feed us and get a room, assuming we can find a decent one that won't ask for a credit card."

Zach stood, shoved his hands in his pockets and faced Lizbeth. "You do this all the time? Are you some kind of professional pick-pocket?"

She surprised Kevin with the ferocity of her response, leaping up with a pugnacious look and pushing at Zach, who didn't move. "No, I don't do this all the time! I never do it. It's wrong and I know it, and I feel like crap about it, but what else was I supposed to do? We're supposed to save the friggin' world, remember? A little hard to do without Caitlin."

Kevin heard the break in her voice when she said Caitlin's name. She turned away and her shoulders slumped. He started to get up, but Zach waved him off and tentatively put his arm around her shoulders. Kevin heard him murmur something, but he couldn't make it out and didn't want to. The whole scene seemed too intimate suddenly and he shifted uncomfortably on the bench. He was so discomfited, in fact, that it almost felt like that old "something's wrong" sensation.

He looked around. A group of teens sat on a grassy landscaped hill. A man walked by with five well-mannered dogs on leashes, each a different breed. On the main sidewalk, the woman who'd been pushing her baby stood talking to a uniformed police officer. She pointed at Lizbeth and the officer turned.

"Um, guys," Kevin said. "Heads up. We're in trouble."

Chapter Twenty

London

At Kevin's warning, Lizbeth took a seemingly casual step back from Zach. The residual scent of his deodorant had been vastly overpowered by the pungency of his body odor. She'd gamely ignored it while he offered her comfort, mostly because of the unexpected feelings she experienced in his loose embrace. Now was not the time to examine those feelings, however.

She raised an arm and casually flipped her hair, surreptitiously taking in the police officer and the woman, who were both looking their way. The three stolen wallets were quickly tucked away in the satchel she used as a purse. She swung it to the ground next to the jumble of their luggage.

"It's nothing to worry about. She wasn't one of my marks."

"Yes, but she heard Big Mouth here," Kevin tilted his head towards Zach, "say that you were off robbing people."

Lizbeth tossed Zach an irritated look, but then produced a careless, tinkling laugh. She stepped in front of Kevin and with her arms behind her back, waved at him to hide the money, which he still held in a limp grasp on his lap.

"You guys are so funny," she said loud enough for the approaching police officer to hear. "Let's find our hotel so we have time to see the Changing of the Guard."

"I'm afraid you've missed it, Miss," the police officer said by way of greeting.

Lizbeth gave the young officer her most disarming smile. "Have we? What time does it usually occur?"

"It's best to get there by eleven in the morning if you want a good spot. You're American. Is that what you lot are doing – sightseeing?"

"Mm-hm." Trying to react as normally as possible, she allowed her enthusiastic façade to fade as the officer dropped his eyes and examined their luggage. Kevin and Zach didn't seem eager to contribute, and Lizbeth had no idea what to say if the officer probed any deeper.

Her brows lifted in quizzical innocence. "Is something wrong?"

"May I see your identification?" the officer asked.

Lizbeth blanched, but tried to cover it with a cough. She lifted her satchel and rummaged inside, keeping the opening away from the officer's prying eyes. There were now four wallets inside the cluttered denim bag, and she squelched a burst of panic as her hand encountered one after the other before finally settling on her own, larger wallet. She produced it with a flourish and murmured something inane about Mary Poppins' bottomless bag. Thankfully, the officer laughed.

She handed him her driver's license, confidence returning. This was a routine exchange. That woman may have overheard Zach say something *gallingly stupid*, but Lizbeth doubted the officer had cause to search them further. Assuming things worked here abroad as they worked on American television, that is.

The officer looked at the license. Something about the way his face froze, and his eyes flicked up to her face made her unease rush back.

"Excuse me," the officer said. His steps were crisply militaristic, all business, and they took him far enough away that she didn't hear what he said into his radio.

Lizbeth wished she had Caitlin's knack of seemingly reading minds, because it sure would come in handy right now. Why had her license caused the officer to call in? *Not the license*, she thought in sudden comprehension. *My name*. If Caitlin was under arrest for terrorism, the authorities surely knew who she'd traveled with.

"This is not good," Kevin said quietly.

Zach replied without moving his mouth. "If he asks for our I.D.'s, too, I want you both to run. I'll take care of him."

"What?" Lizbeth whispered frantically. "You can't assault a cop! And where are we supposed to run to? What about our luggage?"

Zach's face was expressionless. "Just do it."

She knew he was right. Len had assured them that Caitlin wouldn't be in jail for long. Lizbeth had gotten the distinct impression that her freedom would not be facilitated by a lawyer. She doubted Caitlin would be in a position to help if the three of them got arrested, too. With shaking hands, she lifted the strap of her satchel over her head, pulled it across her chest and adjusted the bag in the small of her back. Luckily, she had her runners on. She bounced unconsciously on the balls of her feet.

The officer fastened his radio back on his belt. Before he got within earshot, Kevin said, "Back the way we came, behind the movie theater." Zach nodded.

"Here you are, Miss," the officer said. He held out her license. She tucked it into the pocket of her jeans.

"Alright then. Go about your business." The officer nodded and walked away. Lizbeth let her breath out in a rush of air. She hadn't realized she'd been holding it.

"Does anyone else sense there's more to it than that?" Kevin asked.

Lizbeth grasped the handle of her rolling suitcase and tilted it for an easy getaway. "Let's make ourselves scarce."

Zach put his arms through the straps of his backpack and picked up one of her bags. She noticed a wry twist of his lips and suspected he was disappointed that there hadn't been a fight.

"Where to?" she asked, looking down the sidewalk. People were slightly thinner on the ground now and she figured the lunch crowd was making its way back to work. Two men in uniform just rounding the corner caught her eye. They were walking and talking casually, but she said, "Guys?"

"I see them," Zach said.

Kevin relaxed his grip on the suitcase he'd been about to pick up. "Two more coming from the opposite way."

Lizbeth swung around and met the eyes of the officer who'd stopped them. He stood maybe twenty yards away with his hand on his belt.

"The little weasel was calling reinforcements," she said.

Chapter Twenty-one

London

Zach set Lizbeth's bag down and unzipped it. He selected the first item of clothing that came to hand, a white cotton button-down shirt.

"What are you doing?" Lizbeth snapped.

"When I say 'now,' run into that building," he replied, nodding to the closer of the two high rises. "Do not stop running. They won't shoot with all these people around, even if they say they're going to. Head for the back entrance. I'll be right behind you."

Lizbeth had been right to remind him what a bad idea it would be to assault a police officer. They were in trouble, but as long as Zach did nothing to compound it, the authorities would have to let them go once they realized they weren't terrorists. Assuming they got caught. The furthest officers could potentially be avoided, but the one who'd radioed in was too close. Zach needed to slow him down – nonviolently.

He held the shirt against his chest and quickly folded it in a specific sequence until he held a tight wad of material in his right hand. The other officers were closing in, and the first one, thank goodness he was young and clearly inexperienced, seemed to gain confidence from their proximity. Zach watched him straighten his shoulders and start towards them.

"Now!"

Lizbeth immediately outpaced Kevin as they sprinted for the high rise. Two strides into his own flight, Zach took aim and hurled his missile, the folded shirt, at the first officer. The shirt flew straight into the officer's face and when it hit, it burst open and covered his head and shoulders. Zach raced past. Behind them, the officers shouted "Stop!" Ahead, Lizbeth opened the mirrored glass door and held it for

Kevin. Just before Zach reached her, she ducked in. Zach bolted through the narrow opening before the door closed.

Inside, the high-ceilinged lobby had a great, curved information desk with a lone occupant standing open-mouthed behind it. There were only two choices, right or left, and Kevin had gone right. As soon as Zach rounded the corner, sneakers squeaking on the marble floors, he realized it was the wrong choice. Ahead of them was a bank of elevators on one side and a door with the universal symbols for a unisex bathroom on the other, but nothing else. No back door.

Several people waiting for the elevator swiveled their heads as the three of them charged up and were stopped cold. Zach heard the officers shouting again, presumably asking the information desk clerk which way they'd gone. The elevator dinged and Lizbeth looked like she was going to shove her way onto it, but Zach herded them into the bathroom instead. Luckily, the open room, with its one handicapped-friendly toilet, was unoccupied, and it had a lock.

"Oh, great!" Lizbeth burst out. "This is your big plan? To lock ourselves into the bathroom until they find the key and capture us?"

Zach inspected the room. There were two white plastic grates in the ceiling, both too small for a human body. The floor was covered with black and white tiles slanting slightly to a drain in the middle. The walls were painted glossy white. He tapped the back wall and smiled grimly. Wallboard.

The door handle rattled as someone from the outside attempted to open it. A moment later, a man's voice shouted, "Come out with your hands in the air!"

"That's not going to happen," Zach muttered as he eyed the back wall. Extending his arms, he relaxed his body and mind into a calm state as he focused his concentration on the target. His arms crossed briefly before coming in as fists and he stepped forward onto his left leg. Swift and sure, he performed a basic sidekick, feeling his internal power flow freely through his leg and out his right foot as it connected with the wall. Six kicks produced a good-sized hole in the first layer of wallboard between two studs. Six more kicks opened the far side.

Light from the room next to them shone through a cloud of white dust. Lizbeth didn't wait for an invitation. She ducked through the hole. Zach gestured that Kevin go next and then he followed suit.

The room was large, with a long conference table occupied by about twenty businesspeople with surprised faces.

"I say…" began a white-haired man standing authoritatively at the foot of the table. He waved the pointer he held in a vague circle.

"Pardon us," Lizbeth said, scooting past the nearest chairs and heading for the wall of windows. The door onto a terraced patio opened easily and they exited. There were no police in sight, but they ran down a set of concrete stairs and kept going, through alleys and around buildings until Zach deemed it safe enough to slow down. He knew that three people running hell-bent through London would attract more attention than three people walking as if they had a destination and a deadline.

"Where to now?" he asked, brushing at a coating of wallboard dust on his shirt.

The street they were on now was no less busy with people and traffic than the ones before. Lizbeth stepped into the street, raised her hand and pierced the background noise with a long, sharp whistle. A black taxi responded by changing lanes and stopping abruptly before them.

They piled into the back seat and the cabbie turned with a smile and asked, "'Ave you got an address for me?"

Zach's mind was blank. He turned to Lizbeth; whose face had the beginnings of a panicked look on it.

Then Kevin spoke up, in a perfect imitation of an English accent, "That's a bit tricky. We've been separated from our party. Supposed to have met up at the cruise terminal."

"Oh, Tilbury, is it?" the cabbie asked.

"Yes," Kevin said.

Zach took his backpack off and sat back against the seat as the taxi merged into traffic. He had no idea where they were going, but it seemed Kevin did. They couldn't very well discuss it in front of the cabbie, so he closed his eyes and hoped Kevin's plan was a good one.

Chapter Twenty-two

London

Kevin hadn't had time to play tourist the last time he'd been here, but he knew about the international cruise port, and when the cabbie had asked where they were going, it was the only destination that popped into his head. After sitting next to the malodorous Zach for the last twenty minutes, however, he changed his mind.

"Sir?" he asked in his borrowed accent. "Isn't there a shopping center near the cruise terminal?"

"There is."

"Would you drop us there instead?"

"Anything you say, mate. Mind if I turn on the radio? Last I heard, the Chunnel's been closed. Leaks, you know, from all these blasted little earthquakes popping up in strange places, now that the whole world's gone anti-clockwise."

"Sure," Kevin said, wondering what a 'chunnel' was.

The cabbie turned on his radio and tuned it to a news station. Len had mentioned something about volcanoes, and now Kevin and the others were treated to a sobering account of just how bad it really was.

The female announcer said, "Normally, tectonic plate movement over the course of a year is measured in centimeters, but geologists say the latest satellite measurements of the Pacific Plate show that it has moved almost a meter in the last week alone. Earthquakes have literally been too numerous to count, but there have been more than seventy volcanic eruptions along the ring of fire in the last twenty-four hours, more than would normally occur in a month, with hundreds more volcanoes showing signs of activity. Now word has come in that even volcanoes considered long extinct are reawakening. Authorities in the U.S., Canada, the Philippines, Mexico, Indonesia – indeed, most of the affected countries –

are calling for mass evacuation in some coastal areas. Ash clouds are interfering with air travel and causing health hazards. Damage has been immeasurable, with whole towns lost, and the death toll–"

The cabbie switched the channel then, muttering something about finding local news. Kevin met Zach's eyes and then Lizbeth's. As Caitlin had warned, the situation was getting worse. He set his jaw, grimly determined to find a way to help, with or without Caitlin.

Not long after, the cabbie announced that they'd reached the shopping center. "I'll drop you here on the pavement."

The building that housed the mall had a tall, windowed central structure over the front entrance. As soon as Kevin paid the driver and they exited the cab, Lizbeth asked, "Why did you tell him to come here?"

"Where else are we going to go?" Kevin asked. "At least we can buy what we need now that our luggage is gone."

Lizbeth made a beeline for a door on the left, framed with the familiar golden arches of a McDonalds. Once they'd eaten, they wandered into the indoor mall. The store names were mostly unfamiliar. Kevin pointed to what looked like a department store, a place called Marks & Spencer.

As soon as they stepped inside, a saleswoman approached.

"May I help you?"

"Um, pants?" Zach said.

"Blokes or ladies?"

"For me."

She led the way up the aisle and after a few turns, pointed to the men's underwear section. Zach started to correct her, but Kevin interrupted with a quick, "Thanks."

After the saleswoman was out of earshot, he said, "Things are different here, dude. 'Pants' probably means 'underpants.' Besides, I'm guessing you could use a fresh set of drawers."

They selected socks and underwear for Zach, and after a short discussion, decided each of them needed a new shirt. The police would have confiscated their luggage; therefore any description of the three fugitives released to the media would include their current attire. As Kevin was making the purchase with the stolen cash, Lizbeth took off. She returned moments later to set a stick of deodorant on the counter. She and Kevin changed into their shirts and waited on a wooden bench while Zach escaped to the men's room to wash up in the sink and change.

Kevin watched her face as a wet-haired, fresh-smelling Zach emerged in his new blue, long-sleeved shirt, appearing confident and, not that Kevin spent a lot of time evaluating other guys' looks, handsome. There was a softness around Lizbeth's eyes when she looked at Zach that reinforced Kevin's suspicion that something was developing between his two companions.

Zach said, "I guess we should look for a hotel and hide out until Caitlin finds us."

"How?" Lizbeth asked. "Hotels need I.D. and credit cards, right?"

Kevin thought back to the beginning of summer, when he'd first arrived. He'd spent less than twenty-four hours in England before he'd boarded the drilling vessel. Dr. Weinstein had checked into the hotel for them, so he had no frame of reference to offer advice. Then something occurred to him.

"I know where we could stay. Getting there might be a problem, but I'm sure he'd put us up."

Lizbeth looked relieved. "Where?"

"On the drilling vessel."

Zach and Lizbeth said in unison, "What?"

"Bill Masters is looking for someone to work the iridium, and we need a place to hide out."

"Great idea." Zach's tone said the opposite.

"I think that's the last place Caitlin would want us to go," Lizbeth said.

Kevin snorted. "Even if we do manage to find a safe place to stay, are we really going to wait for Caitlin to somehow break out of jail and find us before the police do? And before the gossamer sphere destroys the world?"

"Nice speech," Zach said. "I agree with you, though. We should take some kind of action instead of hiding like cowards, but I'm not going to walk up to Caitlin's *enemy* and ask him for help."

"If they worked together looking for the crown, then they weren't always enemies." Kevin looked out at the passing shoppers. No one seemed to be paying them any attention. "What do *you* think we should do?"

"We need to find survivors from *The Gossamer*, the ship that salvaged the crown from Titanic. Time is running out. We need to find that crown."

"And do what with it without Caitlin?" Lizbeth asked. "We don't even know what it's for. No. Caitlin was looking for the survivors when she got arrested. Maybe the police set a trap for her."

"Come *on.* She dropped us off at Simon's and he told us to run like an hour later. How long do you think it took the cops to catch her? She didn't have time to find any of the survivors." Zach stood and swung his backpack, bulkier now with the addition of his soiled clothes, onto his back. "If we can't get a hotel, let's at least find an Internet café. I need a connection."

He said it like he needed a fix, and Kevin smiled.

The mall was huge and the directory confusing, since the first floor to Brits was the second floor to Americans and on up. Still, it didn't take them long to find a cybercafé. There weren't many patrons, so they had their pick of tables. Zach chose a secluded spot near the back and sat with his back to a faux brick wall.

Kevin escorted Lizbeth to the counter to order coffee and scones, leaving Zach to boot up his laptop. When they got back to the table, Zach was hunched intently over his keyboard, rapidly tapping. Lizbeth sat next to him and scooted her chair close to look at the screen.

"Whatcha doin'?" she asked.

"Not having much luck, that's for sure. Can't find anything else about *The Gossamer* or her crew."

Kevin said, "If they all died from contact with the crown, maybe you could search for the symptoms."

Zach glanced up briefly. "We don't know what the symptoms are, do we?"

"Fever, agitation, flushed skin, bleeding conjunctiva," Lizbeth supplied. When Zach gave her a look, she shrugged and said, "What? You saw that lady scientist."

Zach twisted his lips but began typing again. "Okay, here. Looks like we have Ebola or Dengue Fever."

"Try searching for the symptoms plus the word shapeshifter," Kevin said.

Zach's expressive face told him what he thought of that suggestion, but he tapped the keys, waited a second and said, "Hm, that's weird."

Lizbeth leaned closer, and Kevin noticed their shoulders were now touching.

"What?" she asked.

From across the table, Kevin couldn't see what Zach was pointing at on the screen, so he got up and came around.

"I just looked at this website this morning," Zach said, clicking on the link.

When the site loaded, Lizbeth said, "Seamus the Bard, huh? Oh, look! What's this? Click on 'The First Shapeshifters.'"

Zach obliged, and a long block of text appeared, with illustrations in the border that looked like woodcut prints from a classic fairy tale storybook. Lizbeth read aloud in her soft voice:

"Wyn of the Grove was a young queen who ruled a minor clan in the land that would come to be called Ireland. Just outside the Grove's border was an abandoned mine, feared by all. Legend had it that a deadly affliction struck any who extracted the ore. The old mine had become lair to a vicious wild boar with blood-red eyes and tusks the size of a man's forearm. The boar had encroached upon the Grove, so Aedn, the clan's bravest warrior, requested permission from the queen to subdue it. Although the beast attacked in an erratic, agitated manner, the fight was long and fierce, and Aedn lost two of his finest hounds. Just as the monster gored Aedn in the leg, the warrior defeated it with a spear-thrust down through the heart. That night, the queen's household feasted on succulent wild boar.

"Tadg the Small convinced his queen if the boar could live in the mine, the danger was only superstition. She agreed to let him lead a group to scout it for workable veins. When the party returned with reports of great wealth to be had, elation soon turned to sorrow. Six of the ten men who'd gone to the mine grew gravely ill. At first, they thought the boar meat had been tainted, but none of the sick men ate at the queen's table. The clan shaman concluded from their symptoms that they suffered the same illness as the boar, with feverish skin and bleeding eyes, and the affliction was brought about because they offended the evil spirit haunting the mine. Tadg was charged with the miners' deaths and banished to live within the mine one year for each of the dead. Alone in the mine, it wasn't long before he unearthed a strange lump of metal, surrounded by iron hematite. He spent much of his penance carefully experimenting with the metal, deducing that it imbued unique and wondrous powers to whatever living thing survived its touch.

"At the end of six years, Tadg returned to his clan. He approached Aedn, whose injury had robbed him of his warrior livelihood and left him an artisan by trade. Under Tadg's guidance, Aedn painstakingly formed the silvery stuff into a crown and crafted an iron-lined box to hold it. The two men presented it to their queen with the warning that there was something very special and very dangerous about the gift..."

Lizbeth trailed off and then said, "Oh, my gosh."

"He's talking about the gossamer crown." Zach hit his browser's back button and they all studied the photo of Seamus the Bard. Other than the long, black hair pulled back to reveal a sharp widow's peak, he looked perfectly normal.

"I wonder if Caitlin knows him," Lizbeth said.

Kevin thought about Simon and Len, Caitlin's highly colorful acquaintances, and figured this Seamus guy, with his flamboyant website and imaginative storytelling, would certainly fit in. As Zach clicked on another link to further explore Seamus' site, something niggled at the back of Kevin's mind. He looked up and scanned the cybercafé. It had gotten busy fast. The café's computers were all occupied now and many of the tables had sprouted laptops. He looked out into the mall through the green fronds of a wall of potted plants and saw a security guard who seemed to be looking right back at him.

"I think we better get out of here," he said.

Zach looked up at the plump security guard and made a face that said he'd taken his measure and found him wanting, but he shut the laptop and popped up out of his chair. They left and walked quickly towards the mall exit, weaving in and out of the shoppers. They paused in the bright sunshine by a line of grumbling, exhaust-spewing buses. By unspoken mutual decision, when the guard stepped outside, too, they got on the nearest bus. Kevin thought it ironic that when the bus pulled out of the parking lot and got on the highway, it took them back towards London.

Just in case it wasn't paranoia and the security guard really had pegged them for fugitives, they decided to switch buses. They did so two more times, meandering all over the outskirts of London, talking little and looking out the windows at the city's strange little cars and unfamiliar road signs. Finally, when the sun was getting low in the sky, they alighted in an industrial area near a marina on the Thames River.

The marina was big, with several buildings that were not quite seedy looking, although it seemed he and Zach and Lizbeth landed far from the nearest upscale yacht club. At least the three of them could wander into the restaurant off the street without looking out of place. Kevin did all the talking in his faux English accent and wondered if he was fooling anyone. It might be called English in both countries, but there were so many differences between the languages he probably gave himself away with every other sentence he spoke. He doubted American tourists were all that common in this area, though, and it was the best disguise he could come up with.

The friendly waitress called him "duck" and showed them to a booth. Even though Kevin had been sitting on buses for the last three hours, he collapsed onto the bench gratefully. The view out over the Thames was partially obstructed by boats moored in their berths. He'd learned a bit from his time at sea, and it looked as if the marina housed all kinds, from twenty-foot fishing boats to forty-foot yachts to one hundred-foot luxury cruisers.

Lizbeth fiddled with the condiments after they ordered their food. "I feel like a broken record, but – what now?"

Kevin bit his lip and shifted his eyes to the boats. He hadn't seen one person out there since they'd arrived. Other than some gulls, the docks appeared to be abandoned. "Do your skills extend to breaking and entering?"

She nodded. "I can pick just about any lock. Are you thinking about breaking into someone's boat and sleeping there?"

He remembered the nauseating nights aboard the drill ship and reconsidered, but Zach said, "That's a good idea, but what about security? How do we do it without getting caught?"

Kevin shrugged. "You tell me. I've committed more crimes today than I've committed in my entire life."

After they finished their meal, they found a path that paralleled the river and walked along it as dusk began to fall. They hadn't settled on a plan. Kevin felt helpless and dejected.

The river was wide here, and he supposed it must be deep, because a huge commercial vessel slid silently downstream. When they reached the outskirts of the marina, they stopped near the farthest dock and eyed the boats there.

"What about that one?" Lizbeth said, pointing to a classy-looking yacht.

Zach gently slapped her hand down. "You want to draw security a picture about what we're thinking about doing?"

Her bottom lip came out in a childish pout. "My feet hurt and I – I want to go home."

Kevin raised his eyebrows as Zach took yet another opportunity to put his arm around her shoulders. Zach said, "Yeah, home and bed sounds real inviting right now, I know, but we'd probably have to spend a few weeks or months or years in a nice foreign jail bed before we'd get to go home, remember? Not to mention that home and bed might not be there if we don't figure out how to fix things."

Kevin turned away when Lizbeth sighed and leaned against Zach. He took a deep breath of the fresh, cool air and looked out across the water again, aware suddenly of that strange anticipation, the sensation that something was going to happen. In the dying light, he peered at the boats on the water. A barge that looked like a garbage scow moved slowly upriver, a few sailboats headed for the marina, and a big cruiser floated downstream. He focused on the cruiser. It was just close enough for him to make out the name painted on the bow.

The Gossamer.

Chapter Twenty-three

Thames River

Lizbeth saw Kevin's face when Zach put his arm around her – saw his eyebrows disappear into his shaggy bangs and his eyes roll a little. As self-conscious as that made her feel, she couldn't help relaxing against Zach, enjoying his nearness. It was getting cold, and he seemed to radiate warmth, like a furnace. *A tall, handsome furnace with an incredible body.*

A wave of heat swept up her neck and settled in her cheeks and ears. She was glad of the near darkness; it hid her flushed skin, but if she didn't get a grip on her heart rate and breathing, he was bound to notice her reaction. Why it was important that he didn't, she couldn't really say. He didn't frighten her, but his effect on her certainly did. This was not the time or place for a flirtation.

She'd just gathered her wits enough to move away from temptation, when Kevin said, "Look, the ship!"

"What ship?" Zach asked.

"*The Gossamer*! Right there." Kevin pointed to a boat on the water.

Lizbeth knew a little about boats growing up in watery New Orleans, but this one was much bigger than any of the craft she'd piloted on the bayou. The hull of the ship had once been white, but now streaks of rust attested to its age. Like all the boats on the river, it was traveling slowly, and she wondered if there was some kind of speed limit. Even so, if they didn't do something soon, the ship would continue on out to the open sea and be lost to them.

Without conscious thought, she found herself running down the grassy bank. By the time she reached the dock, long-legged Zach had caught up to her. Their footfalls hammered hollowly on the wooden slats as they ran, passing boat after moored boat until Lizbeth reached her goal.

Out of breath from the second unaccustomed sprint of the day, she put her hands on her hips and examined the motorboat she'd chosen. Zach scowled down at it and stepped over to the yacht she'd pointed out earlier as a potential place to sleep.

She shook her head. "That one's too big, I can't drive it. This one's small, it looks fast, and it's so ugly maybe no one will miss it. Get the lines."

Before Kevin had even caught up to them, she was on board and in the driver's seat. She rooted around in her bag for her tools before realizing she hadn't had the foresight to remove the kit from her luggage. It was getting darker. She estimated they only had about half an hour before they'd need a light to see out on the river. For now, there was enough light for her to see that the owners of the boat hadn't left any lock-picking devices lying around.

Zach and Kevin's low voices reached her, as they engaged in a brief argument about how to unfasten the mooring lines. The boat dipped as they climbed in and then rocked as they struggled over who would sit shotgun.

"Will you two knock it off?"

Pointedly, she asked, "Zach, how much do you know about boats?"

Zach conceded the seat to Kevin. The boat began to drift backwards.

Lizbeth took a steadying breath and said, "We have a little situation. Do either of you have anything sharp and thin on you like, say, a bobby pin?"

She sat in frustrated silence as Kevin patted himself down and Zach began unzipping and checking inside all the myriad pockets of his backpack. He produced a pen, she shook her head; he held up a flash drive, she shook her head; he pulled a plastic comb out and she said, "Stop showing me things that are not *sharp and thin*!" The boat drifted past the end of the berth.

"Someone's coming," Kevin said.

Lizbeth glanced up. Two men had just stepped onto the dock. They appeared to be chatting and laughing as they walked, but they were headed their way. Through gritted teeth, she said, "I can't start this thing without a key or a reasonable facsimile thereof."

Zach came forward and knelt between the front seats. He put his hand on the dashboard next to the steering wheel and closed his eyes. His face was so close she felt his breath on her cheek. "What are you doing?"

86

"Caitlin started a truck just by putting her hand on the steering column," he said.

Kevin put his hand on the dash a couple of inches away from Zach's. "Well if we're going to do this, we'd better do it fast. Those guys are going to notice us any second now."

Lizbeth set her hand next to Zach's, too, feeling like an idiot. She believed him when he said Caitlin started that truck, but none of them was Caitlin, despite the fact that she'd chosen them. In her whole life, Lizbeth had never done anything as impossible as start a vehicle with just her, what, mind? Her willpower? She'd learned how to mimic the impossible by perfecting her father's magic tricks. Smoke and mirrors and prestidigitation did not cause motors to start without the cold hard reality of a key.

She closed her eyes. In her mind, she heard her grandmother drumming a voodoo chant. It worked because Granma's clients believed.

I believe.

She *did* believe. The evidence was all over the news. The earth was in very real jeopardy and she believed that Caitlin could stop it. But Caitlin wasn't here.

I believe in me. I believe in me! No matter how fiercely she thought it, it rang false in her mind. Her hand on the dash was cold.

She heard the men's footsteps now. One of them called out, "Do you need a hand there?"

Lizbeth looked at her hand and had an epiphany. She lifted it from the dash and placed it across Kevin and Zach's, creating a bridge. The engine roared to life.

Chapter Twenty-four

Thames River

In the back of the boat, Zach wasn't protected by the narrow windshield and every time the hull hit a rough patch of water, he got a face full of spray. They were slowly gaining on *The Gossamer*, even though Lizbeth drove like an old granny. She'd pointed out that none of the other boats on the water were making much of a wake, which indicated there was a speed limit. The last thing he wanted was to attract the British version of the coast guard, so he swallowed his complaints about the slowness and sat back on the moist cushions. After a few calming breaths, the unhurried pace stopped bothering him.

He thought about the ship they were chasing, about who might be piloting it. The original owners and half the crew had died years ago, presumably from having contact with the crown. His mind conjured an unbidden image of the sick blonde scientist in the ambulance with her blood-red eyes. Was she dead now, too? What about him and Kevin and Lizbeth – did they have enough of the "ancient blood" to protect them if they found the crown? He supposed so, or why else would Caitlin have picked them?

Lizbeth had followed directly behind *The Gossamer*. As they neared, the motorboat bumped along in the bubbly wake. Zach coughed when a cloud of spent fuel from the old diesel-powered ship wafted across the motorboat's bow. Over the rumble of the ship's engines, he heard the motorboat's rpm's increase as Lizbeth changed course to come alongside.

He knew she was going to say it even before she raised her voice to be heard over the noise. "Now what?"

In the near dark, Zach saw Kevin offer a useless shrug. Zach looked at the side of the ship, at a complete loss as to how they were supposed to get aboard. Then a man appeared at the rail, and another. There was just enough light on deck that Zach could see the men wore some kind of uniform. He felt his stomach clench in apprehension.

Lizbeth turned to him with a panic-stricken face. "Why are they dressed like that?"

"Let's hope it's just a formal crew."

Zach heard a faint shout and a third man joined the first two, taller and older, with a cap on his head that gave him an air of authority.

"This may not have been one of my best ideas," Lizbeth said.

"Can we make a run for it?" Kevin asked.

"Not without stopping for gas first," Lizbeth replied.

Moments later, the ship's engines wound down. Once the huge vessel slowed enough, someone on board extended a ladder. Lizbeth flipped the boat's fenders over the side while Kevin tied the mooring rope to the ladder.

Zach went first, emptying his mind of thoughts and emotions with every step. At the top, he swung his legs over the side and dropped lightly onto the deck, ready for anything. To his left stood two men who wore dark jackets and some sort of floatation device with the prominent label "Metropolitan Police." Zach had no doubt they were part of a marine unit, but he didn't give them more than an assessing glance. His full focus was for the older man in the cap, and not just because he was clearly in charge.

Lizbeth and Kevin came aboard behind him and she placed her hand on his waist. "Do you feel it?" she asked softly.

Zach was certain that the man in front of them had the crown on his person or had been in contact with it recently. He radiated the same sort of almost electrical energy as Caitlin. Zach nodded his head once to acknowledge Lizbeth's question and gave her a quick warning look.

The man ran his eyes over the three of them almost dismissively. In an accent that sounded just like Len's, he said, "I'm Chief Inspector Griffey. What is your business with this ship?"

The lights on the ship were reflected in Griffey's eyes like spinning pinpoints.

Zach's plan had vaguely involved storming the ship and fighting his way to the crown, but that was before he knew it was crawling with cops. He didn't have time to muster up a good lie, however, because the Chief Inspector's face suddenly fell into a fierce frown and he stepped towards him threateningly.

"What do you know about the-"

He stopped and his eyes flicked to the officers. Zach noticed his chin came up slightly as he regained control. To his men, he said, "Bring them to the captain's quarters."

If he'd been alone, Zach would have taken out the two officers and leapt overboard. He had no idea if Lizbeth and Kevin could swim, though. Besides, after that display, his interest in the Chief Inspector was piqued and he wanted to hear what the man had to say. His outburst made no sense at all.

The Captain's Quarters were not impressive. Paneled in a dark wood circa 1960, the room smelled like a cross between foreign cheese and a musty old cigar. The Chief Inspector sat at a scarred desk and after Zach and the others were seated in front of him, gestured to his men to leave.

"Who are you?" he asked, looking at Zach.

"Zach Wong."

The Chief Inspector placed his cap on the desk, revealing close-cropped black hair with traces of gray at the temples. His long fingers adjusted the cap just so in the center of the leather blotter, and he smiled, looking anything but amused. In the light of the desk lamp, his green eyes glittered.

"How did you know about the crown?" he asked.

Zach went cold. Either the Chief Inspector was jumping to a conclusion because they'd chased after this ship, or he'd read Zach's mind. Which meant Zach hadn't sensed the crown, he'd sensed *Griffey*.

Zach said, "Chief Inspector Griffey, did you say? *Brian* Griffey?"

"The crown, Mr. Wong. Who told you about it?"

Zach emptied his mind as the Chief Inspector stared him down. He thought of the lotus blossom painting in his mother's parlor and how the light from the late afternoon sun highlighted the dust motes in his bedroom.

"Very clever," the Chief Inspector murmured. "I have to assume we have a mutual friend. An incarcerated friend."

Lizbeth spoke up for the first time. "She thought you died on the Titanic."

Brian Griffey produced a feral grin, and then his nose thinned, his lips plumped, and his hair sprouted almost instantly into curls reaching down to narrow and newly feminine shoulders under Griffey's uniform. In a husky falsetto, he said, "Women and children first."

Chapter Twenty-five

Thames River

Kevin had barely recovered from the shock of the three of them starting the boat without a key when he witnessed Griffey change into a woman. Griffey didn't hold the change for long, and the reformation of his features was even weirder than the original change had been. Kevin shuddered when the shapeshifter's long, black hair silently sucked back into his skull, like enthusiastically eaten spaghetti. The creepiest part was how attractive he'd been.

Once Griffey transformed back to his normal, intimidating visage, he said, "Why don't you tell me about your business dealings with Caitlin."

"We're just friends," Lizbeth said. "Better friends than you."

Kevin wasn't sure what she hoped to accomplish by baiting Griffey. This was a man who'd just bragged about taking some doomed woman's seat in a lifeboat. When Caitlin spoke of him, even though she'd shown little emotion, Kevin got the impression his supposed death had affected her deeply. And yet, here he was, not only very much alive, but a shapeshifter, too, something Caitlin had failed to mention. Plus, Griffey was now a high-ranking law enforcement officer. Did he have something to do with her arrest?

Griffey narrowed his eyes at Lizbeth. "Caitlin doesn't make friends. She has, however, clearly shared some – classified – information with you, and I'm at a loss as to why she would do that. I don't like not knowing things."

There was an implied threat in the words, and Kevin sensed rather than saw Zach go on alert.

"You mean about the crown? Why do you think she told us?" Lizbeth asked. "Don't tell me you haven't noticed the earthquakes and volcanoes."

Griffey blinked, but otherwise didn't react. That one blink and the blank stare that followed told Kevin that Griffey had no idea the crown had anything to do with the current state of the world. He confirmed it when he asked, "Are you saying whoever has the crown is causing it?"

"Can it do that?" Kevin asked. Caitlin had never explained exactly why they needed the crown.

Griffey laughed. "Typical Caitlin. Only tell them what they need to know."

Kevin suspected Caitlin told them what she thought they would *believe*, when they were ready to believe it, but he didn't say as much.

"The crown is going to stop what's happening to the world," Lizbeth said. "And it sounds to me like you know even less about it than we do."

"Well, why don't we pool our information, then?" Griffey said. "First tell me what makes you three so special."

"And give away our advantage?" Zach asked. If Kevin didn't know Zach was bluffing, he'd be convinced by the confidence in his voice.

"Oh, you have no advantage," Griffey began, but his cell phone rang. He flipped it open to look at the display before taking the call. The volume was up so loud Kevin heard the entire conversation.

The tinny voice of the caller said, "Caitlin O'Connor has escaped."

Griffey's lips thinned into a furious line and he hissed, "When?"

"The guard was found in her cell, dressed in her clothes-"

"I didn't ask how. *When*?"

"We don't know. Hours probably."

Griffey snapped the phone shut and stood. "Consider yourselves under arrest."

He posted two officers to guard the door and left without another word.

Zach said, "Did you guys hear that? Caitlin's out."

"I heard. I also hear *that*," Kevin said, referring to the renewed sound of the ship's engines. His stomach lurched a little in apprehension. "We're moving again."

Lizbeth hurried over to a bank of wooden file cabinets against the wall behind the captain's desk. "We probably don't have much time then. Let's see what we can find out."

The cabinets were locked, but the desk drawer had all sorts of junk in it, and it didn't take long for Lizbeth to find a suitable tool. Kevin was impressed by how quickly she picked each of the locks. He and Zach began to look through the files. Kevin kept glancing over his shoulder, expecting someone to catch them at their clumsy snooping, especially after the ship stopped moving again. They'd been digging through what seemed like hundreds of files for over an hour when Zach said, "Here."

He placed a thick file on the desk, and they huddled around it. It appeared to be a crew manifest dating from the ship's maiden voyage to its last. Zach started to read the names out loud, but Kevin held up a hand.

"Shh—what's that?"

The others lifted their heads and listened for a moment. With the cessation of their movements in the cabin, the sounds from the ship seemed hollow and ghostly.

Zach looked back down at the file. "It's just the guards."

Lizbeth went to the door and pressed her ear to it. After a moment she waved them over. Kevin put his head against the cold metal door on one side of Lizbeth and Zach on the other. It was faint, but he could hear the guards' conversation.

One officer was saying, "I don't understand why we're moving this bucket of rust. Ship feels haunted. They say seventeen people died on board."

The other officer replied, "Boat wasn't secure where it was. Griffey thinks there's evidence here someone might try to hide. And those people that died—he's linked it to the new deaths on that drill ship."

"Marine command always jump when Griffey calls?"

"Thames Counter-Terrorist Partnership is a beautiful thing, isn't it? Thank Al-Qaeda."

An echo of footsteps from the corridor heralded someone's arrival. Kevin straightened. "Someone's coming."

Zach rushed to the desk, tore the top pages from the file and stuffed them in his pocket as Lizbeth tossed the file under the desk. They scrambled for their seats and acted nonchalant when the door opened.

Griffey entered, followed by another man.

"I suspect you're all acquainted," Griffey said.

Bill Masters looked directly into Kevin's eyes and nodded.

Chapter Twenty-six

The North Sea

Lizbeth thought she'd been confused before, but when Bill Masters showed up, she became, as Granma liked to say, completely confuzzled.

Bill looked around the Captain's quarters and asked, "Where's Caitlin?"

Griffey gestured to the officer hovering in the corridor to take a position outside the door. He closed it and made a rueful face. "I apologize. I told you she was here, but she's not. Until recently, we've had her tucked away in a high security cell."

"What? Why?" Bill asked.

Griffey stepped back from Bill's vehemence and moved to put the desk between them before answering. "We were holding her for questioning. There were no charges, except of course now her escape has racked up a whole slew of them."

Bill's baffled expression deepened. "Escape...questioning for what?"

"I'm not at liberty to divulge that. Ongoing investigation."

Lizbeth frowned. If Griffey was responsible for Caitlin's arrest, why didn't he know who Lizbeth, Kevin and Zach were? She thought about their panicked flight from the officers in London. If the police hadn't pegged them as terrorist associates of Caitlin's, then Lizbeth's pickpocketing had gotten them in trouble after all. She felt a flush of shame work its way up her neck.

"So why have you brought me here?" Bill asked. He looked down and ran his eyes over Lizbeth and the others.

Griffey sucked air between his teeth. "As we speak, a dozen hazmat-suited officers are searching the drill ship."

Bill looked like he'd been slapped in the face. "Do you have a warrant?"

"It's been served on the captain, but you could save us all some time by telling me where it is."

"Where what is? The core sample?"

Griffey snorted a humorless laugh. "The crown, Masters. I know it was on your ship. You may have convinced the health authorities that those people died from natural causes, but I've seen that illness before."

"The crown has never been on my ship."

"But you do know about it. Are you Guild?"

"What?"

Whatever "Guild" meant, Griffey seemed to take Bill's response as a "no," because he went on to ask, "What did Caitlin tell you about the crown?"

"Enough."

Griffey sighed. "How do you know her?"

Bill spread his hands. "Look. Caitlin hired me to salvage the crown from Titanic, but we were ordered to stop looking and someone else got to it first. I couldn't even tell you what it looks like."

"Then what infected those scientists on board your ship?"

Bill compressed his lips.

Griffey stared at Bill with the same intensity he'd directed at Zach earlier. Lizbeth thought about how Caitlin had spoken to her mind-to-mind that first day, when her father's incantation had echoed in her head. She suspected Griffey, too, had some level of mind-reading ability, and was exercising that skill now. Finally, he said, "Tell me about the core sample."

"You wouldn't believe me."

Lizbeth felt the hair on the back of her neck stir. For a second, she thought Griffey was exuding some kind of energy, but then Zach stiffened in his chair like he was having an epileptic fit, and Kevin muttered, "Not again." She looked at Griffey and saw him wince. It made sense that if they could feel it and Caitlin could feel it, Griffey would, too.

Outside, night became day. The two portholes over the file cabinets changed into floodlights beaming a multi-colored glow into the cabin. It was another sub-space storm aurora. A message was coming in, and the force behind it made her doubt that the changes the gossamer sphere had made thus far to the earth were working. The energy pulses coursing through her body were stronger than ever, and the show this time lasted for several minutes. While everyone in the room but Bill suffered through the discomfort of it, Bill kept asking, "What's going on? What's wrong with you people?"

Finally, it ended. Griffey sat slumped in his chair, breathing hard and staring at Lizbeth. His eyes reminded her of Caitlin's, swirling as if each orb was home to a galaxy of stars.

"Why did you say the crown was going to stop what's happening to the world?" he asked.

Lizbeth exchanged a look with Zach. In her mind, she imagined she heard his voice: *be careful what you say.*

"Maybe you should ask Bill what's going on," she said. "He's the one who set it all into motion."

Bill was leaning back against the door with his arms crossed. "I already said he wouldn't believe me. I don't know how much Caitlin told you, but there's a lot of bizarre stuff involved here."

Zach held a hand out palm up to indicate Griffey. "You mean like shapeshifters?"

Bill's head went back. A small silence passed while he studied Griffey and appeared to absorb Zach's veiled assertion that Griffey was a shapeshifter, too. "Yeah, like that."

The light from the desk lamp cast deep shadows over Griffey's face, emphasizing his craggy profile and the bags under his deep-set eyes. He looked tired, and Lizbeth wondered if he was experiencing negative aftereffects from the message.

She halfway expected him to deny it, but he said, "Caitlin and I were members of an ancient society, only it wasn't ancient when we joined. Recruitment was limited to the young, intelligent and strong. The ritual was simple, but deadly for most."

"Touch the crown," Lizbeth whispered.

Griffey heard her and shrugged one shoulder. "Dozens of people died every year hoping to attain power and immortality. Maybe one out of a hundred survived. Once the Romans invaded our shores, they mistook it for human sacrifice and decided we were barbarians. Before they came, our people were revered. We were the nobles, the healers, scholars, philosophers, judges and teachers for centuries."

"Druids," Zach murmured, and Griffey nodded.

"The Roman Empire persecuted us out of fear, and those who survived went into hiding or left the country. The nobles were in charge of protecting the crown, but they began to die off, one by one, until there was only one left – Caitlin."

A light knock sounded on the door and Griffey called, "Yes?"

The officer stationed outside leaned his torso in and shook his head at Griffey, which Lizbeth took to mean they hadn't found the crown on the drill ship. Griffey nodded curtly in dismissal and once the officer shut the door, rested his chin in his folded hands and glared at Bill.

"Where's the damned crown?"

"I don't know."

"I can have you arrested, you know," Griffey said.

"For what?"

"We've got six bodies on slabs at the morgue. The mere suggestion it was caused by an agent that could be used in a terrorist attack will get you a comfortable cell. Caitlin may have resisted my interrogation techniques, but I assure you, you won't."

Lizbeth gasped when she heard all the scientists had died, but Bill's face didn't change. She looked back and forth between the two men. Caitlin said Griffey had been her friend, but then he'd disappeared from her life only to reappear as a powerful adversary. Lizbeth was pretty sure Bill had been more than a friend to Caitlin at some point, but now they, too, were at odds. At least Bill's motives, if not his methods, seemed honorable; he was attempting to find a different way to stop the sphere, wasn't he? Griffey didn't even seem to know about the sphere, yet he was after the crown with a frightening single-mindedness. He and Caitlin obviously had different plans for the crown, but what did *he* want it for?

"The deaths weren't caused by the crown," Bill said.

"Don't tell him," Lizbeth said.

Griffey's eyebrows lifted, creating three narrow furrows in his forehead. "Make up your mind. You said he set all this in motion. Someone explain to me-"

A commotion from the corridor interrupted what Lizbeth suspected would have become a tirade. Griffey shouldered Bill aside and opened the door.

"Fireballs in the sky!" The officer shouted, even though he was five feet away. "Dozens of them. Asteroids or missiles!"

Griffey followed the officer down the dark corridor. Lizbeth and the others exchanged quick looks.

"Let's get out of here," Zach said. Bill was closest to the door and he led the way down the corridor and up the ladder to the deck. The sky was lit up again, only this time, bright balls of white flame streaked through the atmosphere. Some trailed away and disappeared, some rained down. Lizbeth instinctively ducked as a loud whoosh preceded a fireball that exploded in the ocean mere miles from where they were anchored.

Griffey was nowhere in sight. One of the officers ran up and she thought he was going to make them go below, but he attempted to get past them. Bill grabbed his arm and asked, "What's happening?"

"Command says it's satellites! They're crashing to the ground all over the northern hemisphere! They've lost communication with the space station!" The officer yanked his arm away and rushed off.

Lizbeth remembered what Caitlin had said, "The sphere has been struggling to receive messages for some time now. Climate changes caused by greenhouse gasses, space cluttered with orbiting satellites and junk, all have interfered."

She stared around her at the hail of fire, convinced that the last aurora must have been more than a message.

Chapter Twenty-seven

The North Sea

The afterimage from the last big fireball hadn't yet faded from his retinas when Zach heard a sibilant whistling that rapidly gained in volume. Another satellite had entered the atmosphere, and as the flaming ball of wreckage approached, it illuminated the deck of the ship and the ocean all around them. In the eerie glow, he mentally marked the location of the nearby drill ship. The sound grew to ear-splitting proportions as the light became brighter than a white-hot day. One of the officers screamed, *"Incoming!"*

The light was too brilliant for Zach to assess the fireball's trajectory, but it seemed to be coming straight for them. His instinct was to jump overboard, but he had a feeling the odds of survival were slightly better on the ship. Standing next to him, Lizbeth cringed, and he pulled her into his arms and bent over her, even though his body would not provide much of a shield from what was coming.

When it hit a few hundred yards from the bow of the ship, the fireball shot an enormous steaming column of water high into the air. Zach didn't have time to rejoice, because immediately following in the fireball's plume came a barrage of deadly projectiles, penetrating the ship like machine-gun fire.

Someone on the bow shrieked in agony, but the piercing sound was cut off by a cascade of hot seawater raining down on them. The water tore Zach's footing out from under him and swept him along the deck. Submerged in the flow, he and Lizbeth clutched each other as the waves tumbled them up and over the rail. He lost hold of Lizbeth in the fall, and with the light from the fireball effectively extinguished, he couldn't see anything. He tried to tuck his body into a ball as he fell, but he hit the water awkwardly. It slammed into his shoulder, neck and the side of his face. Immersed underwater, he floated in a cold cocoon, silent but for the ringing of his ears.

Lizbeth!

Zach kicked for the surface but panicked when he realized he didn't know which way was up. He needed to help himself before he could help her, so he relaxed and trusted his training. His open eyes saw blackness all around. He had a lungful of air, and his body should be floating upward, but he was too disoriented from the fall to sense any movement. As his lungs began to burn, he put a hand in front of his mouth and released a stream of bubbles. They trickled along his cheeks up into the hair at his temples. He swept his arms in a wide breaststroke and frog-kicked desperately in the direction of the bubbles. Two kicks, three, four – finally his head broke the surface and he gulped in ragged breaths of air.

"Lizbeth!" he yelled when he'd barely caught his breath.

"Zach? I'm here."

"Where are you guys?" It was Kevin's voice. He'd been swept overboard, too. Zach closed his eyes in relief.

When he opened them again, he realized there was a light source somewhere, since he could see the rusty hulk of *The Gossamer* about twenty yards away. He tilted his head back to look at the sky but saw only fading streaks of light. Dropping his gaze to the side of the ship, he noticed a reddish glow emanating from on deck.

Someone treading water nearby called, "The ship's on fire."

The male voice didn't belong to Kevin, so Zach asked, "Who's there?"

"It's Bill. We need to get away from here. With all that water, I'm guessing the only thing that could be burning right now is oil or fuel."

Zach toed his shoes off and joined the others as they swam toward the drill ship through the now calm sea. He looked over his shoulder several times during the long, taxing swim to watch the fire grow larger. When they reached the drill ship, Bill hollered to the crew and within minutes they were safe on board. The captain met them on deck and shook Bill's hand heartily.

"We saw the asteroid hit and thought you were done for."

"You and me both," Bill replied. "But it wasn't an asteroid. Apparently, we've lost all our satellites."

"Bloody hell. That explains a lot. We've got a real muddle in the control room."

Zach looked at *The Gossamer*. Three rescue boats had arrived, maintaining a safe distance from the ship. Two of the boats shot narrow streams of water at the fire. The third swept the sea with searchlights.

"I suggest we put some space between us and that." Bill jerked his head at the flames.

"Right," the captain said. "Can't go far without functioning equipment, though."

Someone brought a stack of blankets, and Zach draped one over Lizbeth's shivering shoulders before wrapping one around himself. Beyond the burning ship, the coast of England seemed peaceful and unaffected by recent events.

"Let's get you kids below deck and see if we can find some dry clothes," Bill said.

Zach had barely begun the motion to turn away from *The Gossamer* when the aft deck exploded in an immense cloud of fiery black smoke. Reflexively, he ducked, as the concussive boom blasted them with scorching heat. Once the rolling smoke cleared, he saw that the three rescue boats appeared to be unharmed. The third boat joined in pumping water on the fire.

Lizbeth leaned into him. "I wonder if Griffey made it."

Zach detected a note of sympathy in her voice, so he deliberately reminded her who Griffey was. "He's probably the only woman in the lifeboat."

Chapter Twenty-eight

The North Sea

Kevin sat on his old bunk and rolled up the cuffs on a borrowed pair of work pants. The claustrophobic space brought back memories of his nausea-filled summer. He was frankly surprised he hadn't had to make a run for the bathroom yet.

Zach had flopped on the top bunk and was bemoaning the loss of his laptop. "I had everything backed up to thumb drives, too, most of which were also in my backpack, which has now been blown to smithereens."

"I think we have more important things to worry about, dude," Kevin said.

Legs appeared over the side of the bunk. Kevin stared at bare ankles poking out of too-short jeans and the battered sneakers Zach had been given to wear. When Zach slid off the bed, Kevin braced for another confrontation. By now, he knew Zach could kick his butt, probably without much effort, but he wasn't intimidated. Zach had been a jerk from the get-go, and now that he took every opportunity to flirt with Lizbeth he was really getting on Kevin's nerves.

A light tapping on the door interrupted whatever Zach had on his mind. He opened it and Lizbeth slipped into the cabin.

"Like my duds?" she asked, pirouetting in the minuscule space. "One of the scientists bailed on some of her stuff."

There wasn't much to comment on about the plain black slacks and baggy t-shirt, but Zach said, "You look great."

Kevin recognized the t-shirt with its faded concert logo. One of the less formal of the scientists had worn it often under her lab coat. She'd left the ship at the same time as Kevin, before anyone had gotten sick. According to Bill, none of the scientists were left on board, and none of the crew was allowed to leave under the terms of the quarantine. Griffey had broken the rules when he transported Bill to *The Gossamer*, but then, as he'd said, he knew the sickness wasn't contagious. He just didn't know it wasn't the crown that caused it.

"She wasn't one of the ones that died," he said.

Lizbeth turned wide, horrified eyes on him as if it hadn't occurred to her that she might be wearing a dead woman's clothes.

Zach snorted in laughter. "Smooth as usual."

"Yeah, but your outfit belonged to one of the first to go," Kevin lied.

Zach pulled a face at him and Lizbeth said, "Cut it out, you two. Maybe we should brainstorm where Caitlin might be."

"Personally, I'm about twenty hours behind on my sleep," Zach said. He vaulted up onto the bunk. Kevin couldn't see him, but from the sound of it, Zach was stretching out and making himself comfortable. First one, then the other shoe thumped to the floor.

Lizbeth looked disappointed, but she said, "That's a good idea, I guess."

Kevin took pity on her. "You don't have to leave if you don't want to. We can talk."

Her eyes flicked up to the top bunk and back. "That's okay. I'm tired, too. Zach's right – we should rest up so whatever tomorrow throws at us won't be...well...alright, tomorrow's probably going to be just as crazy, if not worse, than today. But sleep is good."

Kevin thought her sudden babbling proved her need for sleep, until he caught another wistful look towards the top bunk and realized she must really want to spend time with Zach. Zach must have noticed, too, because his legs reappeared, and he jumped off the bed. Kevin looked away when he placed his hands on her shoulders and dipped his head. He heard it though, a quick, light pecking sound, and suddenly he was infuriated that Zach would kiss her like that, right in front of him.

As Zach leapt confidently back onto the bed, Kevin couldn't help but sneak a peek at Lizbeth's flushed and pleased face. She stumbled out and he sat there for a long time staring at the closed door.

Up until now he'd been exhausted, but he knew he wouldn't be able to sleep until he resolved his anger, something he wouldn't be able to do in the same room with the source of that anger. Zach, who'd been so critical of *his* snoring, was doing a fine imitation of a slowly drawn hacksaw on wood.

Before Kevin knew it, he'd left the cabin and made his way down the silent corridor to the lab. Everything looked exactly the same as when he'd left. Somehow, he imagined that the departing scientists would have packed up the equipment, but it was all there, neatly laid out on pristine stainless-steel counters. The lab was as cold as ever, like the frozen food aisle at the grocery store. Deep glass-fronted refrigerators and freezers took up one whole wall of the large space. Inside were long tubes containing core samples, stacked and labeled.

Even though he knew the lab was empty, Kevin looked to his right and left before moving toward the freezers. He'd typed and labeled most of these core samples himself, so he knew the system. The only one he hadn't labeled, the last sample containing the iridium, wasn't where it should be. Had Griffey's hazmat-suited men confiscated it? But then, why would they? Griffey hadn't known about the core sample.

Kevin looked around the lab until he spotted the refrigerator in the corner. It was a regular kitchen-appliance type refrigerator where slices from the core samples shared space with the scientist's lunches. His borrowed sneakers squeaked with every step across the linoleum floor. The refrigerator was empty. The freezer compartment, however, held a large plastic tub of vanilla and orange sherbet ice cream. The tub was semi-transparent, and the "ice cream" was much darker than it should be. He started to reach for it but stopped.

He may be descended from a shapeshifter, but after Caitlin's dire warnings he wasn't fool enough to think that would protect him from the horrible consequences of touching it. He went to the drawer where they kept the latex gloves and wrestled a pair onto his hands. The tub was heavier than he expected. The weight strained the plastic handle and he'd just decided to put it back and try picking it up from the bottom when the handle snapped. The tub landed on its side and the lid burst open, shooting half the contents all down the front of his shirt. He shoved the tub back into the freezer and stepped back, frantically brushing at his clothes, stopping only when he tasted salt on his lips. Specks of the moist deep-ocean silt had sprayed his face and now he'd even consumed a minute quantity.

His heart began to pound, and he broke out into a nervous sweat. Core samples were normally solid, as weight from successive layers compressed it, eventually forming rock. Despite the fact that this sample was loose and sandy, he had no doubt that he'd just inadvertently exposed himself to the final core sample. Disgusted with his clumsiness and not a little frightened, he found a broom and began to sweep up. He would have to tell Bill what he'd done so no one touched the refrigerator or the floor around it until it was decontaminated.

He peeled the gloves off his clammy hands and tossed them on the counter. No point worrying about protection now. Kneeling, he swept the dark sand onto a dustpan with his hand. Immediately, his palm began to tingle. He looked down and saw that it was covered in a silvery metallic sheen. Without conscious thought, he placed his hand over the mound of sand on the dustpan. A rush of something like and yet unlike pleasure crawled up his arm and settled somewhere in his head. He stared at his hand with unfocused eyes as the sensation increased.

"To me," he murmured, instinctively concentrating on drawing the metal out of the sand. And it came.

Chapter Twenty-nine

The North Sea

After Zach had gone out of his way to give her that sweet peck on the cheek, Lizbeth thought she wouldn't be able to fall asleep. The rocking motion of the ship and her bone-deep exhaustion combined to work its magic however, and she woke feeling refreshed, if not exactly fresh in her borrowed clothes.

She had no idea what time it was when she cracked her door and peered out into the corridor. They were supposed to all meet with Bill sometime this morning to figure out the next move.

The door to the cabin across the way opened and Zach leaned out. He held a finger to his lips and swept his other hand for her to join him inside.

"What?" she whispered.

"Come in and tell me if you notice anything different about Kevin," he said softly.

As soon as she crossed the threshold, she sensed it. Kevin was a lump under his utilitarian grey blanket; the only part of him visible was his distinctive mop of brown hair. Lizbeth felt him, though, just like she felt Caitlin and Griffey. It was as if overnight he'd obtained the same sort of tingly aura the shapeshifters had.

"Kevin!" she said loudly.

He flipped around under the covers and fought with them briefly before rolling out onto the floor. On all fours, he looked up through the hair hanging in his face. Lizbeth laughed. He looked like a shaggy dog.

He got to his feet and raked the hair out of his eyes with his fingers. "Thanks a lot."

"What happened last night?" Zach asked.

Kevin averted his eyes, shoved his hands in his pockets and mumbled, "Nothing." He forced one foot after the other into his sneakers without bothering to untie them.

"You must think we're stupid," Zach said. "Did you find the crown?"

"Huh? No. I wouldn't keep that from you."

Lizbeth put her hand on his shoulder to prevent him from turning away. "What *are* you keeping from us?"

He stood there with his head down for a moment and then pulled something from his pocket. Pinched between forefinger and thumb, he held up what looked to Lizbeth like a melted quarter or a spent bullet. "This is the iridium from the core sample."

"What?" Lizbeth exclaimed at the same time Zach thrust out his hand and demanded, "Let me see it."

Kevin curled his fingers around the metal lump. "Why don't we wait to make sure I don't get sick before anyone else touches it?"

"How did you get it?" Lizbeth asked.

He told them about his accident in the lab, and how he put his hand in the sample and the microscopic iridium dust separated itself and congealed into a solid mass seemingly of its own volition. He hadn't been able to stop until he'd gone to the freezer and gathered all the iridium in the lab.

"On a good note, the lab's probably not dangerous to normal people anymore," he said.

Lizbeth stared at him in consternation. "Why did you do it?"

"I don't know. I didn't mean to, but it felt like I was supposed to, if that makes sense."

Zach puffed mockingly. "It makes as much sense as anything else."

They found Bill in the lab. Caitlin was with him. Lizbeth was so happy to see her that she ignored the possibility that Caitlin would repulse her and ran forward for a hug. To her surprise, Caitlin hugged back. When Lizbeth stepped away, Caitlin said, "Kevin."

It was obvious to Lizbeth that Kevin was reluctant to meet Caitlin's eyes. When he did, they maintained a steady gaze for several seconds. Lizbeth imagined she heard whispers of conversation in her head. Kevin looked for a moment like he was going to cry.

"They're all safe," Bill said. "Like I told you."

Caitlin turned to him. "Thank you."

"I'm not sure I had much to do with it. They're pretty resourceful."

"Did he tell you about Brian Griffey?" Zach asked.

"He did. We'll discuss it later. Right now we need to get to a safe location."

"You can't leave yet," Bill said. Lizbeth hadn't noticed before, but he wore latex gloves on his hands. He opened the freezer compartment of a refrigerator, lifted out its only contents, and set it on the counter next to Caitlin.

"Yum, ice cream for breakfast," Zach said in an aside to Lizbeth. Even though she knew the container had sand in it, she had to admit it sounded good. They hadn't eaten since the restaurant at the marina.

Bill removed the lid, but Caitlin began shaking her head. "No, Bill."

"You can't say that," he said, sounding agitated now. "Don't you know what I went through to get this for you? Six people – six of my *friends* died!"

"I never asked for this. I told you it wouldn't work. Any biometal in that sample is microscopic. The iridium sank too deep for the drill to reach."

Lizbeth started to tell Caitlin that the iridium wasn't even in the sample anymore, when Kevin placed a hand on her arm. She heard it for certain this time, his voice in her mind. *"Don't say anything."*

"We can get more. And you've got help now," Bill swept his hand towards Lizbeth and the boys. "They can help make you a new crown."

Caitlin's voice went cold. "They can't and they won't. Take your bucket of sand and drop it back into the ocean."

Bill removed the latex gloves and grasped Caitlin by the shoulders. He searched her face, which looked to Lizbeth to be made of marble.

"I love you," he said in a tormented whisper, before shoving her backwards and plunging his hands into the core sample. He lifted fists full of the sandy silt and shook them in the air.

Lizbeth felt the sting of tears, but Caitlin seemed unmoved.

Bill's arms fell to his sides and he looked at Caitlin with something like happiness. "Now I'm either going to join you or die."

Chapter Thirty

The English Channel

Zach didn't know which was harder to believe, that Bill had risked his life for love, or that Caitlin left him standing in the lab with only two handfuls of sand to show for it.

She wanted them to leave right away, but Lizbeth begged her to stop by the onboard laundry room so they could get their own clothes. Caitlin waited outside while they hurriedly changed; Zach and Kevin in the laundry room proper, and Lizbeth behind an open closet door.

Zach raised his eyebrows at Kevin. "Do you believe what he did?"

"What he *thinks* he did."

"He must really love her."

"Can you imagine loving someone enough to die for them?" Kevin asked.

Zach thought of Lizbeth and almost said yes but balked. He didn't love her; he hadn't known her long enough. No, he was just fascinated with her because she was different, like him. He said, "Nope."

Lizbeth appeared from behind the door, expression haughty. "Oh, really?"

Zach hadn't yet put on his shirt, but he didn't think she was in the mood to appreciate his sculpted chest and abs, so he quickly pulled it over his head. He offered her a grin and replied, "It's hard to imagine something you've never experienced."

"You've never been in love?"

Pleased that he'd so effortlessly distracted her, he let his gaze linger on her face for a moment before saying, "Not yet."

Her shoulders relaxed a bit. "Neither have I."

"Hurry up," Kevin said in a gruff voice. He joined Caitlin in the corridor, followed by Lizbeth.

On the way out, Zach noticed the wad of paper he'd pulled out of his pocket the night before. He'd set the sopping wet pages of *The Gossamer's* crew manifest on top of the dryer before tossing his pants in the washer. Even though he supposed the ink had melted away and the pages would be stuck together like a lump of paper mâché, he reached for it on the way out. In the heat of the laundry room, it had dried into a solid clump.

Bill was nowhere in sight when they descended the ladder to board a motorized yacht not unlike the one Zach had tried to convince Lizbeth to steal from the marina. After detaching the mooring lines, they went down into the cabin. It was paneled from floor to ceiling in a rich, dark wood and had been designed to fit all the amenities of home into a very small space.

Caitlin took the helm and started the powerful motor. Zach noticed she had a key.

"There's food in the cooler," she said.

Lizbeth beat them to the mini-refrigerator and handed out a six-pack of soda and several prepackaged deli sandwiches. Conversation was light as Zach and Lizbeth devoured the meal. Kevin didn't eat much.

Replete, Zach leaned against the cushions backing the bench seat and looked out one of the narrow rectangular portals. The yacht was moving at a rapid clip, hugging the coastline.

"Where are we going?" Lizbeth asked.

"To see a friend," Caitlin replied. She twisted around and said to Kevin, "Let me see it."

Zach wasn't surprised Caitlin knew about the iridium. In the lab, he'd been certain Caitlin and Kevin were communicating telepathically. What would have been amazing and unbelievable to him a week ago, he now took in stride.

When Kevin stood in the swaying cabin to show Caitlin the lump of metal in his pocket, instead of holding it out to her, he slapped his hand over his mouth and made a sound like, "Urgle."

Caitlin pointed. "The head's there."

Kevin nodded vigorously and rushed into the tiny bathroom. The noise of the motor and the drumming of the waves against the hull almost blocked out the sounds he produced. Zach looked at Lizbeth and they both started laughing. It provided a much-needed release from some of the strain they'd been under, but he felt bad for doing it. Which kind of surprised him.

Lizbeth stopped snickering first. "Poor Kevin."

With mild censure, Caitlin said, "His people were miners. He's someone you'll want to have with you if you're ever in a cave."

Rather than putting a damper on their merriment, the statement set Zach and Lizbeth off again. By the time Kevin came out, though, looking sheepish and rather green, they were inspecting what was left of *The Gossamer's* crew manifest. Lizbeth's nimble fingers had separated the pages, revealing two dozen or so still-legible names. Zach hoped he'd have access to a computer wherever they were going so he could research the names, even though the chance any of them meant anything was slim.

Caitlin slowed the engine and turned the steering wheel toward the rocky coast. "I need to understand something. Why didn't you stay with Simon, as I asked?"

Zach said slowly, "Be-cause he told us to leave. Told us you'd been 'taken' and that we had to hide."

She looked over her shoulder with the faintest trace of bewilderment. "Exactly what did he tell you?"

"That's pretty much it, but Len told us-"

"*Len?*"

"Yeah," Zach said, not sure by her reaction if she knew him or not. "Horizontally challenged? Raven for a pet?"

"Where did you meet him?" She fired the question at him.

"Simon told us to go to his pub. Len took us to London in his toy car."

Caitlin abruptly shifted into neutral, letting the engine idle as she left the helm. She stood before them without speaking for a moment, eyes shifting around as if chasing her thoughts.

Finally she sighed and said quietly, "Simon reveals his true affiliations. I'm surprised they didn't kill you."

Zach suppressed a flash of dread. "Who is he? Len."

She took a deep breath. "He's Guild. During the centuries when the church held Inquisitions, if the folk weren't careful enough, they were caught and accused of heresy. Torture was often sanctioned. When one of us was clapped in irons, confessions were obtained. The existence of the crown became known. Members of the Guild continue to this day to hunt us down. They profess to want to keep the crown out of the wrong hands. I had a run-in with Len soon after Bill and I began our salvage efforts on Titanic. Suffice it to say, if Simon sent you to Len, he's no friend of mine."

"So this Guild wants the same thing as you. To protect the crown," Lizbeth said.

"No. I was its guardian, to make sure it didn't fall into the hands of someone like, say, Hitler. The Guild wanted to remove the crown from *anyone's* influence. They would destroy it, if they knew how."

"Uh, I don't know," Lizbeth said. "The gossamer sphere crashed into the earth, right? Sounds like it's not that easy to destroy."

"There is one element that the biometal is vulnerable to. It's why I presumed the sphere was meant to strike a different planet in our solar system. This planet is rife with it."

Zach thought about high school chemistry. He'd done poorly memorizing the periodic table of elements. He'd been too busy doodling pictures in the margins during class. If his teacher had tested him on mythology and fairy tales, he would have gotten an "A." There was only one element fabled to injure mythical creatures; the main element presumed to be at the core of the earth, and the one Caitlin told them iridium was attracted to.

"It's why they talked under torture instead of shapeshifting and escaping," he said. "Chains are forged out of iron."

Caitlin nodded. "Yes. It prevents the biometal from joining the grid, effectively containing it, and it disrupts the abilities the biometal gifted us with. Chained, we cannot shift, we cannot read minds. The Guild knows it hurts us. Whether there is some way to use iron against the crown itself, I do not know, and I pray it has not already been accomplished."

Caitlin sat back in the drivers' seat and reached for the controls, but Kevin asked, "So today, when we—talked—how did that work?"

"Just like the sphere controls the earth's magnetic gossamers," Caitlin replied, "we simply harness the magnetic fields produced by electrical activity in the brain. I've tested it using an MEG, a magnetoencephalography machine, on my own head. Most people have very weak fields that can be measured with MEG. Mine were more like the gossamers, stretching as far as ten meters, reaching out towards my assistant's head. When I read his mind, the MEG showed my magnetic fields merging with his."

She shifted out of neutral and eased the throttle forward. Zach noticed Kevin swallow convulsively a few times at the renewed movement. He'd been exposed to the biometal. Zach thought about the story they read, about Tadg the Small, and how six of the ten miners died.

"Caitlin?" he asked.

"Yes, Zach?"

112

"I get it that descendants of shapeshifters are more likely to survive the biometal, but how did their ancestors become shapeshifters in the first place if they were just normal people? Why didn't it kill everyone?"

In reply, Caitlin said severely, "I will say only this: there are some things it is better you do not know."

Chapter Thirty-one

The Isle of Wight

If Kevin hadn't experienced the same level of nausea on the drill ship this summer, he'd think he was dying. After kneeling miserably in front of the john on his third trip to the tiny bathroom, he struggled to stand on shaky legs and blearily inspected his eyes in the mirror mounted over the sink. The whites looked inflamed from the strain of repeated vomiting, but they weren't blood-red like Astrid's. He didn't know how soon after exposure she'd developed symptoms.

In the main cabin, Zach seemed to avoid him while Lizbeth kept casting sympathetic looks his way. He sat at the bench and tried to limit the movement of his body, as if that would somehow offset the relentless bumping and bouncing of the speeding yacht. Zach must think he was a flaming wimp.

When Caitlin announced that they'd almost arrived at their destination, he cautiously lifted his head from where he'd anchored it to the table and looked out the front windshield. A green island rose from the sea.

Caitlin got on the radio to contact the "lock control tower," but Kevin was too miserable to pay much attention to the procedures for gaining entrance to the harbor.

"Where are we now?" Lizbeth asked.

"The Isle of Wight," Caitlin replied.

A car waited for them in the marina parking lot, and after a short drive, Caitlin pulled into a circular gravel driveway lined with hedges that had been trimmed into fanciful dragon shapes. The stone house looked very old to Kevin, something like a castle on a much smaller scale.

Before they got to the age-darkened and scarred front door, a huge, mangy-looking dog galloped around the side of the house and jumped on

Caitlin. Its paws hit her in the shoulders and nearly knocked her to the ground.

The door opened, and a lavender-haired old woman in a velour jogging suit appeared on the stoop.

"Wolfdogge! Leave it."

The dog immediately dropped to a sitting position, its head rotating so adoring brown button eyes could take in both Caitlin and its mistress.

"Still getting out of the kennel?" Caitlin asked.

The two women hugged, and Kevin sensed a strong affection emanating from Caitlin.

"I'm so tickled you called," the old woman exclaimed.

"How are you, Grandmother?"

The old woman laughed, a merry cackle that brought an answering smile to Caitlin's face. "Dinna call me that, now, or you're sure to confuse the young ones. They'll think me your real granny and get their minds all in a boggle."

The old woman shaded her eyes from the afternoon sun and looked them over. Her lips turned down when she saw Kevin.

"Ooch, laddie, you're lookin' mighty peaked. Come in, come in!" She stood aside as they obediently trooped into the cool foyer. "I'm Felicity. Caitlin was married to Victor O'Connor, me great-grandda, many, many moons ago."

Kevin didn't have time to absorb that statement, because Felicity kept on talking.

"There's no telly, but the radio says once some of the satellites from the southern hemisphere are realigned, things will get back to normal. Shame about the space station, all those brave astronauts."

"Is the Internet working?" Zach asked.

Felicity gave him an incomprehensible look. "The what now?"

Zach's horrified expression set her off into peals of laughter. When she got control of herself, she wiped a tear from her eye and said, "That was precious, and so worth it."

Zach didn't hide his disgruntlement very well, but it didn't last. Kevin saw his mouth drop open when Felicity led them into a large room interspersed with wide, carved beams that held up the wooden roof, also beautifully carved with scrolling Celtic patterns. Natural light from leaded glass skylights flooded the room and hundreds of hanging crystal figurines sent sparkling rainbows everywhere. From the furnishings, the area served as living room, dining area and kitchen.

Felicity pointed with an arthritically crooked finger. "Computer's there, young man. Top o' the line, have at it."

Zach made a beeline for a heavy old desk against one wall. Lizbeth spun in a slow circle and said, "Do you mind if I look around?"

"Please, by all means, do. No point constructin' a showroom if no one looks at it."

She put her hand on Kevin's arm. "Come, lad. Seasickness, is it? I've just the thing."

In the kitchen, she set a copper tea kettle to boil and made some foul-smelling tea. He'd already begun to feel better once he'd stepped off the boat, but he sipped the tea and tried to look freshly hale and hearty.

"This isn't a social call," Caitlin said.

Felicity rolled her eyes. "Oh really? I hadn't noticed the world's gone crazy. What are you goin' to do about it, then?"

For the first time, Kevin saw something in Caitlin's eyes that belied her perpetual air of assurance.

"We're looking for something that was stolen from me. Its power is the only thing that can stop the destruction."

Felicity nodded once, sharply. "You'll be needin' the hounds. I can send them straight away. Do ya have a photo of the thief?"

"I don't. This isn't a task for Wolfdogge's kind."

"Then why come to me?"

"I escaped from jail. There's a warrant out."

Kevin thought Felicity didn't look surprised in the slightest.

"Ah. And how was it?"

"I preferred the Tower," Caitlin said, straight-faced.

"You're welcome here, you know that. Anythin' you need."

"I need to get back to the mainland. The police will be looking for my car."

Felicity pressed a set of keys into Caitlin's hand. "Take mine to the ferry."

"Thank you. My boat's at the marina, but it's a risk to continue using it, as well."

Lizbeth wandered into the kitchen area and wrinkled her nose in the direction of Kevin's cup of tea.

"Just one thing," Caitlin said to Felicity. "The next time you see me, ask me about Victor. If I don't know who he is…sic the hounds on me."

Felicity's eyes widened. "You're not the last after all?"

116

"No."

"Hey!" Zach called from the living room. He was looking at the monitor and had a finger pressed to the pages of *The Gossamer's* crew manifest. "What's Simon's last name?"

Caitlin said, "Why?"

"It must be a popular name in England. There's two of them on this list. One named Simon Finster and one Simon R. Allen."

The air left Caitlin's lungs as if she'd been punched in the gut. She whirled and ran for the door, throwing over her shoulder, "Change of plans. If Simon was on *The Gossamer*, he knows where the crown is. Keep them safe!"

Chapter Thirty-two

The Isle of Wight

Lizbeth stood frozen in disbelief. Caitlin left them behind. They were supposed to help her save the world. How important could they be if she kept treating them like a liability to be protected?

She glanced over at Kevin, who stared morosely into his tea, and to Zach, who'd already turned to the familiar comfort of the computer monitor. Suddenly, she desperately wanted to feel her mother's arms around her. She couldn't call her on her cell, since she'd lost her satchel in the ocean after being swept off *The Gossamer*.

"Felicity?" she asked, hating the warble in her voice. "Does your phone work?"

"Connection's spotty, but you can try. Oh, wait, is it long distance? Of course it is. I'm afraid not, then."

Lizbeth nodded. To hide the tears that threatened, she shuffled over to the sliding glass window that overlooked a flourishing garden. The view was beautiful, but she may as well have been staring at a parking lot for all the pleasure she got out of it.

This whole impossibly far-fetched quest had taken her on such a thrill-ride – one she hadn't signed up for in the first place. They'd encountered so many wonders and so many setbacks, and they seemed no closer to finding the crown than when they set out. Had it been only a few days ago? Conflicting emotions welled up and sent wetness spilling down her cheeks. She missed her mother and grandmother so much. If Granma were here, she'd chide Lizbeth out of this funk with one of her nonsensical sayings. When Lizbeth had realized there wasn't enough money for her to attend even the local community college, Granma said, "Spit in one hand and cry in the other. Which hand helps you solve the problem?"

She lifted her hands as if the solution would be in one of them. Instead of searching her palms, she placed them on the cool glass. The garden blurred as her eyes refocused on her own faint reflection. To one side she saw Kevin's worried image, and on the other, Zach's. She hadn't heard them, but she knew when they'd arrived to stand beside her.

Before either of them spoke, Lizbeth caught a glimpse of something beyond the garden, past the low picket fence and behind a length of tall, unruly bushes.

"Did you see that?" she asked.

She felt Zach's hand settle lightly on her shoulder. "Looked like some guy."

Felicity's voice came from behind them. "I've got neighbors neither near enough, nor rude enough to traipse through my garden."

"There!" Kevin pointed further down from where Lizbeth had spotted the flash of something dark, but Lizbeth didn't see anything. Whatever they'd seen was either gone or hiding. She heard the slight swish-swish of Felicity's velour stretch pants and looked around to see the old woman pull a shotgun out of a cabinet.

"Step back from the door." Felicity held the gun confidently in her left hand and had just reached out for the sliding glass door handle, when over the far fence bounded Wolfdogge. The hound ran straight for the back door, his tongue flopping out of his mouth in a silly doggie grin.

"Och, I forgot to put you back in the kennel with your brothers, didn't I?" Felicity opened the slider and the dog rushed in, wagging his tail. Instead of shoving his snuffling wet nose at the visitors as Lizbeth expected, he took a turn around the big room and settled on a floor cushion across the room near the arched opening to the foyer.

"Well," Felicity said with a smile, "at least we know there wasn't anybody out there fool enough to take on Wolfie here. Musta been the dog you seen."

"Is he good protection?" Lizbeth asked, eyeing the dog, which sat alert and still, looking back at her with bright, intelligent eyes.

Felicity placed the shotgun back in the cabinet. "The best. Me dogs are the last of a dyin' breed. Not your average canine. Very special talents, you might say."

So far Lizbeth had encountered a giant, a little person who was the closest to a leprechaun she'd ever seen, and an eerily clever raven. Not to mention the shapeshifters, but she wasn't sure if they were supposed to be fairies or elves or what. At this point, she wouldn't be surprised if Wolfdogge stood on his hind legs and danced a jig.

"Something's not right," Kevin said, voice low and serious.

Lizbeth expected Zach to launch one of his Kevin-bashing quips, but he must have finally learned to trust Kevin's intuition, because he asked, "What is it?"

Kevin slipped his hand into his pocket and pulled out the nugget of iridium. "I didn't feel it when we saw Wolfdogge before, but it's there now. Felicity, you may want to ask your dog if he knows who Victor is."

Chapter Thirty-three

The Isle of Wight

Zach had no idea what Kevin was talking about. Ask the dog about some guy named Victor? He must have missed something while he was on the computer and they were talking in the kitchen. The old lady said it was a special mutt, but Zach doubted it could talk.

Kevin, Lizbeth and Felicity were all staring at the dog as if they were waiting for it to do just that, however, so Zach said, "Hey Wolfdogge. You know Victor? Yeah, me neither."

He started to laugh, but Lizbeth jabbed a sharp elbow into his ribs. "Can't you feel it?"

That's when the dog changed into a man.

Zach had about half a dozen questions about the whole shapeshifting process, but after watching the fascinating full-body morph of Wolfdogge to Brian Griffey, one question at least had been answered. A shapeshifter turning back into a human apparently *did* have to run around naked. Griffey shifted from furry dog to naked man in under ten seconds. As he changed, he rose from all fours clutching the big pillow he'd been laying on in front of him. Zach didn't let the ridiculousness of the situation lower his guard.

Griffey began to walk over, but quick as a whip, Felicity had the shotgun back in her hand. She braced the butt against her shoulder and pointed it at him. He stopped in the middle of the room, eyes on the hand Kevin still held out.

"That's a piece of the crown, isn't it?" he asked. "I can feel it from here."

Zach tried to recall the conversation between Griffey and Bill Masters on board *The Gossamer*. He didn't think Bill really said anything about the core sample other than that it existed, but he was also pretty sure

121

Griffey had attempted to pick Bill's mind apart. He must not have learned much if he thought Kevin's iridium nugget was part of the crown.

"Except…" Griffey trailed off. "Bill did say the deaths weren't caused by the crown."

He took a step closer, but Felicity made a sharp sound like she was correcting one of her dogs, *"Eh!"*

He stopped, held one palm out in a placating gesture and seemed to reconsider his tactics. Since intimidation wasn't going to work while the old lady had a bead on him, Zach expected him to try the friendly approach. He wasn't disappointed.

"Last night was pretty wild, wasn't it?" Griffey asked, lips stretching in a smile.

"Do you think we're stupid?" Lizbeth snapped. "Trying to sneak in here disguised as a dog. As if we couldn't sense you."

Griffey's eyes widened. For the first time, it occurred to Zach that he really had no idea who they were.

"Of course," Griffey said, voice full of wonder, speaking directly to Kevin. "I get it now. That hunk of metal in your hand is from Masters' core sample. All those scientists died because it's the same stuff the crown is *made* out of."

To forestall Lizbeth from any more bursts of information Griffey could potentially use against them, Zach said, "You've got it all figured out, huh?"

Griffey laughed. "But this is marvelous. She's rounded up a bunch of initiates, hasn't she? And you can *sense* me. Only the strongest of us can sense each other. You kids are the next generation. Caitlin's goals appear to be closer to my own than I ever dreamed."

"And what goals would those happen to be?" Felicity asked. She waved the barrel of the gun through the air as if to remind him he was still in her sights.

Griffey's delighted smile faded, and his usual sly expression returned.

"If she were here, we could discuss them. The plates on the car out front are hers and the engine's warm, so I clearly just missed her. Where did she go?"

Zach saw Griffey's eyes go all swirly-sparkly again.

"Pizza!" he shouted, hoping the noise would somehow drown out the answer that had to be right there on top of Felicity's mind for Griffey to pluck. His diversion attempt backfired as Kevin, Lizbeth and Felicity looked at him as if he'd lost his mind.

122

Griffey's laugh held ridicule this time. "You've got a lot to learn. Caitlin must want to keep you well in hand if she hasn't told you the things you need to know. I'd like nothing more than to offer you fledglings some guidance, but I've got to hurry if I'm going to catch Caitlin at the ferry."

"You'll be crossing the Solent with buckshot in your arse if you take one more step," Felicity said.

"No I won't, my dear," Griffey said with a dismissive wave of his hand. "You see, I know the gun's not loaded."

He turned quite deliberately to leave, dropping the pillow carelessly. Lizbeth averted her eyes, but there was no way Zach was going to stand still and let this psycho get to Caitlin, naked or not. He cleared his mind of all the myriad distractions in the room and calculated how many steps it would take to cross it. Before Griffey disappeared under the foyer arch, he leapt into action.

Zach had no idea what Griffey's training might be, but he wouldn't underestimate it, nor would he assume the shapeshifter would fight fair. For all Zach knew, Griffey could throw lightning bolts out of his fingers, so he decided to disable him rapidly and efficiently. He caught up to him and bent to grab one of his ankles. When Griffey stopped to frown down at him, he grabbed the other. A swift jerk backward and Griffey toppled like a tree. He threw his hands out in front of himself to break his fall, leaving Zach free to enclose his neck in a chokehold with his forearms.

Under normal circumstances, the unimaginative wrestling hold was very effective, but not, as Zach discovered, when your victim changed into a snake. Zach was almost relieved at first that he was no longer grappling with a buck-naked guy, but he was soon too busy fighting to worry about it one way or the other. He still had a good grip on Griffey, and kept applying pressure to his now scaly neck, but the 180-pound python flipped him around on the floor until it had Zach's torso and legs tightly in its coils. Zach quickly realized that in a wrestling match, the snake would win. Griffey had Zach's face pressed against the wood floor and his entire lower half was rapidly taken out of commission. Despite the steady pressure Zach continued to apply just below its head, the snake didn't seem to be in danger of passing out any time soon. If he released his hold, there was no guarantee that Griffey the Snake wouldn't simply continue squeezing him to death.

Griffey's reptilian eyes were mere inches from Zach's mouth. Just when Zach came to the conclusion that his teeth were his weapon of last resort, he heard Lizbeth scream, "Have some of *this*!"

Zach didn't know what she'd done, but the python writhed violently, partially releasing him from its hold. In seconds, Griffey had changed again, this time back into the Wolfdogge visage. He slipped out of Zach's grasp and bolted past the others, who were all standing over Zach. Lizbeth held an old ornamental dagger in one hand.

At the sliding glass door, Griffey became himself again. Zach struggled to his feet and started to go after him, but Felicity stopped him.

"He's missed her! By the time he finds his clothes and gets there, the ferry will have gone."

With one hand pressed against his bleeding side, Griffey left without a parting word.

Zach looked at Lizbeth, who still held the dagger in a trembling hand. There wasn't a lot of blood, so she probably hadn't done Griffey much damage, but her attack had certainly distracted him and saved Zach. He wasn't sure what to make of that.

Lizbeth handed the dagger to Felicity. "I saw it earlier hanging on the wall. I figured with the rust on the blade it was probably iron."

Chapter Thirty-four

The Isle of Wight

Less than a minute after Griffey left, an earthquake rocked the old house. Kevin followed Felicity's advice and crawled under the kitchen table with Lizbeth. The rhythmic back and forth movements quickly brought back his nausea, and the flashes of zigzagging rainbow light from all those hanging crystals didn't help. When it finally stopped, Felicity called out from wherever she'd taken shelter, "Everyone okay?"

After Kevin crawled miserably out from under the table, Lizbeth popped up and like a chirping bird said, "Just like any other day in Alaska."

Zach climbed out from under the desk and checked Felicity's computer. "Wow! Internet's still up."

"Amazing," Kevin said, trying to sound sarcastic, but he was afraid it came out sounding as weak and shaky as his knees felt.

Felicity gave the walls and foundation a cursory once-over and said, "It'll take a lot more than that to topple this old house. I'd best check on the dogs."

She took a moment to load the shotgun and took it with her into the back yard. Kevin found his mug of tea and downed it, hoping the concoction would settle his stomach.

"You okay?" Lizbeth asked.

"Fine," he muttered.

"Hey, you guys," Zach said casually, as if the fight and the earthquake hadn't happened. "Come look at this."

He showed them a YouTube video he'd made a few days before he met Caitlin. Kevin was kind of embarrassed watching the normally composed Zach appeal to his fellow San Franciscans to prepare for the big one. The video was definitely cheesy, but he understood why Zach had felt compelled to make it. Things had gotten pretty weird for Kevin, too, before Caitlin showed up and offered an explanation – of sorts.

"So, yeah, I know, it was a dumb idea," Zach said, "but look how many hits it got."

The video had over two-hundred million views. There were over seven million comments. Zach chose one at random and said, "Everybody thought I was crazy before the big one really did hit, and now look. Most of these people want me to tell them what's going on. Like they'd believe me."

"What's this?" Lizbeth asked.

"That's the Video Responses."

"I know, but this one looks like a news report."

Zach clicked on it. It began with a heavily made up female reporter from a Sacramento channel sitting behind a news desk. On the video display behind her head was a photo of Zach from his doomsday YouTube video. The reporter said, "They are the subject of ridicule in cities across America, mentally ill people standing on street corners trumpeting their paranoid message: the world is coming to an end. So what happens when the world really does seem to be coming to an end? Were the crazy predictions coincidence, or was there a grain of truth? Cynthia Perkins has the story."

The scene changed to a ten-second sound bite from Zach's video, one that made him seem particularly unbalanced. Kevin glanced over and saw him wince. Then a blonde reporter standing outside a large two-story house said, "Zach Wong lives in this quiet, upper-class neighborhood in San Francisco. He's been described by family and friends as a normal, if slightly off-beat eighteen-year-old. So what would prompt an otherwise apparently mentally healthy young man to post such an inflammatory video on the popular site YouTube? And how, in less than a week, did it become one of the most-watched, highest-rated Internet videos of all time?"

The story showed brief clips of the reporter interviewing a few of Zach's friends, one of the scientists he'd called attempting to discuss the electromagnetic pulses, and finally, a clip of his mother claiming he had da zhuang.

"I can't watch this," Zach said. He reached for the mouse, but Lizbeth stopped him.

"Hush! This is good reporting."

"How would you like it if your grandmother got on there and started chanting voodoo curses?"

Felicity announced from the far side of the room, "Annette Moreau would never curse anyone."

Lizbeth spun around, looking astonished. "You know Granma?"

Kevin noticed Zach take advantage of the distraction by closing the YouTube page. He didn't blame him.

"We met at your parents' weddin'."

"That's right, they did get married in Ireland. Was Caitlin there? She used to help my dad with his magic act."

"Of course she was there."

Zach said, "If Caitlin is your great-grandmother that means you're like us, right?"

"No, we're not related at all, actually. She was Victor's second wife, after me great-grandmother died of the cholera, you see. Back then, a young woman, even if she just *looks* young, had to have the protection of an 'usband. My grandfather was Victor's first-born, and Caitlin, well, she only ever had the one son – who survived, that is."

"What does that mean?" Kevin asked.

Felicity hesitated before answering, as if mulling over her words. "The legends say that fae folk switched their sickly babes with healthy human ones. That may have a basis in fact, I'm afraid. Those who touched the crown couldn't have children together. Even if the father or mother was normal, the babes seldom survived."

Kevin thought about the iridium nugget in his pocket. His own mother had abandoned him. Every time he'd considered having kids, sometime way in the future, of course, it was with the conviction that he'd be a good dad. Now it sounded like that was no longer an option.

"That's horrible," Lizbeth said, placing a hand on her abdomen.

"It was the price they paid," Felicity replied. "As you can imagine, Caitlin never talks about it."

She sat in the middle of the sofa and patted the cushion. "Come sit with me."

Kevin and Lizbeth complied, but Zach stayed where he was near the monitor. Felicity opened a chest that doubled as a coffee table, removed a thick, leather bound volume and set it in her lap.

"Caitlin came to visit me a few months ago so we could reminisce. Mind you, she didn't bother to tell *me* what was about to happen with the world, but I know now, don't I?

"At any rate." She opened the book to reveal pages filled with neatly labeled pictures. The first few pages had color photos. She flipped further into the book where the photos became black and white, and even further to show copies of painted portraits from another era. Beyond that were just handwritten names, staggered like in a family tree. "She kept this book to try and keep track of, well…these are your ancestors. Other than yourselves, everyone in her book of memories has passed on."

Stunned, Kevin asked, "She knows who my parents were?" but Zach waved his hand in the air and said loudly, "Uh – *Chinese* here. I still don't see how my family was supposed to be descended from a bunch of red-headed Irish druids."

Felicity turned the pages of the album until she reached one that had a grainy photo of a man with distinctively Chinese features. She gave Zach a crafty little grin and he finally seemed interested enough to make his way over to the sofa. "Your father's family came from a long line of warriors, did you know that?"

Zach's eyebrows lifted and he shook his head. "I don't know anything about my father's family. Don't really know much about *him*, either. All I know is he was born in China, became a U.S. citizen and died in the Gulf War when I was a baby."

Kevin sat back to wait impatiently for Felicity to explain Zach's lineage so he could ask again about his own.

"Caitlin, in her long life, has travelled the world. As the story goes, she and Victor were in China just after the Second Opium War broke out. Qing soldiers arrested and imprisoned them, and confiscated all their belongings, but the entire garrison died of some mysterious illness. All but one soldier."

Felicity tapped the photo and Zach leaned in to get a closer look. "Wong Ming, 1863," he read. "So this guy is my however-many-greats grandfather?"

"Actually, he *was* your grandfather. You know that Caitlin is very old. Legend says that when a human steps into the fae world, they stay for what feels like a day but when they go home, their children have all grown up and died. The reality is simply that the folk live longer, maybe forever if they aren't killed. He married your grandmother and when she grew old and passed on, he couldn't bear it. That's how so many of them went, with broken hearts.

"This," she turned to the front page of the album and pointed to a handsome, unsmiling Asian man in a U.S. Marines uniform, "is Ming's only child, your father."

"Yeah, that's him. I mean, Mom has plenty of pictures. Okay, so I get it that these soldiers all died because they took the crown from

Caitlin. What I don't understand is how my grandfather survived if he was Chinese."

Felicity smiled. "That's the irony. Caitlin and Ming traced his ancestry and you really were descended from a red-headed Irish druid. Well, maybe he wasn't red headed, but he fled the Roman Empire and ended up in China. Caitlin kept track of all the folk she could in this book, but there were more who went out into the world and blended in. Their children and their children's children could be anywhere."

Kevin thought about the nugget again. "And what about the children's children? How closely related to the shapeshifter does a person have to be to survive the crown?"

Felicity bit her lip. "All I know is the initiates who were most likely to survive were the progeny of the fae and a normal person. Caitlin herself was one such. I don't know how many generations removed a person can be and still be safe."

"Hey, there's my dad!" Lizbeth said, jabbing her finger at a postcard with a magician on it.

Kevin opened his mouth yet again to ask about his parents, but Lizbeth was apparently more anxious to find out about her roots because she demanded, "Show me *my* grandparents."

"Why would Caitlin put a picture of herself in the book?" Felicity asked.

The silence that followed was so profound, Kevin finally understood the phrase, "You could hear a pin drop."

Chapter Thirty-five

The Isle of Wight

So many thoughts skittered through Lizbeth's head that she was unable to funnel any of them through her voice box. Years ago she remembered asking her mother about her father's family. All her mother would say was that they had gone to heaven, but then she'd said under her breath, "or wherever their kind go." Lizbeth knew her mother hadn't intended for her to hear the derogatory comment, but it stuck in her head. When she'd asked her grandmother what it meant, the older woman shook her greying head and asked, "You know how your mom feels about my occupation?" Lizbeth's mother had even less tolerance for Annette Moreau's 'voodoo nonsense' than Lizbeth did. "Well, some people," Granma had said, "are afraid of things they don't understand, and your father's folks were very different souls."

Lizbeth was vaguely aware of Zach sitting on the side of the couch and putting his arm around her, but she didn't acknowledge him.

One thing puzzled her. If her mother was so leery of Caitlin that she led Lizbeth to believe she was *dead*, why did she agree to let her accompany her in the first place? She wished she still had her cell phone, wished the phone lines were working. She'd call Granma and get some real answers. Then something occurred to her: she hadn't had an opportunity to even speak to her mother before Granma and Caitlin packed her up and rushed her to the airport. Granma told her that her mother was on board with the whole crazy scheme, but maybe that was, as Granma would say, "a rubber-band truth."

Felicity interrupted her thoughts with a gentle nudge. "You didn't know, did you?"

Lizbeth blinked and her memories faded away. Suddenly, it was the last topic on the crumbling earth she wanted to discuss. She looked past Felicity into Kevin's concerned face. "What about Kevin? Who were his parents?"

"I don't know," Felicity said.

"What?" Kevin burst out. "But you said – the book-"

She heaved a sigh and closed the album with a musty-smelling puff of air. "Caitlin knew about Lizbeth, of course, and she knew about Zach. I suspect the real reason she came to see me was to search through the album for your parents, Kevin. She met you, you see."

"I never...oh," he said. "Who was she?"

"At the time she was posing as your professor to get close to the project director of the scientific drilling vessel."

"Bill Masters."

"Yes. I gathered she, ahem, didn't want him to know she was interested in his activities."

Lizbeth knew it was an inappropriate time to pry, but she couldn't help herself. "Were they, you know..."

"Lovers?" Felicity asked, with a teasing gleam in her eyes. "I believe so. They had a falling out over whatever project he was working on."

Zach's hand was still on Lizbeth's back. He'd been making small circles with his fingers throughout the whole conversation and she'd become rather self-conscious about it.

"She spoke to you, Kevin, in the guise of the professor, of course, and whatever you told her very much piqued her interest."

Kevin stood and stepped away from the sofa, slipping his right hand into his pocket. Lizbeth suspected he got some kind of comfort from contact with the nugget.

"Okay," he said. "Okay, yeah. I think I know when she did it. Right before we boarded the ship, Professor Weinstein was supposed to have been taking a nap in the hotel room, but I ran into him having fish and chips with Bill. As soon as I started to ask him how he managed to get to the restaurant ahead of me, he interrupted and invited me to join them. I did notice the conversation got a little weird. The professor kept asking questions that he should have known. Bill was answering like he thought Weinstein had Alzheimer's, you know, and I remember thinking maybe he should have taken that nap."

Felicity pursed her lips. "But it was something you said that made her wonder who you really were."

Lizbeth saw a look of comprehension cross Kevin's face. He gave a short laugh, and his cheeks darkened a shade. "I said...I mean, the professor was talking about the enormity of the project, how he thought maybe we were messing with something we shouldn't, and I agreed with him. Then they both looked at me like I spoke out of turn and I got all flustered. I told them I was, you know, drawn to the idea of exploring Silverpit Crater, but I had a feeling something bad was going to happen."

Lizbeth frowned at Zach's snort. "That's it?" he asked. "Caitlin came to see Felicity based on one of your feelings?"

"No."

Lizbeth heard the mild resentment in Kevin's tone, and it irritated her that Zach had reverted right back to tossing sarcastic remarks his way. She knocked his arm away to stop the incessant rubbing over the same spot on her back.

Kevin said, "I don't think it was what I *said*. I remember wondering if Weinstein really was sick or something because his eyes looked strange. Caitlin and Griffey strange."

"She was reading your mind," Lizbeth said, "but you didn't know anything about being descended from shapeshifters."

Zach got up and went over to the computer again. "Yeah, but Griffey said the strong ones can sense each other. He obviously couldn't sense us, but I'll bet Caitlin can."

"Is that who it was – Griffey? That sounds familiar." Felicity opened the album again, rapidly turning pages and muttering, "Griffey, Griffey."

Felicity was running her finger down the names on one of the pages. "Oh, here he is! Brian, is it?"

Lizbeth squinted at the black and white photo of a short, bearded man with a broad nose. "That's not him."

"You mustn't assume the person he's shown you is his real face."

Lizbeth frowned. "I didn't think of that."

"What does this mean?" Kevin asked. He tapped his finger on a notation written in a neat hand next to the photo. The letters D.O.D. and April 15, 1912 were crossed out. Next to it was Kevin's own name.

"Oh, dear," Felicity said, tapping a finger against the tip of her nose and looking sideways at Kevin's pouting face. "I think perhaps she thought you were related to our Mr. Griffey."

"Yeah, but that would mean Caitlin knew he was still alive," Lizbeth said.

Zach produced another snort. "Wouldn't be the first time she lied, now would it?"

Chapter Thirty-six

The Isle of Wight

After suffering through the angst of Felicity dropping the ancestral bomb on everyone, Zach was glad when she and Lizbeth went into the kitchen area to make something to eat. Kevin had stretched out on the couch and closed his eyes, so Zach read more comments and looked at several video clips from his YouTube page. There were a few in particular that got his attention.

A thin woman with short brown hair and horn-rimmed glasses living in western Washington said she'd experienced the electric-like sensations, too, right before Mount St. Helens blew its top for the second time in recent memory. An elderly Filipino woman in Manila, with translation help from her grandson, described the "fits" she'd suffered before Mayon erupted. Her grandson shyly admitted to feeling it, too. A Japanese man who spoke barely intelligible English gave a serious account of the two major and eighty minor earthquakes that nearly leveled Tokyo. He claimed to have predicted each one before it hit because, "The ground spoke me it going to shake."

Zach thought about what Felicity had said, how Caitlin kept track of as many of the children of the underground druids as she could, but there were more out there. How many could there be, though, if so few of the infants survived? Still, were these people in the videos like him and Lizbeth and Kevin? Could they sense the gossamer sphere's intentions, or were they the crazy ones? He had to admit none of them seemed crazy. Heck, *he* had seemed more like a lunatic on his stupid video than the people who'd responded to him. He decided to check out more of Seamus the Bard's site, but when he clicked on the link his screen told him the page could not be found. He tried refreshing it, and closed and reopened his browser, but it appeared the Internet had gone down. Banging his hands down on the desk, he exclaimed, "Augh!"

Kevin groaned and Zach saw him pull a cushion over his head.

"Is that your plan, dwarf-boy? To hide from what's left of the world?"

"Zach!" Lizbeth said. "Leave him alone already."

Zach was still smarting from her earlier rejection, after she'd slapped his hand away when he only wanted to comfort her. Now she'd spoken to him with the kind of scorn he got from his mom when he stayed up too late working on his art or didn't pick up his room. Lizbeth sure spent a lot of energy defending Kevin, who had curled up in the fetal position on the couch, still hiding under the cushion. *The wuss.*

Felicity asked calmly, "Has the Internet gone down?"

"Yeah," Zach said. "Now we can all just sit here and fester while we wait for Caitlin to tell us what we're supposed to do."

As if he weren't sitting within hearing, Felicity commented to Lizbeth, "Not so level-headed when he doesn't get 'is way, is he?"

Lizbeth rolled her eyes and it infuriated him even more. With a major effort, he stopped himself from going off on her. Instead, he checked the browser again. Felicity's home page, a website for Wolf Hounds, obligingly popped up. He went straight to Seamus' site.

"What are you doing?" Lizbeth asked. She'd come to stand behind him. When she placed a hand on his shoulder, his eyes closed involuntarily as a rush of longing flowed through him. He endured it for a moment and then shrugged her hand off.

"Nothing," he mumbled.

"Is this that bard website?"

"Yeah." The banner across the top had changed. It now said, "Children of the Boar: Cast off your Shrouds and Come Forth."

"What's this?" Lizbeth pointed to a heading that read, "The Last Noble." He opened the page and read silently alongside Lizbeth:

"In her long life she's been called many things, but she was named Caetl in the year of her birth 47 AD, the only child of the Chief of a powerful clan and his Druidess wife. When Caetl was fourteen years of age, a rival clan raided their holdings, taking her hostage. Her father rallied his people and besieged the enemy, the survivors of whom had no choice but to escape by sea, taking Caetl as insurance. A storm arose and forced her captors' vessel ashore at the island of Anglesey, the stronghold of druid priests and priestesses. Her mother, the Druidess, changed into a pelican and upon seeing where the storm was blowing the raiders, flew ahead and waited on shore to greet them with an escort of armed Druids.

"Times were dire for the inhabitants of Anglesey Isle. The captured raiders were given a choice: die or swear allegiance to the druids, who needed aid against the Roman army poised to cross the Menai Straight. The raiders were more fearful of the druids than the invading army, so they capitulated. The next morning, the commander of the Roman legion gave the order and catapults began hurling missiles from one bank to the other as his soldiers crossed on flat-bottomed boats and his infantry swam the low tide.

"The wildly painted Druids and their supporters put on a frightening show for the soldiers, dancing and shrieking and casting curses, but their numbers had been decimated from years of resisting their conquerors. Those who had not been killed outright had fled, either deep into the Irish countryside like Caetl's mother, or for parts unknown. Anglesey was the last stronghold, and it soon became obvious it would not hold much longer against this enemy. The druids could have abandoned their people and saved themselves, but they stayed, fought and died.

"On the far side of the island, away from the horror of an invader that left no one, not even women and children alive, Caetl's mother and two other noble High Priestesses bundled Caetl aboard the raider's boat to escape with the Druids' most treasured artifact: The Gossamer Crown."

"He's talking about Caitlin!" Lizbeth said. "Kevin! Come look at this."

When he didn't respond, she went to the couch and lifted the cushion. He winced and pulled it quickly back over his face, but not before Zach saw his eyes.

Lizbeth swung around, her face horrified, and Zach jumped up to pull her into his arms.

"Don't tell him," she whispered in his ear, and he nodded. Zach may not like Kevin very much, but he never wanted him to die.

Chapter Thirty-seven

The Isle of Wight

Kevin had never been all that fond of bright light. Huddled on the couch with his face buried in a cushion, he supposed it made sense, now that he knew his ancestors were mine-dwelling, darkness-loving dwarves. First, he'd been sick on the boat, then the earthquake set it off again, and now the interior of Felicity's house, illuminated with its abundance of skylights, had become too much for his burning eyes to bear. There was nothing wrong with his hearing, however, and since the cushion wasn't blocking his ears, Lizbeth's anguished whisper reached him clearly.

He lifted the cushion enough to ask, "Tell me what?" and then heard an unsubtle, "Shh!" from one of them.

Zach said quietly, "It's not like he won't notice when he looks in the mirror."

Even through his misery, that got Kevin's attention. He sat up and replaced the cushion, blinking against the brightness. "What are you guys talking about?" His voice was hoarse.

Felicity walked into the room, saying, "I've got three kinds of dressing – oh! Dear Lord, what happened to your eyes?"

Kevin's empty stomach clenched. "Are they red?"

"Very much so! I could imagine Zach here, after the squeezin' he got from Griffey, having some burst vessels in 'is eyes, but you…"

Kevin got unsteadily to his feet and put his hand in his pocket. His fingers automatically caressed the misshapen lump of iridium. He heard it again, a strange sound that had been plaguing him for the last half hour, a faint buzzing voice in his head talking nonsense, as if his fillings were picking up a foreign radio station.

He squinted at Zach, who was holding Lizbeth in his arms – again. Both of them looked stricken.

A hand on his shoulder pulled him around and Felicity's lightly wrinkled face appeared so close he couldn't focus. He tried to open his eyes long enough for her to get a good look.

"Must be from the strain of vomitin'," she said softly.

"It isn't," Lizbeth said. "It's that nugget."

Kevin pulled it out of his pocket and let it rest in his palm. Felicity reached for it, but three voices in unison stopped her, "*No!*"

Her eyes went round as she took an affronted step back. "For goodness sake, tell me what's wrong."

Kevin started to slip the nugget back into his pocket, but Lizbeth twisted away from Zach and grabbed Kevin's arm.

"It's the nugget."

Felicity shook her head. "You already said that, dear."

"Kevin, stop touching it," Lizbeth said. She let go of his arm and crossed her own tightly against her stomach. "Let's put it away somewhere safe."

He made a protective fist around the nugget and immediately heard the strange voice, hissing loudly in his ears this time. Disoriented, he shut his eyes and dropped his chin to his chest. He didn't know how long he stood there, but a sudden sharp pain in his forearm forced his hand to open involuntarily. The noise in his head abated as the nugget clattered across the tile floor. Had Zach hit him? He wanted to snatch the nugget back up again, but he was so tired. He stumbled to the couch and collapsed on it.

Through a haze of exhaustion he heard Felicity say, "So, if I'm understandin' this rightly, that chunk of metal there is not part of the crown, as Mr. Griffey originally thought, but a bit of the same material it was made from?"

"Yes," came Zach's voice. "And Kevin's been messing with it for almost 24 hours."

"That's got to be why he's sick, right?" Lizbeth still sounded worried. "The ritual was to touch the crown. Maybe prolonged exposure is dangerous."

Kevin opened his eyes and looked at her. The room didn't seem quite as bright as it had before.

"Now that, I can't say," Felicity said. He watched as she went to a curio cabinet on the wall and took something from a shelf. "Here's a box you can put the bit into. It's got a secure enough latch, I would think."

Between them, Zach and Lizbeth managed to get the nugget into the box without touching it. Kevin didn't see what they did with it after that, because he closed his eyes and must have dozed off.

When he opened them again, it was dark in the room and his stomach was rumbling. He sat up, waiting for the room to spin, but nothing happened. He felt fine. Standing, he turned toward soft voices from the dining area.

"Kevin!" Lizbeth rushed over and studied his face in the light from the dining room chandelier. "You look better. Thank goodness. How do you feel?"

"Where's the nugget?"

Zach spoke from the table. "You're not getting it back, dude. Look what it did to you."

Kevin shrugged one shoulder in annoyance. "Yeah, alright. I just – it just…talks to me."

"Seriously?" Lizbeth asked.

"I don't know how else to explain it."

Lizbeth patted him on the back. "Well, once Caitlin gets here, we'll ask her about it. Hey, maybe while she's gone she'll find the crown and we can do whatever it is we need to save the world."

"*Find* the crown?" Felicity asked. Her downturned mouth hung partly open in shock. "Is *that* what she's lookin' for?"

Chapter Thirty-eight

The Isle of Wight

Felicity seemed like such a kind-hearted and wise woman, despite her familiarity with the shotgun, that her distressed pacing around the big room made Lizbeth uneasy.

"That horrible thing!" Felicity cried. Lizbeth had never seen someone literally wring their hands before.

Zach leaned towards Lizbeth and asked quietly, "What, the crown?" but Felicity heard.

"*Yes*, the crown! It ruined her life. Everything she does is in service of that bloody crown. I thought she was finally rid of it, but now you say it has enslaved her again-" She broke off, stomped around a bit more and then stopped in the middle of the room. She inhaled and let it out slowly.

"If only we knew who had it, then the Cú faoil could help her find it."

"What's the Cú faoil?" Zach asked.

Felicity took another calming breath and said, "Let me tell you a story."

Lizbeth was looking at Felicity and projecting an air of polite interest, but she suspected Zach had performed his signature eye-roll, because Felicity said, "Don't fret, it's a short one, and it might help you understand why Caitlin likes to go it alone.

"Wolfdogge's kind are the Cú faoil, bred for their bravery in battle and cunnin' at huntin' wolves. It's said his ancestor was the Cú Sith, a monstrous, red-eyed supernatural dog from the Scottish Highlands, dreaded by all. Me family's been raisin' these hounds for centuries.

"Wolfdogge doesn't need to get the scent off what he's searchin' for, you see, because unlike other dogs, he hunts by sight, and because of

139

his ancestry, his sight is keener than what he can see with his eyes, if you know what I mean.

"The Cú faoil were bred for kings – by law, none other were allowed to keep them. When he was a young man, Victor raised a fine specimen from a pup. Ooch, how he loved that dog. But the dog was meant to go to a noble household, and go it did."

As Felicity's "short" story stretched on, Zach shifted from foot to foot next to Lizbeth.

"The great estate that got the dog was nearby Victor's ancestral lands, and the dog, well, he kept escapin' his pen, much like Wolfdogge. They're hard to contain, they are, bein' as how they're so intelligent. At any rate, one day Victor was leadin' the dog back to its home when he saw a certain beautiful young redhead runnin' across a field, chased by an armed man on horseback. Victor didn't know what she'd done, but he feared for her, and told the dog to attack. It pulled the horseman from the back of 'is mount midstride, for that's what they were bred to do in battle, don't you know.

"The nobleman was furious, as it turned out Victor had set his own dog on him. 'Get her, you fool, she's a thief!' he shouted, but when Victor set the dog to follow her, it went barkin' after a poor sheep mindin' its own business in a nearby field. Victor had never seen the dog do such a thing, and the nobleman thought it had gone daft and told Victor to take it back, which he was quite pleased and willin' to do."

Lizbeth noticed that Zach was no longer fidgeting. He'd given Felicity his rapt attention.

"All that week, Victor thought of nothin' but the beautiful girl, wonderin' who she was, what she'd done, where she'd gone. He was so besotted that he even sketched her likeness, rememberin' every detail of her face and hair. Then he sat with the dog and showed it the drawin' and set it the impossible task of huntin' the girl down."

Felicity went into the kitchen and began washing dishes as if she'd finished the story.

"Is that it?" Zach asked.

"Well, you know me great-grandfather and Caitlin ended up together," Felicity said, and Lizbeth saw her lips curl in a devious little smile.

Zach yawned and ran a hand through his hair. "What's the point of the story, though?"

"The point is: Wolfdogge can find anyone."

"And Caitlin knows it," Kevin said.

"Exactly."

"So why didn't she take you up on your offer to have Wolfdogge help her?" Lizbeth asked.

"As I said, the Cú faoil are sight hounds," Felicity replied. "It's a special kind of sight, but they need to know who to look for. Caitlin wouldn't be likely to ask for help anyway, for the same reason she's gone and left you three here with me. She knows how much I love Wolfdogge and wouldn't want to put him in danger. The stubborn wretch. Please understand that Caitlin has seen so many of her friends and family die, many of them to violent ends, like-"

She stopped and concentrated on scrubbing a dish that looked perfectly clean to Lizbeth.

"Like Victor?" Kevin asked.

"No. Me great-grandda was an old man when he passed. Caitlin stayed with 'im 'til his final hour, aging herself to match him wrinkle for wrinkle."

Lizbeth had a feeling she knew who Felicity had been about to mention. "How did my father die? Mom told me it was in a car crash."

Felicity bobbed her head up and down several times. "With the crown at the bottom of the Atlantic Ocean, she was finally free of that crushin' obligation. Then they began salvagin' Titanic, and she became obsessed with findin' it before anyone else, for obvious reasons. She asked your da to help her. He did die in a car wreck, on his way to the airport. Your mother never forgave her."

"Mom told me she was dead."

"I'm not surprised. I'm sure your mother had her reasons, but I still remember how she treated your granny, her own mother, at the weddin'. Your granny dressed herself in a perfectly lovely gown, quite colorful, it was. I overheard your mother beratin' her, shamefully, about how her choice of dress was too flamboyant. And this from a daughter of the fae."

"What do you mean?" Lizbeth asked.

"Caitlin was certain your granny's got a bit o'the blood in her. Makes you extra special, I think."

Lizbeth thought about her grandmother, recalling the other evening when Granma, too, felt the electric sensations from the aurora. Granma had always said Lizbeth was destined for great things.

She looked over at Zach, who'd picked up a dishtowel. He selected a plate from those Felicity had set in the rack. As he dried it, he asked, "When Caitlin mentioned to you that something had been stolen, didn't she say it could stop the destruction? Wouldn't that tell you what it was?"

Felicity's lips puckered in offense. "Not at all, young man. The crown has no other power but to turn ordinary souls into fae folk. None that I'm aware of, that is."

Lizbeth felt sorry for Zach as he sputtered an apology, but Felicity's good nature prevailed and she said, "Never you mind. We all know Caitlin keeps to herself. If she withheld information, we'll just assume she felt she had a good reason."

After the dishes had been washed and dried and the food put away, Kevin mentioned he was famished. It was the sort of awkward thing Lizbeth had come to expect from him. When he'd eaten and his dirty dishes were resting unwashed in the sink, Felicity assigned them each a place to sleep. Kevin got the couch, where he'd taken his restorative nap. Zach got an inflatable twin mattress that was too short for his height and was located in a spare bedroom jam-packed with junk. Lizbeth, to her discomfort, was told she'd be sleeping next to Felicity in her musty queen-sized bed. It was apparent from Felicity's casualness about the arrangement that she didn't see any reason why Lizbeth would balk at bunking with her.

"Here's a nightdress for you, dear," she said, handing Lizbeth a long, white cotton gown. "The loo's right through there."

Lizbeth took the opportunity to take a quick shower. When she removed her jeans, she felt something in her pocket and remembered Kevin's nugget. She'd tucked the little box Felicity had given them into her pocket for safe keeping. She pulled it out and set it on the back of the toilet, then turned on the bath faucets, adjusting the hot and cold until the water was comfortable.

She hadn't ever really gotten a good look at the nugget. Figuring there was no harm in looking, she lifted the box and flipped the tiny hook. The lid came open faster than she'd anticipated, and the box slipped between her wet fingers. In a reflex reaction, she jerked her hand to keep the box from falling and the nugget popped out. Her free hand shot out and caught it before it dropped into the open toilet bowl.

With shaking hands, she placed the nugget back in the box, fastened it, and set it back down before closing the toilet lid and stepping under the shower spray. She scrubbed her hand with a bar of Felicity's sweet-smelling soap until it hurt.

Once she joined Felicity under the crisp white sheets, she laid face up, stiff and uncomfortable until the old woman began to snore softly. Even then she couldn't relax, not because of the incident in the bathroom, which she'd firmly blocked from her thoughts, but because her mind insisted on poring over the other events of the day. Not that she blamed it.

So much had happened. So much had changed, illustrated by the fact that Zach had been in a life-or-death struggle today and they hadn't even talked about it. And who knows what would have happened to Kevin if they hadn't realized the nugget was making him sick? The truth was, while she was safe in this strange bed, people all over the world were *dying*. Lizbeth, Zach, Kevin – any one of them, or all three at once, could be next.

Caitlin was out there trying to carry the weight of the whole world on her shoulders, while the three of them just…waited. Suddenly it became essential that she convince the others to go find Caitlin. What if she was in trouble? Were they going to just passively wait for her until the world ended?

Lizbeth slipped out from under the covers and made her way down the dark hallway to the spare bedroom. The doorknob made clicking noises and the hinges squeaked as she entered. She stubbed her bare toe on a box and swore under her breath. She heard the soft sound of Zach's laughter.

"What are you doing?" he asked.

She shut the door and felt her way in the dark to the mattress on the floor. It was chilly in the room. "If Caitlin isn't back by morning, we need to go find her."

"I know. I was just thinking the same thing. Is that your teeth chattering? Sounds like you're typing on a keyboard. Come here."

She moved closer and felt his hands at her hips. He guided her down onto the mattress and tucked her under the covers. She lay on her side with her back to him and he snuggled close with one arm around her mid-section.

"I'm just going to sleep," she said, although she knew he didn't need the clarification.

"Well, whatever you're wearing would make anything else impossible."

She giggled a little and relaxed into the warmth of the cocoon they'd created.

"Goodnight, Lizbee."

She didn't even ask him where he'd come up with Granma's nickname. "'Night."

Chapter Thirty-nine

The Isle of Wight

When he woke the next morning, Zach knew right away he'd slept in one position all night. He couldn't feel his right arm at all, and a slight turn of his head told him he had a crick in his neck. Lizbeth had rolled towards him at some point and was sprawled all over him; her head rested on the numb arm, her hand was on his chest and one leg hooked around his legs. As soon as he realized that in order for her leg to get that way, her nightgown must've ridden way, way up, he decided he'd better sever all contact and find a cold shower – fast. She obligingly rolled away when he tried to extricate himself, and he was glad, since he hadn't known how he was going to get the dead limb out from under her.

He shook his arm and flexed his fingers as he walked down the hall, soon discovering that Kevin had beaten him to the bathroom. It looked like that cold shower was a reality whether he liked it or not.

Once he'd finished up and redressed, he headed for the main room, passing Lizbeth in her white nightgown on the way. She gave him a shy smile and he returned it. He hadn't so much as kissed her, but somehow it felt like so much more had happened between them.

"Mmm, something smells good," he said as he entered the kitchen.

Felicity glanced up. "Eggs and sausages."

He sat at the table across from Kevin and studied his face. The whites of his eyes were almost normal. "Dude, you used up all the hot water."

"That's not his fault," Felicity said. "The water heater is old. We should be grateful the plumbin' hasn't burst with all these earthquakes."

Zach was grateful Felicity didn't say anything about Lizbeth sleeping with him. She had to have noticed Lizbeth's side of the bed hadn't been slept in. They were lucky Felicity hadn't panicked upon

144

finding her missing and searched the house for her. Just thinking about it made his face burn. He wanted to tell Felicity that nothing had happened, but there was no way he'd do it in front of Kevin. Not that he wanted Kevin to think that something *had* happened. He just didn't want him to know at all.

Lizbeth came out just as they were digging into the hearty breakfast Felicity laid before them. "Just eggs and sausages" turned out to include potatoes, brown bread, fresh strawberries and a rich coffee with heavy cream.

Over breakfast, Lizbeth broached the subject of finding Caitlin. To Zach's surprise, Felicity was all for it.

"I assume you know where she went?" she asked.

"Sure," Zach said. "Simon's house."

"And where exactly might that be?"

Zach looked at Lizbeth; she shook her head. He looked at Kevin, who shrugged.

"Ahh, well, we…were there, but none of us knows how to get back or what the address is."

"That settles it, then. You'll be taking Wolfdogge," she said with a finality that did seem to settle it.

Once they'd eaten, Zach sat at Felicity's computer and opened Seamus the Bard's website. He'd lain awake last night, holding Lizbeth, thinking about how awful it would be if she died and trying to come up with some other way to stop the sphere. What if the crown was lost to them forever? Were all of Caitlin's abilities—the shapeshifting, the mind-reading, the electrical bursts that came in so handy whenever they needed to steal a car—useless without the crown? Would the whole quest be a waste of time if they couldn't find it? He thought not. What was the point of them having all these impossible powers if they couldn't use them to shut the sphere down? He'd formed a nebulous plan after Lizbeth's breathing became soft and regular in sleep. Caitlin may have spent her long lifetime keeping her secrets, but maybe it was time to abandon that mindset.

On Seamus' home page, Zach read the lines below the prominently displayed heading, "Children of the Boar: Cast off your Shrouds and Come Forth." The message was short and cryptic: "The age of hiding is done; the time for action is nigh; we must come together as one; Sound the battle cry!"

He clicked on Seamus' link labeled "Contact Me," made note of the email address, and opened his own email provider. Felicity was bustling around preparing for their departure, so he had to hurry, but he'd already mentally composed his message: "Dear Seamus, you probably won't believe this, but I'm in England right now with the last Noble looking for the crown. It was stolen from her a long time ago, probably by the Guild. It's the only thing that can stop the gossamer sphere. Can you help us? Do you know of anyone who claims to be the descendant of a real shapeshifter? Please answer ASAP. Zach." He included a link to his YouTube page and after a brief pause to consider the ramifications of going behind Caitlin's back, hit send.

Felicity gave them all the cash she had on her and brought Wolfdogge in from his kennel. The dog looked to Zach to be as tall as a Shetland pony.

"Here's his food," she said, handing Zach a heavy knapsack. "Be sure he has access to plenty of water. There's a picture of Caitlin in the bag. Show it to him once you get across the Solent, tell him to 'find,' and be sure to keep a tight hold on his leash."

Wolfdogge sat calmly by his mistress, tongue lolling out of the side of his mouth. Zach said, "I don't get it. We're going to have to take a taxi-"

"He'll tell you which way to turn," Felicity said.

Despite her assurance, he remained skeptical and hoped the dog didn't turn out to be one big hairy, slobbery obstacle.

"If he can find Caitlin that easily, why can't he find the crown?" Lizbeth asked.

"Even if a picture of the crown existed, he can't find things, just people."

Zach thought about his laptop with the digital image he'd created. It was either at the bottom of the sea or floating in the burnt-out hulk of *The Gossamer*.

"It was silvery, and had," he said, walking around one of the huge wooden posts in the living room, "one of these in the center of it." He tapped his knuckles on a triple-spiral symbol carved into the age-darkened wood.

"The Celtic triskele?" Felicity looked impressed. "It's one of the oldest symbols there is. Scholars have speculated for centuries, but no one really knows what the symbols represent."

Lizbeth came to stand next to Zach. She ran her fingers over the spirals one by one. "I feel like I should know what it means."

"Ask Caitlin," Felicity said. "When you find her."

146

The morning was cold, the sky an unnatural brownish grey. Tiny particles floated in the air; drifting volcanic ash. Lizbeth had borrowed one of Felicity's jackets, but the old woman had nothing suitable for Zach or Kevin. After hugging them each as if she'd known them all their lives, she put them in Caitlin's car.

"Drive carefully," she said. "Caitlin was afraid to be on the road in this car for good reason. Griffey recognized the plates, so you must assume the police are lookin' for it."

Since Caitlin had the keys, they had to do their car-starting trick. Kevin drove, but only because he'd spent marginally more time in England than the others, which somehow made him more qualified to drive on the wrong side of the road. Zach sat in back next to Wolfdogge, who reeked of that pungent doggy odor, and his breath smelled like the sausage Felicity had snuck him for breakfast. At least he was well behaved. Zach petted him tentatively, and never once did the dog try to lick him on the face, even though they sat eye to eye.

The ferry ride was uneventful but getting a taxi driver to agree to take what amounted to a small *horse* along proved more difficult. The only taker was a friendly Indian man who lavished attention on Wolfdogge as soon as he saw him.

Zach felt like a complete idiot showing the dog the picture of Caitlin, but he surreptitiously held it up for Wolfdogge to see as soon as the driver asked them where they were going. Nothing seemed to happen.

"Do you have an address for me?" The driver repeated.

Lizbeth, sitting in the front seat, suggested Zach roll down the window so the dog could get some air. As soon as Zach complied, Lizbeth said, "Find!" and Wolfdogge thrust his head out and barked. His nose pointed east.

"We don't have an exact address, but we can direct you, if you don't mind," Zach said.

"Whatever you say," the driver said in his heavy accent.

Just before every turn, Wolfdogge let out one bark and stiffened his body like a hunting dog giving away the location of its quarry. Several times he threw himself across Zach and Kevin to get to the opposite window. Zach kept intercepting amused looks in the rearview mirror from the driver, who said, "That's one smart dog. He knows the way home, doesn't he?"

It was a long drive, but the landscape finally began to look familiar to Zach. When they pulled up in front of Simon's house, he looked at the scruffy dog sitting next to him and shook his head in amazement. They paid the driver and got out. As the taxi drove off, Wolfdogge began to pull on his leash and whine.

"Maybe we shouldn't have come right up to the door," Lizbeth said, sounding nervous.

The house was silent; the only sound the cawing of a nearby raven.

It sounded to Zach like the bird was saying, "Cú faoil, Cú faoil!"

At the end of the leash, Wolfdogge became more insistent. Zach was strong, but the dog began pulling him toward the house. Then the front door flew open and Caitlin appeared on the step. Zach was so startled to see her looking pleasantly inquisitive that he relaxed his grip enough to allow Wolfdogge to pull free. The dog bolted away, but instead of throwing himself at Caitlin, who stood twenty yards away, he disappeared around the side of the house.

"Zach," Lizbeth said quietly, with warning in her voice.

"I know," he replied. "But we need to find out where she is, so let's smile and pretend we're happy to see her."

Chapter Forty

East of England

Kevin tried to produce a sincere smile. If he believed in the dog – and after the taxi ride he was certainly convinced of Wolfdogge's abilities – they weren't walking toward the real Caitlin. She wasn't wearing the same outfit she'd had on when she left Felicity's house; the jeans were so long she'd had to roll them up at the cuff, and although she was her normal height, it looked as if she'd put on about fifty pounds overnight.

Kevin paused on the stone walkway and said loudly enough for the fake Caitlin to hear, "I better go get that dumb dog."

Zach shot him a quick look. "Yeah, good idea."

"Don't worry about that," Caitlin said. "Come inside, I've got something important to show you."

"I'll bet," Kevin said under his breath, thinking, *the business end of a gun, probably.*

Griffey, assuming that's who it was, went back into the house, but Kevin, instead of following behind Zach and Lizbeth, made a split-second decision to go after Wolfdogge. Zach could handle whatever Griffey wanted to "show" them, and if he couldn't, then they'd need Caitlin that much more.

He ran around the side of the house, leapt over a low rock wall, and sprinted across the grassy field. The growth was heavy with morning dew and his shoes and the bottom of his jeans were soon soaked through. He looked over his shoulder as he ran. No one pursued him; the house looked abandoned and lonely against the grey sky. The only sound was the staccato cawing of a raven.

He slowed, panting, and began to walk. His illness had taken more out of him than he'd known if he couldn't even run a couple hundred yards.

Wolfdogge was nowhere in sight. Kevin whistled, made kissing noises, clapped his hands and called, "Here doggy!" with no response. A glance down at a patch of muddy ground showed recent footprints, small ones a petite woman like Caitlin might make, and big ones, so big they had to belong to Simon. On top of one of the big prints was a paw print, smeared as Wolfdogge ran, his claws digging deep. Simon and Caitlin's prints pointed to the west, at a right angle to the house and in a different direction from the oak grove and the old church foundation. However, Wolfdogge seemed to have been headed directly for the trees.

Puzzled, Kevin went in the direction of Caitlin's prints. A little further on, he spotted more evidence that they'd come this way, although this time the prints could have been made by his own rather average size eleven shoe. The grass got thicker and bushes obstructed his progress. He pushed his way through the shrubs, worried now that he was taking too long. A prickly branch scratched him, but he bent it out of the way with little regard for the pain. Passing between two thick bushes, he stopped cold at what he saw.

His first reaction was to recoil in horror at the sight of two bodies lying prone in the grass, but before he'd even formed a thought, a whistling wind brushed the side of his face. Startled, he ducked a little as Caw landed on his shoulder. The bird cocked its head and regarded Kevin with its odd blue eyes. It made a sad kind of rattling chirp in his ear.

Kevin didn't want to look, but he forced himself to examine the bodies. Neither was wearing a coat and each had a streaked spot of reddish-brown discoloration on the shirt. It looked as if they'd been shot and then left out in the rain. Simon's corpse lay face down in the grass, and Len – thank goodness the mud-prints hadn't been Caitlin's after all – lay on his back, eyes open and unseeing. Caw launched himself from Kevin's shoulder and landed on Len's chest.

Tears sprang to Kevin's eyes as the bird began pecking at a button on Len's shirt. He backed away, allowing the bushes to once more conceal the crime from casual view. He looked back at the house, a slow fury building within. Griffey would have access to a gun – he was a police officer, after all. At this very moment he could be holding Zach and Lizbeth at bay with it.

Kevin fought his way out of the bushes, oblivious now to the thorns, and broke into a run again, straight for the oak grove. He prayed as he ran that he wouldn't find Wolfdogge holding vigil over another body.

Under the canopy of leaves, the ground was not as wet, but when he began to navigate the treacherous root system, he lost his footing on more than one occasion. He clambered around tree after tree, calling just loudly enough not to be heard at the house, "Wolfdogge! Caitlin!"

He heard something, was it a response? The sound was high-pitched, like a dog's whine, only it echoed strangely. Even listening carefully, he couldn't discern its location. It was as if Wolfdogge were trapped at the bottom of a canyon.

He looked down at the deep black shadows between the roots under his feet. Had Wolfdogge fallen into one of the clefts under the oak trees? And if so, how was he supposed to find him without a flashlight?

Caw flew into the grove and alighted on one of the twisted limbs branching from the tree that towered over Kevin. The raven gave voice to a raucous cry, "Cú faoil, Cú faoil!"

"Yeah, I'm looking for him, thanks," Kevin said, knowing he'd just imagined that the bird had spoken the Irish name for wolfhound. Caw glided down and perched on Kevin's shoulder again, so close that Kevin had to bend his head back to focus on the bird. He wasn't worried that Caw would peck him in the eye or anything, in fact, he had the strongest feeling that the bird wanted to help. He stared into Caw's blue eye. "You wouldn't happen to know where the Cú faoil is, would you?"

Caw cocked his head, and then flew to another tree. Instead of landing in a branch this time, he landed on a thick root. Kevin scrambled over. At the base of the enormous tree was a gaping chasm. He heard it clearly now, Wolfdogge's distressed whining.

Without thinking, he braced his hands across the divide and lowered his legs into it. They swung unimpeded. He didn't speculate on the depth of the hole – just dropped down into it. The fall was considerable; comparable perhaps to jumping from the roof of Simon's Victorian house. He landed on a thick mat of old leaves and rolled, striking his head sharply on a root.

"Ow," he said, looking around. He might have expected his eyes to take some time to adjust to the near pitch-blackness, but there appeared to be sufficient light from the holes at the base of the trees. He blinked in wonder at the vast network of roots, serving as roof to the place as well as structural support. The underneath of the entire grove was hollow.

Inhaling the pungent scent of fertile earth and rotting leaves, he thought how wonderful it smelled here, like and yet very unlike home. Another deep breath almost made him giddy with pleasure.

An emphatic bark got his attention. Wolfdogge sat not far away, wagging his tail. Then Kevin saw her.

She was sprawled in the mulch next to a free-standing root with her pale, thin arms wrapped around it. He rushed to her side and saw that her hair was matted with blood. He reached out but didn't touch her.

"Caitlin?"

She lifted her head and waved her arm through the air. "Is that you, Kevin?"

Couldn't she see him? Her eyes were open, but they appeared unfocused.

"Did Griffey do this?" he asked, clenching his jaw.

She nodded, but the movement must have pained her because she laid her cheek wearily against the root. "The trees will heal me."

"What?" Her head wound must have muddled her mind.

"This place," she said, and her words came out as barely a whisper, "is an ancient place of healing."

"How long have you been here?" He thought that the healing couldn't have begun yet if she looked this bad. The ugly wound on her head had soaked the top of her shirt in blood.

"I don't know. It's dark."

"It's not that dark, Caitlin. I can see you clearly."

A grating sound came from between her lips. It took him a moment to realize she was laughing. "You can see, can't you? I'm so glad you're coming into your heritage."

He suddenly understood. The familiar smell of the place, the feeling of homecoming. He'd spent his life above ground, when his heart had always been below. He placed his hand on the ancient oak root and instantly felt a powerful presence, like a choir was silently harmonizing in his head. Disconcerted, he dropped his hand.

"Did you find the crown?" he asked. "Does Griffey have it?"

"No. Simon told him Werka took it away." She reached out blindly and grasped Kevin's arm. Her voice sounded stronger to him when she asked, "Where are Zach and Lizbeth? He's much too dangerous for them to take on alone."

Kevin sighed. He didn't want to leave Caitlin here, but if Zach and Lizbeth needed him...

Then Caitlin astonished him by getting to her feet. Wolfdogge moved to her side and she grasped his scruff, allowing the dog to support her. "Let's go."

"You can't-"

"I can. Humans were not the only ones affected by the biometal. This oak grove must have been home to druids long ago. The trees have given me back my strength. They did it the moment you gave them communion."

Chapter Forty-one

East of England

With trepidation, Lizbeth entered the dark interior of the house behind Zach and closed the front door behind them. So far, "Caitlin" seemed unaware that Kevin had run after Wolfdogge.

Instead of following Caitlin into the room with the gruesome taxidermy display, Zach positioned himself in the doorway, effectively blocking Lizbeth from getting past him. She pushed, but he resisted, and she thought she understood. The longer they hid the fact that Kevin hadn't come into the house with them, the better. If they lingered here, "Caitlin" would assume Kevin was standing in the gloom behind them.

Caitlin turned and in a very un-Caitlin-like manner asked, "Are you kids alright?"

Lizbeth panicked as it occurred to her that whoever was posing as Caitlin didn't have to wait for a response. She could easily read their minds and find out for herself if they were "alright."

One of the first magic tricks Lizbeth had ever learned came to mind; misdirecting the audience to look at one hand while the other palms a coin. If she could misdirect the fake Caitlin long enough to prevent her from reading their minds, maybe Kevin would find the real Caitlin in time.

"Actually," she said loudly, "We're not so great. After you left Felicity's house, her dog came in, but it wasn't her dog, it changed into *Brian Griffey* – the guy who was supposed to have died on the Titanic – *right before our eyes*, and then he found out that you were taking the ferry because he read Felicity's *mind*, but before he could go after you, Zach went after *him* and they got into a fight, but then Griffey *changed into a snake*!"

Halfway through her dramatic rant she stopped to take a breath. Zach turned to her with an appalled look on his face.

154

"Lizbeth," he said, but she ignored him. Her misdirection must have been convincing enough so far, because Caitlin's eyes still looked normal.

She launched into another effusive run-on sentence. "Then Zach was having a hard time because he had a huge green *monster* wrapped around him, so I took this dagger off the wall and *stabbed it*, and it turned back into a dog and ran across the room and then *left,* and then there was this *earthquake*, and-"

"Yes, well, I wanted to talk to you about Mr. Griffey," Caitlin said. "He and I had a disagreement, but we're quite over it now, and I want to be sure you show him the respect he deserves."

Over Caitlin's shoulder Lizbeth saw out the dining room window that Kevin had run into view. He was headed straight for the old oak grove. To ensure that Caitlin didn't get distracted and turn around, Lizbeth barreled on.

"Oh, and poor *Kevin*," here she looked to the right as if she could see him standing there out of Caitlin's sight, "found out that Griffey is his *father*. Or maybe his grandfather, we're not sure, because Felicity-"

That did the trick. Lizbeth had Caitlin's full attention now, as she burst out, "What?"

Lizbeth turned to the phantom Kevin again. "Wait, Kev, I'm sorry!" Then she looked back at Caitlin and said by way of clarification, "He went upstairs. Yeah, he's all torn up about it."

A sneak peek at Zach told her his initial confusion at her misdirection tactic had been replaced with admiration. In her mind, she clearly heard the words, "*I think I love you.*"

She didn't take time to ponder whether he really meant it or if he was simply expressing approval for her strategy, because Caitlin sank down on the stiffly upholstered sofa.

"It can't be," she said quietly.

Lizbeth felt safe enough to step fully into the room now that "Kevin" had gone upstairs. She sat next to Caitlin and put her arm around her. "Why not?"

Caitlin winced and scooted a few inches away on the sofa. Lizbeth trailed her fingers softly across the back of Caitlin's shirt before dropping her arm. There was a raised bump under the fabric, probably a bandage from where Lizbeth had stabbed her. It was definitely Griffey, although Lizbeth had never doubted it.

Caitlin-Griffey took a deep breath and tugged his collar as if it were uncomfortable. "Ah, well, Mr. Griffey couldn't have been his father."

"So who was?" Zach asked.

To forestall Caitlin-Griffey from denying any knowledge of it, Lizbeth prompted, "Felicity said you knew."

"There was a woman once," Caitlin-Griffey replied, with a sideways shift of the jaw. "She died of an infection a few days after childbirth and Griffey's name was on the birth certificate. He took care of the kid for a week, but it got sick and he didn't know what else to do. He drove to a hospital in another state and left it there."

"That's terrible. Felicity said babies between fae and humans rarely survived," Lizbeth said.

Caitlin-Griffey, eyes downcast, nodded. "I – he thought it was going to die. He couldn't risk sticking around while the doctors tried to figure out why."

Lizbeth thought Griffey's actions were indefensible, but she didn't want to agitate him, so she said, "It wasn't his fault. What else was he supposed to do?"

Caitlin-Griffey lifted his eyes. They were swirling. Adrenaline flooded Lizbeth's system, but before she could move, he clamped a hand on her arm. Within seconds, the Griffey they were familiar with was sitting next to her.

He said, "I won't hurt you. I promise. Just give me a few minutes to go upstairs and talk to my son."

At that moment, Lizbeth was simply grateful that Griffey's eyes were normal. If he were still reading her mind, if he used his abilities to reach out for a Kevin who wasn't there, they'd never get this chance again. The chance to run.

She and Zach stood by the door as Griffey trudged slowly up the staircase. There were three rooms he'd have to look inside before it became obvious Kevin wasn't up there. As soon as she lost sight of him on the landing, Lizbeth opened the heavy front door. Zach held it for her as she slipped out.

They ran in the direction Kevin had gone, around the house and across the field toward the oak grove. As she ran, she saw ahead of her that Kevin had found Wolfdogge, and more importantly, the real Caitlin. He had his arm around her and seemed to be supporting her as they walked. A little closer and Lizbeth saw why – Caitlin's shoulder and shirtfront were covered in what looked like blood.

Over the rhythmic sound of her feet hitting the grass, Lizbeth heard a strange thumping noise coming up fast behind them. She glanced over her shoulder and did a quick double-take. A bounding kangaroo was rapidly gaining ground. She stumbled and fell in the grass. Zach stopped and put himself between her and the kangaroo, taking a defensive martial arts stance. But the unmistakable growling scream of a big cat shredded the air and the kangaroo leapt past them to meet the white jaguar head on.

Chapter Forty-two

East of England

From the amount of blood he'd seen on Caitlin's shirt, Zach doubted she'd be in any condition to fight, even in the guise of a jaguar. She pounced, but the kangaroo shifted his weight to his thick tail and kicked out with a vicious swipe to the jaguar's injured head.

Zach bared his teeth, furious. If Griffey wasn't going to fight fair, there was nothing stopping Zach from doing the same. While the jaguar shook her head and backed off, Zach ran straight for the kangaroo. He launched himself into the air with his left leg, spun around in midair and kicked down on the kangaroo's back – right where he'd spotted the oozing wound Lizbeth had given the snake. The force of the kick sent the kangaroo lurching forward on his powerful hind legs. By the time Zach came around 360-degrees and landed on his feet in the tall grass, Wolfdogge joined the fray.

Felicity told them that Wolfdogge's kind had been bred for battle, trained to pull armored knights from their steeds. The dog would have never seen a kangaroo, much less know how to fight one, but after Zach unbalanced the big marsupial with his kick, Wolfdogge bit down on one of its forelegs. With snarling ferocity, Wolfdogge shook his head, tugging and grinding on the kangaroo's undersized arm. For a moment, Zach thought the dog had gotten the upper hand. Then, in a flash, the kangaroo shifted its weight to its thick tail and kicked out at Wolfdogge's underbelly with its wickedly sharp hind claws.

Emitting a high-pitched yelp, Wolfdogge released the kangaroo's arm and toppled backward in the grass. Zach only got a glimpse of the dog's horrible wound, but with a twist of his heart, he knew it was fatal.

As Wolfdogge fell, Caitlin went in for the kill. She knocked the kangaroo sideways to the ground, jaw clamped at his throat. For a moment, Zach thought the kangaroo was going to attempt to disembowel Caitlin, too. Instead, he changed back into Brian Griffey, lying naked under the jaguar, breath wheezing through his constricted windpipe, arm bleeding from the wound Wolfdogge had given him.

"Caitlin!" he cried hoarsely. "I surrender."

The jaguar, claws digging into Griffey's chest, hesitated. Zach saw her eyes, swirling as she probed for the truth. Finally, she must have been satisfied that Griffey had really given in, because she backed away and began to morph into her true self.

As soon as her transformation began, however, the liar Griffey too began to shift. Zach readied himself to strike. Before yesterday, he never imagined he'd fight a python or a kangaroo. Now, as Caitlin became herself, crouched down in the grass, Griffey changed into a beast with the oversized head and wings of an eagle and the hindquarters of a lion. As a long-time player of online fantasy computer games, Zach recognized a mythical griffin when he saw one. He didn't have time to marvel that a shapeshifter could become a nonexistent creature, because Griffey was instantly upon Caitlin.

"No!" Lizbeth screamed from somewhere behind him. The quality of the scream changed at the end to sound like the piercing, distressed cry of an eagle. Zach looked over his shoulder to see another, smaller griffin, one wing beating ineffectively at the air while the other was tucked tight to its side holding the remnants of a shirt. It lurched awkwardly forward, tripping over a pair of jeans, head tilted to look at its own claws as they opened and closed spasmodically, all the while filling the air with its plaintive cries.

Thankfully, the appearance of the newcomer was enough to distract Griffey from Caitlin. He tilted his head to turn a fierce eye on the stumbling little griffin.

Zach took advantage of the momentary distraction. He had little useful knowledge of a griffin's anatomy, but all vertebrates were vulnerable at the neck. His left hand shot out, gripping Griffey's wing above the wrist. Griffey jabbed his sharp beak into Zach's forearm at the same time Zach's stiffened right hand chopped down with enough force to snap a plank in half. The vertebra at the base of the eagle's head gave off a sickening crunch. The griffin stiffened, but before his body could collapse to the ground, Kevin came roaring in from the other side, tackling the feathered and furred creature like a defensive end. As they rolled to a stop in the grass, Zach grasped Kevin by the collar and hauled him off the now limp shapeshifter.

His eyes cut to Caitlin. She'd donned her bloody shirt and pants and staggered to the flailing little griffin with eyes whirling madly. "Lizbeth! Be still!"

Out of the corner of his eye he saw movement, but it was only Griffey's body changing again, this time not into the tall, distinguished Chief Inspector, but into the stocky, coarse-looking man from Caitlin's album. His original form. Cautiously, Zach bent to press his fingers to one side of Griffey's windpipe. He felt a weak pulse and Griffey's eyes fluttered open, the pupils dilated so that even in the sunshine, his brown eyes looked almost black.

Through lips that barely moved, the dying shapeshifter asked, "Where's my son?"

Kneeling several feet away, Kevin's face had gone hard, but he said, "I guess that's me."

"Come closer. Can't move. Neck's broken." Griffey's voice was thin.

Zach stepped back, not convinced that the threat had been eliminated.

Kevin crawled forward and sat back on his haunches, staring at Griffey dispassionately.

"Didn't know…you'd survived," Griffey said.

"Good," Kevin replied. "My parents raised me right. You would have screwed up my life."

Zach glanced up as Caitlin came up next to him, leading a shocked and quivering, but no longer griffin-shaped, Lizbeth. She was dressed, but her shirt and Felicity's jacket must have torn during the transformation, because she held the tatters together in front of her chest. He pulled off his own shirt and looked away as she put it on.

Caitlin touched Kevin on the shoulder. He got to his feet and walked off towards the oak grove. She sat cross-legged next to Griffey and clasped his unmoving hand between hers. To Zach's astonishment, tears flowed freely down her face.

"It's come to this," she said, bowing her head.

"Our race does not have to die," Griffey whispered. "The crown can bring back our glory."

"The price is too great, Brian."

"Science can determine who will survive!" Spittle appeared on Griffey's bloodless lips.

"And war between the races would soon follow, just as it did in the past. Even if the crown's purpose was to create a race of shapeshifters, it won't matter if the earth is uninhabitable."

The sound of the wind in the grass was louder than Griffey's voice. "What other purpose does it have?"

Caitlin lifted his hand to her lips. Zach saw his eyes turn lifeless just before she responded, "To speak with the gossamer sphere."

Chapter Forty-three

East of England

Kevin had never liked dogs. They were slobbery creatures that shed hair all over the place and smelled bad. He'd barely even known Wolfdogge, but the sight of the brave canine lying so still in the grass made him want to sob out loud.

He walked stiffly away and stopped just outside the oak grove with his hands jammed into his pockets. With one thumb, he rubbed the side of the little box with the nugget inside. He'd found it in Felicity's bathroom. No one knew he'd taken it, but he suspected it didn't matter either way. He'd survived the sickness and wouldn't make the mistake of touching the nugget directly again. Still, even in its box, the iridium comforted him.

The trees, the same ones he'd "communed" with earlier, towered before him, leaves flickering in the breeze just like any other grove of trees.

For years he'd dreamed of finding his real parents, but nothing he'd imagined came near to the truth of it. He didn't understand what Griffey meant when he said he hadn't known Kevin survived, but he assumed it had something to do with his abandonment at the hospital. Maybe Caitlin could tell him. Maybe he didn't really care anymore.

He looked over at them. Zach held Lizbeth protectively as Caitlin sat next to Griffey, rocking back and forth as if in mourning. He frowned. Was she actually sad that he was dead? Griffey killed Simon and Len, and he'd tried to kill Caitlin. Why was she so upset that a monster like him had gotten what he deserved? He shook his head, thinking about how cold she'd been to Bill Masters, someone who wasn't perfect, but who probably deserved better. Kevin certainly didn't understand women.

He sighed. As much as he wished he could shapeshift into an ostrich to hide his head in the sand, he knew he had to join the others – find out what, if anything, was left for them to do now.

When he reached them, Caitlin stood. Her tears had washed thin lines into the blood on her left cheek. The partially scabbed-over wound in her scalp glistened. She brushed her hands down the seat of her pants and faced Simon's house.

"Is Wolfdogge dead?"

Kevin nodded.

"That's it then," she said. "We'd best find Werka. Last I heard, flights are still coming and going out of Heathrow. She could be anywhere."

"What about him?" Zach asked, jerking his head toward Griffey.

Caitlin began walking. "We don't have time to bury him. Or the others. It goes against everything I believe in, but the crown comes first."

"What others...?" Lizbeth asked in a small voice, but Caitlin was out of earshot.

"Len and Simon," Kevin gestured to the patch of concealing bushes.

Lizbeth went extremely pale under the creamy light-brown skin of her face. In a tearful voice, she asked, "He killed them?"

"Yeah." Kevin didn't need Zach's stern look to regret that he'd mentioned it. He tried to change the subject. "Are you okay? That was pretty cool, the griffin thing."

"I don't want to talk about it. Let's just-" she stopped. Her eyes drifted to Griffey's toes sticking up out of the grass. Her lips parted and her mouth slowly dropped open as she stared. Pulling away from Zach, she went and stood over Griffey, looking down at him with arms crossed tightly over her ribs. For a panicked moment, Kevin wondered if Griffey had come back alive, but then Lizbeth said, "Can you feel him?"

He didn't want to look. "No. He's dead, isn't he?"

"Yes. *Yes!* Don't you get it?" she practically shouted the last few words.

Zach reached out for her, but she ducked away. In an unexpected move, she began to run, not for the house, but toward the trees.

Kevin and Zach exchanged perplexed looks. Zach shrugged and loped after her while Kevin called out to Caitlin. She looked around. With a sweeping wave of his arm, he gestured to the oak grove. Lizbeth had just disappeared into the shadows, with Zach close behind.

Caitlin made her way back to where Kevin was standing, weariness in every step. Together, they walked across the field, navigated the tree roots, and came out on the far side. Kevin had a sense of déjà vu when he saw the place. It looked the same: the four stones marking where the old church had been, the line of trees along the creek. More powerfully than ever before, he felt the sensation that something was going to happen.

Lizbeth and Zach had pulled the clumps of sod away again and were standing next to Richard Allen's gravestone. As Kevin got closer with Caitlin, she suddenly gasped and pressed a hand to her breastbone. Her steps quickened into a hopping, stumbling gait. Concerned, Kevin stayed right on her heels in case she collapsed.

At the gravesite, she fell to her knees and pressed her face to the stone.

In addition to Caitlin's powerful presence, Kevin felt what he'd felt before, something emanating from Richard Allen's grave. He and the others had wrongly assumed that the long-dead occupant of this plot had been a shapeshifter. As soon as Lizbeth had pointed out to Kevin that he couldn't feel Griffey anymore, he should have realized.

"It's here," Lizbeth said. "The crown was here all along."

Chapter Forty-four

East of England

Richard Allen's gravestone was too heavy for even the four of them together to lift, so Lizbeth waited with Caitlin in the overgrown graveyard while Zach and Kevin went to look in the barn for digging utensils. The boys had been treating Lizbeth like a porcelain doll. She'd seen violence before, and not just on television or at the movies. Once, a gator attacked a deer on the bayou not ten yards from her boat, and on two occasions Granma gave refuge to the neighbor lady whose husband regularly beat her to a pulp. Even so, Lizbeth had never seen a dead person, much less watched someone die.

It wasn't Griffey's death that made her so fragile, though.

Shapeshifting had been a horrifically disorienting experience. She'd been standing there, helpless to contribute to the awful scene being enacted before her. Caitlin had fallen for Griffey's ruse and changed back into herself. Then Griffey began to take on the guise of a griffin. In all Lizbeth's seventeen years, she'd never felt such an overpowering desire to be someone else – someone stronger, faster – not a useless spectator. She'd focused intently on the way Griffey changed. First, pointy pinfeathers appeared all over his head and arms as his hair receded, fur began to coat his legs and a tail budded. Then he rocked forward onto his toes as his feet elongated and his thighs shrank into the flanks of a lion. The pinfeathers on his arms grew long and thin and suddenly popped open into full-fledged feathers while his eyes migrated down the sides of his face and his jaws expanded forward into a huge, curved beak.

It all happened so quickly that she'd had no idea the change was occurring simultaneously in her own body until she heard the sound of her own clothes ripping. Thinking about it now, it bothered her. How could she not feel something that traumatic? Was she going to start morphing uncontrollably at random without even realizing it? Caitlin had talked her through the process of changing back by saying, "Lizbeth, you must listen to my voice! Imagine you're looking in a mirror. See your face, see your body, see your arms and legs and hands and feet." Changing back had been effortless.

"Caitlin?"

A wasp whizzed by and a songbird warbled. The sun had broken through the hazy clouds and shone down on the pretty glen as if the brutality of the day had never happened.

"Yes?"

With all the questions Lizbeth had, about shapeshifting, about Caitlin being her grandmother, about the crown, the one that came out was, "How could I become a griffin when there is no such thing?"

"They used to exist," Caitlin replied. "Like a lot of other things. Brian always did enjoy using that form. It was his family crest. What I would like to know is how you shifted without touching the crown."

"Kevin's nugget. It was an accident. I just held it for a second. The guys don't know."

Lizbeth waited for Caitlin to chastise her, but she didn't. The silence stretched. Lizbeth wanted to sit down, but there wasn't enough room next to Caitlin and she knew from the prickers in her socks that the weedy grass wouldn't be comfortable. In the distance, she saw Zach and Kevin hurrying back, each carrying a shovel.

Another wasp, or maybe the same one, buzzed by. It advanced and retreated in that drunken way wasps have, hovering around Caitlin's head. She seemed unaware of it, so Lizbeth shooed it away with a few waves of her hand. The wasp persisted, however – there was something about Caitlin that was really attracting it. Just as it occurred to Lizbeth that it was the blood in her hair and on her shirt, a black ball of feathers shot past, snatching the pesky insect out of the air.

The raven glided up and around full circle before flapping back toward them. There wasn't any place flat for it to land, so it came straight for Lizbeth. Instinctively, she held out her arm and braced for impact. The bird landed easily, turned around to face forward and settled its wings, glossy black feathers fluffed up as if it were ill. It stepped sideways up her arm, foot to foot, stopping only when it reached her shoulder.

166

Lizbeth didn't need to see the blue eyes to know it was Caw. "This is Len's bird. He looks so sad."

"It's hungry," Caitlin said.

Caw snuggled up next to Lizbeth's cheek, his feathers tickling her.

"Well, I think he's special," Lizbeth said, watching Caitlin out of the corner of her eye to gauge her reaction. "I read that ravens are kept at the Tower of London because there's a legend that if they ever leave, the tower and the kingdom will fall."

Caitlin gave a weak laugh. "Who do you think started that legend?"

Lizbeth shrugged, disturbing Caw, who uttered a small squawk.

"We did," Caitlin said, and Lizbeth assumed she meant the druids. "There's an old Irish poem that goes, 'The raven lit upon the crown, its eyes went red as fire, but when the fever cooled, it sang a song and played the lyre.' Humans were not the only ones who had contact with the crown. We used the ravens at the tower for centuries to keep track of who was imprisoned."

"What about Wolfdogge?"

"The hounds, too."

"So can they talk? The ravens?"

"They communicate to some extent. Just like us, it's who your parents are. I'm surprised Len would keep one, but perhaps he was unaware of Caw's heritage. We don't know the extent of the Guild's knowledge of us."

"Kevin said Len was dead. And Simon."

"Brian couldn't let them live. Had the advantage been Simon or Len's, rest assured they would have killed him first. I wish I had known."

"How did they hide the crown from him? Didn't he read their minds? Wouldn't he have found out where Simon hid it?"

"Be wary of what you learn from someone's mind, Lizbeth. Since we merge our brain's magnetic field, our gossamers, with theirs, we can only pick up what they are currently thinking. We cannot distinguish between truth and lie, even in thought. Brian was able just now to convince me he truly had given in. Len and Simon, as Guild, would likely know it was possible to fool a shapeshifter."

Zach and Kevin arrived with the shovels and four plastic bottles of water. Kevin loosened the lids and handed a bottle each to Caitlin and Lizbeth. Zach was wearing a shirt that looked exactly like the one she'd first seen him in. Smelled like it, too.

167

"Check it out," he said, pulling a backpack from his shoulder. He unzipped it and inside, Lizbeth saw his laptop.

"That's *your* backpack? Where did you find it?" she asked.

"Griffey's car is in the barn. He must have rescued it before the ship went kablooie."

Caitlin moved off the gravestone and said, "Dig."

Using the shovels as leverage, Zach and Kevin were able to flip the heavy stone onto the grass. Surprised bugs wiggled frantically away from the sunlight. The boys began to dig and within minutes, they hit something. Kevin tried to pry a square, wooden box out of the soil with his fingers, but it was held fast by a root of some sort that had grown around and around the box. Lizbeth's eyes were drawn to the nearest oak tree. Zach lifted his shovel, but Kevin stopped him. He touched the stubborn growth and closed his eyes. Moments later, he lifted the box easily and handed it to Caitlin. She brushed the dirt off the top, revealing a Celtic triskele carved into the wood.

"Let's go," she said, turning toward the house.

"Wait a minute," Kevin said, holding up a finger. "Something's going to happen."

Zach scrunched his face. "I feel it."

The ground began to rumble and shake. It was probably a coincidence that another earthquake hit moments after they found the crown, but Lizbeth shivered anyway as she waited for the ground to settle.

Now that they had the means to stop it, would the gossamer sphere, an entity that had controlled the earth's magnetic field for millions upon millions of years, cooperate?

Chapter Forty-five

East of England

Back at the house, Caitlin wanted to get started right away, but Zach flat-out told her he wouldn't participate in whatever she had in mind unless she washed up, put on fresh clothes and bandaged her head wound. He expected an argument, but she said, "Wash your own wound," and disappeared upstairs with the crown still in its box. He wondered if she was going to take it into the shower with her.

After going to the kitchen sink and cleaning the gouge Griffey had pecked into his arm, he plugged in his laptop and sat at the kitchen table. While it booted up, his mind conjured an image of Griffey lying in the grass. Zach knew his blow had killed him, but he also knew if he hadn't delivered it, the shapeshifter would have killed Caitlin. Might have even killed them all. As awful as it was to realize his first kill at eighteen, Zach felt little remorse. He'd known from a young age that his path would lead him to bloodshed. As long as the opponent deserved his fate, Zach wouldn't lose much sleep over it.

On his laptop, he discovered to his irritation that Griffey had deleted the file with the digital artwork of the crown. Not that it mattered anymore, but he'd worked really hard creating it. Simon's Internet connection was working, so Zach's second item of interest was to check his email. His mom's computer skills were fresh from the Stone Age, but she'd borrowed a friend's email account and sent him an update on the family and begged him to respond. He fired off a quick reply assuring her he was okay.

Lizbeth came and sat next to him as he scanned the remainder of unopened emails in his in box. He ignored the spam, scrolling down until he found what he was looking for.

"That's from Seamus," Lizbeth said.

169

"I see that."

The email read: "Zach, thank you for your email. I followed the link you sent and watched your video on YouTube. Only Children of the Boar can feel the pulses. Your video indicates that you have no idea what is happening, and yet in your email you mention stopping the gossamer 'sphere.' What is this sphere? The lore does not mention such a thing, but if you are indeed in the company of the last Noble, and she is intent on stopping it, I must presume it is the cause of the current state of the world and I am therefore entirely at your service. You may find me at the Ritz London. I await further instruction."

"You emailed him?" Lizbeth exclaimed.

"Yeah. It seemed like a good idea at the time, but now we won't need his help."

"How's he supposed to help? He's just a wannabe bard who doesn't even know what the gossamer sphere is."

"Of course he doesn't. Griffey didn't know, either. Caitlin didn't even figure out what it was until recently. Anyway, it doesn't matter. We have the crown and here comes Caitlin. Let's rock and roll."

Caitlin came down the stairs, wearing a blouse she must have borrowed from Werka's closet. The flowered polyester hung almost indecently off her shoulders. Her wound was neatly bandaged, and she looked refreshed. She tossed a sweatshirt to Lizbeth, who went into the kitchen and changed out of Zach's shirt.

Caitlin placed the triskele box in the center of the coffee table and said, "It's time. Come sit."

Zach shut his laptop with a flutter of anticipation in his gut. He had no idea what they'd be required to do, but this was the moment they'd been preparing for since the quest began. His inner critic scoffed at the picture the four of them made; dirty, exhausted and injured. It wasn't at all the dignified ceremony he'd expected it to be. Without a word, no chanting or singing, Caitlin opened the box and removed the crown. It looked exactly like he knew it would. She set it on her head and reached out. They took each other's hands, forming a circle. Caitlin closed her eyes.

He waited for something to happen but felt nothing. He heard the breath whistling faintly in and out of Kevin's nostrils and saw beads of sweat form on Caitlin's brow, but that was it. After a few minutes, Caitlin hissed, "Bugger all!" which he knew was some kind of Irish foul language.

"What do you want us to do?" Lizbeth asked in a small voice.

Caitlin opened her eyes. Zach's heart sank at the hopelessness on her face.

"I should have known," she whispered.

Zach met Lizbeth's and then Kevin's eyes and saw his worry reflected there. "What's wrong?"

Caitlin removed the crown and held it between her fingertips. Her beautiful features were ravaged by despair. "How can we contact the sphere – if it's broken?"

Chapter Forty-six

East of England

They tried several more times. During each attempt, Kevin thought he caught the faintest whisper of something at the edge of his mind, similar to the buzzing he'd heard at Felicity's house when he was sick. None of the others seemed to notice it, so he dismissed it as residual iridium sickness, maybe brought on by his continued proximity to the nugget in its box in his pocket.

"That's it, then," Caitlin said after the final try. She put the crown back in its box.

Lizbeth jumped up, fists clenched at her side. "Is that all you can say? That's it? How do you know? There's got to be something else we can do."

"I know because I am the crown's guardian. I know because its creator told me what it can do. There were three in the beginning. Three shapeshifters. A queen and her two subjects, who became fast friends. Over time, they allowed more to join their ranks, carefully selecting only those they knew would survive. Most were good. They became the druidic people, revered by all. But people are unpredictable, especially under the extraordinary circumstances of gaining immortality and power. Some of them got greedy. They misused their power, going outside the Grove and offering their services to the warring clans—for a price. It wasn't long before those clans began to envy the peace and prosperity of the Grove. In desperation, the queen placed the crown upon her brow, and with her two most trusted friends by her side, implored the gods for a solution. The response was nothing like what they expected, and before the backlash of contacting the sphere killed Queen Wyn, the others saw what it was and knew its purpose. They buried her under a monumental cairn attributed now to some other queen, and the two remaining friends added the triskele symbol to the crown to commemorate their friendship.

"So, yes, Lizbeth, I do know there is nothing else to be done. The sphere did not respond. I would have gladly given my life, as my grandmother did, to accomplish this task. But it is not to be."

She pulled a set of keys and a billfold from her pocket. "We'd best deal with the remaining issue at hand."

Within moments, she'd shapeshifted into a slimmer version of Werka.

"Take my rental car to London and get a hotel. I'll contact the police as a distraught Werka who was knocked unconscious and woke up to find her husband and his friends murdered. Dispose of your shoes. As Werka, I can offer the police a logical explanation for your fingerprints being here, at least."

The police would find their shoe prints all over the property, so dumping the shoes made sense, but Kevin didn't understand something. "Griffey's car is in the barn. He doesn't exactly look like the Chief Inspector anymore."

"Let the police sort it out. Given the possible scenarios, Werka is unlikely to be considered a suspect. Besides, soon they will have better things with which to concern themselves."

Like staying alive, thought Kevin.

"You should all make arrangements to fly to your homes if you can. I'll call and make reservations at the Marriott on-"

"No, put us at the Ritz," Zach said.

Caitlin, in the guise of Werka, raised an eyebrow, but the movement must have hurt her wound because she flinched a little. "If you wish. I'll try and meet you there, but if I cannot...know that you each have my gratitude."

Kevin saw Lizbeth move in for a hug, aborted when Caitlin lifted the triskele box. "When the police arrive, this must not be here." She handed the box to Lizbeth. "If I do not come, the crown is yours. Keep it in the box. Protect it."

"I'll try, Grandmother."

Caitlin gave her a curious look. "Felicity told you."

Lizbeth nodded. "She told us a lot of things. Except—how could you have been Brian Griffey's friend? I mean, he was horrible." She shot an apologetic look at Kevin, who twitched his shoulders in a minute shrug to let her know it didn't matter what she said. The guy meant nothing to him.

"He wasn't always," Caitlin said. "Immortality tends to change a person. Brian wasn't the first to go a little insane—with power as well as from the grief of losing loved ones. He and I met at the summer solstice initiation two years after the druid stronghold on the island of Anglesey was destroyed. Before the Romans came, there were many initiates, but that day there were five who touched the crown. He and I, as the grandchildren of two of the original shapeshifters, were the only survivors. It bonded us."

"Let me guess," Zach said. "You were obviously the granddaughter of Queen Wyn, which would make Brian the grandson of Tadg the Small?"

Werka's plain face showed Caitlin's surprise. "How on earth did you—Felicity? I didn't think I'd ever mentioned them to her."

"It wasn't Felicity. There's this website that has a bunch of stories about shapeshifters. There's one all about someone named Caetl."

"I haven't heard that name for a very long time," she said softly. "It seems some of the lore survived. Well, it's of no consequence now."

Caitlin, normally so guarded about her privacy, suddenly didn't seem to care who knew the truth. Kevin thought, *because there's no reason to hide anything anymore.* They were all doomed, and the past didn't matter. Still, he had one thing he wanted to know about the man, the *druid*, who was his father.

"Why was Griffey on Titanic with the crown? You said it was stolen and then you said he was bringing it to you."

Caitlin smiled sadly. "It was he who convinced me the crown was untouchable locked up in the safe with the Irish crown jewels. That turned out to be far from the truth, as the man entrusted with the jewels was quite careless in both his friends and duties. No one ever found out who opened the safe or where the jewels went. It was as if a ghost had spirited them away."

"Or a shapeshifter," Kevin said.

"Indeed. Five years the crown was missing. Victor was long gone by then and with no clues as to its whereabouts, I was unable to even begin to search for it. I started a new life in America. Out of the blue, Brian contacted me. Said he'd purchased the crown from Shackleton and was coming to America on Titanic. It wasn't long after the ship sank that I began to suspect he'd lied. It's highly unlikely Shackleton wouldn't have touched the crown if he'd had it in his possession all that time. It would have killed him. Later I realized it could not have been a coincidence that the name of the salvage ship that found the crown was *The Gossamer*. I was unable to determine who had financed the ship's salvage effort, but it was clear whoever it was knew what they were looking for. And Brian was the only one besides me who knew where to look. However, it wasn't until I met you, Kevin, that I knew for certain he was still alive."

"How?" Kevin asked.

"I knew you were his son. I sensed your power, and you look exactly like his grandfather, Tadg. It's uncanny, really." She straightened her shoulders then and announced, "It's time."

Kevin didn't know why he expected her to offer Lizbeth some gesture of affection, an acknowledgment of their relationship, but she didn't. Instead, she handed Kevin the car keys, a wad of cash, and simply looked at all of them for a moment before saying, "Go. Be blessed."

Outside, the sun had disappeared again behind some ominous-looking clouds. As they walked the gravel drive to the barn, Caw flew down and landed on Zach's head.

"Not you again," he said. To Kevin he added, "Could you get this for me?"

Kevin offered the bird his forearm. Caw stepped on, making a scratchy sort of noise with his beak. Kevin had no idea where it came from, but he mimicked the noise back perfectly.

"We should take him with us," Lizbeth said.

"Yeah, he'd blend right in at the Ritz," Zach replied.

"He'll starve if we leave him."

"No, he'll learn to eat roadkill like all the other scavengers."

Kevin thought about the four bodies lying unprotected in the field behind the house and shuddered. He made another soft noise and reached tentatively toward Caw, who held still and allowed him to wrap his hand around the bird's body. Caw's feet released their grip on his arm, and he lay passively in Kevin's hand.

"We could hide him," Kevin said.

"I doubt Len trained him that well."

Kevin went behind Zach and unzipped his backpack. He formed a series of squawks in his throat and put Caw inside, partially zipping it back up. The bird stayed put, poking his head out of the opening.

"So now you talk to birds?" Zach asked.

Kevin shrugged. He didn't think he'd actually "said" anything to Caw, but the sounds he'd made did seem to get the bird to cooperate.

Lizbeth bumped into Zach and said, "Quit griping. Caitlin said Caw is special, like us."

They piled into Caitlin's rental car and headed out. Kevin drove, watching the old house get smaller in the rearview mirror. The uppermost branches of the oak trees, just visible past the roof, swayed in the wind as if waving farewell.

On the way, they stopped at a petrol station and asked for directions to the Ritz. Kevin had serious doubts about whether three rather scruffy people would be allowed to register at the upscale hotel, but they didn't have any problems. Maybe the concierge was used to the new generation of grungy rich and famous and assumed they were in that class.

Caitlin had reserved two rooms. They hung out in Lizbeth's and ordered room service for a late lunch. Kevin got a hamburger and fries just for Caw. None of them seemed to want to discuss the failure of their quest, so they watched television while they ate. Most of the channels had continuous coverage of what some enterprising reporter had dubbed "The Cataclysm." The temblors that had rattled the United Kingdom had thus far been mild, but with so many of them, damage was beginning to add up. Hundreds of businesses had closed shop. Crime skyrocketed. A few neighborhoods had been looted by mobs of frightened citizens. Hardest hit were the home improvement and sporting goods shops as people attempted to stockpile survival gear. The worst news of all: Heathrow had finally been forced to stop all incoming and outgoing flights due to runway damage. Crews were working around the clock to fix the broken tarmac, but each new earthquake just contributed more.

"Well." Lizbeth stood and brushed the crumbs off her pants. "Let's buy some new shoes so we can dump these ones."

From his lounging place on the bed, Zach asked, "Why bother? I doubt the police are even going to investigate. Didn't you see the news? Half the police force has abandoned its post and the other half is busy keeping the riots under control."

"Let's just do what Caitlin said, okay?"

"Why? She's not the boss of us anymore. This whole stupid scheme was a bust. We'll be lucky to save ourselves now."

Kevin, who'd been sitting at the little table feeding bits of hamburger to Caw, got to his feet and faced the bed. "Why don't you shut up?"

Zach laughed. "Make me."

"Why are we here then?" Lizbeth asked in a raised voice.

Kevin looked at her. "What do you mean?"

"At the Ritz." She glared at Zach. "You picked this specific hotel for a reason."

Zach got off the bed. "Yeah, alright, so what? Let's get some new shoes and go find that Seamus guy."

Chapter Forty-seven

London

Zach waited with the others for the desk clerk to conclude a phone call, wiggling his toes impatiently in his new shoes. The uniformed young man finally looked up and offered an apology.

"How may I help you?"

Zach opened his mouth to ask about Seamus but stopped. He swiveled around and scanned the luxurious lobby, counting seven people, none of whom looked like Caitlin.

Lizbeth spoke quietly. "She must be in disguise."

Kevin said, "There she is," and nodded in the direction of a black-haired man in jeans and a black polo shirt standing under the archway to the grand staircase.

Zach's heart sped up. "Guys…that's not Caitlin."

The last shapeshifter they'd encountered other than Caitlin turned out to be a psychopathic killer who would have done anything to get to the crown. They'd left it upstairs in Lizbeth's room. This Seamus character knew about the crown, knew they'd been looking for it.

"Can we trust him?" Lizbeth asked.

"We might not have a choice."

"Here he comes," Kevin said.

Seamus sauntered over, all friendly-like, and held out his hand. Guardedly, Zach took it. Seamus was about his height and breadth, with a strong, calloused hand. He said, "It's good that you're here, Zach Wong." Then he smiled at Lizbeth and shook Kevin's hand, too, saying, "Brother, Sister, we've never met. I probably left Ireland before you were initiated. Lucky I had the wanderlust – got out before the empire started their campaign against us."

178

Zach frowned. Seamus must be strong if he could sense that Lizbeth and Kevin were like him. He had no way of knowing they'd only just come into their power. To prevent Lizbeth and Kevin from revealing the truth, Zach said, "I got your email. You said you could help."

"Sure I can. How much do you know about what's happening?"

Zach still didn't trust him, so he said simply, "Everything."

"That's more than I can say," Seamus replied with a twinkle in his eye. "Only the Druidecht knew all the secrets."

"So how can you help?" Lizbeth asked.

Seamus spread his hands. "I'm here, aren't I? And there are plenty more where I came from. Most are just kin, but between us, we've got some useful skills. I've been actively recruiting them through my website for some time now. The Internet is a powerful tool. Now, tell me: how do you plan to stop this bloody 'gossamer sphere' from doing us all in?"

Zach was torn. Seamus hadn't mentioned the crown, and Zach was loathe to admit they had it. At least the shapeshifter hadn't tried to read any of their minds—yet.

A flash of lightning lit up the interior of the building. The sky outside had darkened considerably since this morning and the brewing storm had arrived. Looking past Seamus, Zach felt a wave of relief when he saw Caitlin enter the lobby through the main doors, shaking raindrops from a black umbrella. She wore a black knit cap that hid the bandage, and outwardly at least, seemed fine. He watched her cross the marble floor and head for the registration desk where they stood. When she got close enough, she must have sensed Seamus because she stopped cold.

Seamus' chin came up and he turned. Zach saw him stiffen as if in shock. After everything that had happened, Zach's first instinct was to protect Caitlin at all costs. Seamus was solidly built, and his movements were slow and deliberate, which suggested he knew how to fight. When he began walking towards Caitlin with a stiff, jerky gait, Zach followed, prepared to stop him if necessary.

Seamus halted a few yards from Caitlin, who waited in dignified silence. To Zach's astonishment, he dropped to one knee before her, bowing his head.

"It is my greatest honor to serve you, my lady."

Chapter Forty-eight

London

From the moment she'd walked into the Ritz Hotel, *the* Ritz! Lizbeth felt like a princess. Well, a princess in desperate need of a decent shower and a fresh change of clothes, but still. She had no idea how Caitlin had managed to get reservations at such short notice, but if that was a shapeshifter trick, Lizbeth wanted to know how it was done. The guys hardly noticed where they were, despite the opulence all around them. And when Seamus knelt on the polished marble floor before Caitlin, it all seemed like a fantasy.

The last thing she expected was for Caitlin to immediately begin berating him.

"What do you mean, you called them here?"

"Please forgive me. I thought it best."

"And you," she said to Zach. "You emailed this man? Told him I was in London? What were you thinking?"

Lizbeth wouldn't want to be on the receiving end of the look Caitlin gave him when he responded, "Apparently I wasn't."

"The need for discretion is essential to your very existence," Caitlin spat. "The survivors of the last attempted genocide can attest to that."

"With all due respect, ma'am, this isn't the first century," Seamus said.

That slowed her down for a moment as she considered it, but she shook her head. "Regardless. Your followers won't be of any assistance. The sphere is malfunctioning. We did not succeed."

Seamus hung his head. "I am a simple bard. I do not pretend to understand the ways of the Druidecht, but the lore I remember well. Was the crown not inscribed with the triskele symbol to commemorate the three? They were powerful alone, and more powerful together. Whatever you are attempting to do can only benefit from the united strength of what is left of our people."

Caitlin said something unintelligible, a contemptuously delivered phrase in a guttural language. Lizbeth turned to Kevin, who surprised her by saying, "She said Seamus is overstepping his bounds."

"How did you know that?" Caitlin asked. "That language has been dead for centuries."

Kevin shrugged.

"Milady, please consider my proposal." Seamus shook his head, eyes pleading. "The folk are here and willing to do whatever is necessary. The rest of the world may not be aware of the earth's impending fate, but rest assured, they are. If, with their power combined with yours, we can stop this sphere…"

Lizbeth was completely convinced by Seamus' argument. Caitlin's face, as ever, gave nothing away. Lizbeth held her breath.

"How many are there?" Caitlin asked. "What clans?"

"Almost a hundred, but most are descendants of the folk, with nominal gifts. I won't deceive you: there are sworn enemies among those who have given me allegiance in this, and only this, endeavor. I would like to believe old griefs have faded away, but either way, I give you my oath that I will die protecting you."

Caitlin sighed. "Such a gathering will surely call attention to us."

Lizbeth started to raise her hand as if she were in school but dropped it before anyone noticed. "I think everyone's kind of busy with other things at the moment."

"Besides," Kevin said. "I know exactly where we can go – should go – to make this work. No one will see us there."

Chapter Forty-nine

The North Sea

Kevin felt sorry for Bill Masters. It had been pathetically easy for Caitlin to convince him to take them out to Silverpit Crater on the scientific drilling vessel. Technically, the ship wasn't even his to take. It was owned by some huge conglomerate, but since it had been officially quarantined, it'd just been sitting offshore, fully crewed, until the authorities released it. Bill didn't hesitate.

The "folk" arrived at the pier in cars and vans, taxis and buses. To Kevin, other than the fact that they were forced to walk bent double against the wind and rain, they looked absolutely normal. There were men and women young and old, and even a few children, some solemn, some excited as they boarded the ship. They carried their luggage, coolers of food and drink, and sleeping bags. He sensed only a few as full shapeshifters, and each of those took his measure as they went by.

The trip out to the crater in the storm was wretched. Kevin spent it in the cabin with Caw, who stayed glued to his shoulder except during the worst bouts of vomiting, when he perched on his back and made soothing bird noises. By morning, the engines had quieted, indicating they'd arrived some time during the night. The rough sea hadn't let up, but he'd gotten some sleep and felt marginally better. Zach must have come in late and gone before Kevin woke, or more likely, he'd bunked with Lizbeth again. They probably thought Kevin didn't know about it, but after his long nap on the couch at Felicity's house, he couldn't sleep. He'd heard Lizbeth sneak into the spare room and didn't hear her come back out.

He ran into Seamus on the way to the head. The bard flashed a quick smile, and Kevin, not one to trust a person before knowing him, thought he might like this man.

Seamus lifted his chin, looked down his impressive nose and said, "You've got the look of him."

Kevin raised his eyebrows. Was he talking about Griffey? From the glimpse Kevin got of his birth father's real face after death, he'd have to disagree.

Seamus smiled again. "And you've got no idea who I mean. It's hard to believe there're new druids among us. It's Tadg the Small I'm talking about."

"Oh," Kevin said. "From the story. Did you know him?"

Seamus nodded. "I had the privilege. You're a bit taller, but if you gelled your hair up into a Mohawk, you'd be the spitting image."

"So I hear—well, except the part about the Mohawk. I take it he's dead?"

"That he is lad, and an ignoble death it was. The clan always suspected he'd been jumped by his rivals. Who would have guessed tossing his body in the bog would preserve him for future generations to discover? When this is over, when we've succeeded, look up Clonycavan Man. Tadg's killers went overboard to make sure he was good and dead. Split his skull, the bloody murderers."

Kevin recoiled, but said, "Thanks. I'll be sure and look that up. If this works."

"It will. It has to." Seamus clapped a hand on his shoulder. "See you on deck."

After visiting the head, Kevin found Caitlin in the lab. Piles of luggage and rolled-up sleeping bags were everywhere, but the only other person was Bill. Kevin hesitated in the doorway, not wanting to interrupt their conversation. He cleared his throat, but it went unnoticed.

"So who is he?" Bill was asking.

Caitlin held still as he changed the dressing on her head wound. On the counter under her hand was the triskele box. "His name is Seamus, but that's irrelevant. I just met the man."

"I thought there weren't very many of you left and that you knew them all."

"I tracked the ones I could, but I've always known there were more out there."

Bill made a noncommittal "huh" sound. "So how do you know when you meet one?"

"Some of us can sense each other," Caitlin replied.

Kevin started to back away because the scene seemed somehow intimate, but he stopped when Bill asked, "Can you sense me?"

"What do you mean? Oh."

"I didn't get sick!" Bill finished with the bandage and placed his hands on her shoulders, sliding them down in a caress. Then he gripped her upper arms and shook ungently. "I touched the core sample. By this time, I should have been delirious like all the others, but I'm not!"

"William," Caitlin said, "it's not what you think."

Kevin really began to squirm now. He did *not* want to stick around to see Bill's face when he found out he hadn't risked his life to be with the woman he loved after all. He especially didn't want to see the accusation in Bill's eyes when he discovered Kevin's part in it. He took a quiet step back, but Caitlin called, "Kevin?"

Cursing himself, he realized she knew he was there all along. To his immense relief, Zach and Lizbeth arrived, cheeks pink and hair windblown.

"The rain's stopped," Lizbeth said. "Seamus and the others are on deck. I think they want to get started."

Caitlin turned. "Yes, I imagine they do."

She led the way up the stairs and waited until the others joined her. Zach and Kevin flanked her as they made their way to the forward deck, where Seamus had gathered the most powerful of the shapeshifters. Kevin noticed her knuckles go white from clutching the triskele box. There wasn't enough room on the main deck for everyone, and the folk squeezed against the rails to make room as they passed. Many bowed and curtsied to Caitlin, and Kevin noticed some of the women had circlets of what looked like mistletoe in their hair. The atmosphere was hushed and reverent.

They joined the circle, which had four full shapeshifters other than Caitlin and Seamus, and Lizbeth, too, he supposed. He saw how tensely Zach held himself as Caitlin withdrew the crown from the box and set it on her head. The ship pitched and rolled, and his stomach clenched. Caitlin raised her voice above the wind. He expected her to give some kind of ritual speech or something, but she merely said in her ancient language, "Let us speak with the gossamer sphere."

She didn't ask that they all clasp hands, although many of those outside the circle had done so anyway. Her eyes began to whirl before she closed them. Kevin tried to concentrate, but he heard that annoying, buzzing dialogue in his head again. It distracted him because this time he could almost make out what was being said. His hand snaked into his pocket almost of its own accord. The nugget was in its box, but he felt a strong urge to take it out.

184

Unlike the others, he kept his eyes open. Caitlin's eyebrows were scrunched together, and her jaw clenched. The cords in her neck stood out. He sensed it wasn't going well. Her hands balled into fists and she slowly dropped to her knees on the storm-dampened deck, the crown glittering like a live thing. Above them, the sky between the drifting clouds turned purple.

Kevin's urge to touch the nugget overwhelmed him. In his pocket, his fingers flipped the tiny hook and opened the box. The nugget slipped into his hand, a familiar, comforting presence.

And the voices became clear.

It was a language never spoken on earth. Kevin heard it in his mind and understood it, although he doubted his ears would be able to pick up the frequencies or his voice box produce them. His mind had entered a place that was like a river of silver fire. It felt entirely unlike the tentative attempts he'd made thus far to probe other people's minds. Those were like a blade of straw floating in a trickle of water, whereas this—he was an unwilling passenger clinging to a raft in a raging flood of information. At first, he assumed, as Caitlin had said all along, that his mind had merged with the gossamer sphere. He thought he had accessed some central intelligence part of the grid, like a bio-software program controlling the communication system. He struggled to find the key to shutting the sphere down, but his mind was overwhelmed with incoming data, most of which was too technical for him to understand, even if he were more familiar with the language. At some point—he didn't know how long he'd endured the torrent—comprehension dawned.

The information stream was not the sphere itself, but the messages flowing through it, and the stream did not flow one way. He immersed himself in the outgoing current, and it swept him violently away. Where he was going, he did not know, but consciousness was his lifeline and he clung to it.

In a corner of his mind, he thought about what killed Wyn, and knew it was this place. Her gossamers weren't strong enough and they'd snapped, leaving her body a mindless husk on earth. Kevin felt his own gossamers stretch as thin as a spider's web, and as the current ripped him ever outward, he prayed they were as strong.

Finally, suddenly, he stopped. Numb to any tactile sensations of the body, his mind floated in a pool of silver for an eternity, or was it only a moment?

Identify.

Startled, he answered, *Who, me?*

Sector Vactile, intruder alert.

No, I'm just delivering a message!

Identify.

Kevin Guzman. From earth.

Location?

Earth! Um, I—I don't know. Milky Way galaxy? Yellow sun, nine planets—no, wait, eight planets! We're the blue one, third from the sun. Your sphere is destroying our world.

Initiating merge.

What? I-

Kevin felt his head explode like a thousand suns going nova. Mercifully, the pain didn't last, but the alien presence invading his mind went on and on. Whoever or whatever was probing him seemed to have an inexhaustible curiosity. He *felt* the entity access his memories, each one with a different timbre, like a note plucked on a harp. Helplessness gave way to anger. Just like the flow from the sphere to this place, he suspected the contact went both ways. Drawing on the strength of the folk who unwittingly supported him back on earth with his body, he struck back, like a serpent. The presence recoiled, and Kevin struck again, this time with the intention of finding out something about the entity or entities controlling the fate of everyone on earth.

The inflectionless voice sounded in Kevin's head.

Abort merge.

Just before his head exploded again in pain, Kevin snatched something from the entity, a fact or a memory, a glimpse of three star-rich galaxies in close proximity to each other, swirling through gaseous pink clouds against the pitch black of space.

So that's *where you are*, he thought.

The entity responded immediately. *Sever communication.*

No! Kevin yelled.

The trip back through the silver stream was faster than before, probably because he'd gotten a boost from the entity. Kevin used up the last of his borrowed strength to mentally scream a furious final message:

There are sentient beings on this planet!

Chapter Fifty

The North Sea

The message reverberated in Zach's skull, and even after it faded away his head felt like he'd just embraced a ten-foot-tall speaker at a rock concert. He heard excited murmurs from the crowd and opened his eyes. Above them, the sky blossomed with all the colors of the rainbow. He was horrified that he'd ever closed his eyes when he saw Caitlin lying prone on the deck. At first, he didn't know whether she'd been attacked or if the effort of contacting the sphere had been too much for her.

He crouched down next to her and she stirred. Gently, he turned her over and sighed in relief when she blinked. Lizbeth, too, knelt down beside her as Caitlin looked silently up at the sky as if enchanted. Every once in a while, she inhaled deeply and let it out in a long breath. After several minutes, she said, "Kevin."

Kevin? Not quite what Zach expected her to say at such an auspicious moment. Maybe she simply wanted the three of them with her. A flash of fear shot through him – she wasn't dying, was she?

He craned his neck, looking for Kevin, who had been standing right next to him but had disappeared. Then he spotted him, or what he could see of him – his backside – as he leaned over the far rail and retched. "He's a little indisposed."

"Did we do it?" Lizbeth asked.

Caitlin started to sit up, and Zach helped her. She took the crown from her curls and placed it back in its box. "Help me up."

Seamus came forward and between them, they got Caitlin to her feet. Zach heard people on both sides of the ship calling to those lining the aisles, "She's alright. She's okay!" Some applauded.

"I think it worked," Caitlin said with a weak smile. "I hope it worked."

"How will we know?" Seamus asked.

She raised an arm and pointed. Kevin had just turned from the rail. His shaggy hair hung into eyes that had gone blood red again. A collective gasp rose from the people close enough to see him.

"Ask Kevin," Caitlin said.

By now Zach was used to being confused. Why did Caitlin think Kevin had the answer? He saw Kevin shield his eyes from the brilliance of the light show above them before staggering over to Caitlin. "Ask me what?"

"You broke through. Did you receive a reply?"

Zach was flabbergasted. All that talk of da zhuang, and the dwarf with no personality had been the most powerful of them all.

"No. I'm not sure if I will," Kevin muttered, hand still covering his eyes.

Bill Masters and the captain of the ship pushed through the crowd. Bill gave Seamus a hard look and the shapeshifter relinquished his place next to Caitlin so Bill could support her.

"USGS is reporting complete cessation of the earthquakes," he announced. "Starting about ten minutes ago."

Zach thrust his arms in the air and yelled, "*Yeah!*" as the crowd erupted in frenzied cheering. Lizbeth threw herself into his arms and he lifted her in the air. If there'd been more room, he would have spun her around, but as it was, he settled for rocking her back and forth. Her delighted laughter in his ear was quite possibly the most wonderful sound he'd ever heard.

He set her down, wide grin fading as he noticed Caitlin's pallor. She was not laughing or crying like so many of the people surrounding her. Neither was Kevin. In fact, Kevin looked worse than he had at Felicity's house.

"Seamus," Zach said, catching the shapeshifter's attention. "We need to get them inside."

Seamus nodded. The aurora in the sky had almost faded away by the time Zach, Lizbeth, Seamus and Bill herded Caitlin and Kevin through the rambunctious throng into a lounge area Zach hadn't seen before. They sat them on two stiff grey couches while Lizbeth ran to fetch cold drinks. Caitlin held the triskele box on her lap, looking dazed. Kevin slumped down, eyes closed, one hand in his pocket.

Zach realized that Kevin's hand had been in his pocket throughout the entire saving-the-world undertaking.

He grabbed Kevin's shoulder and gave him a little shake. "You have the nugget, don't you, bro?"

Kevin sighed and pulled his hand out. The lump of metal sat in the middle of his palm.

"What is that?" Bill asked.

Caitlin said, "*That* is why you are not a shapeshifter."

Bill's frown slowly changed to a scowl. His gaze shifted from the silvery nugget to Kevin's bright red eyes. "How stupid of me."

"The end result is that you were protected," Caitlin said.

"Protected from what? From you? Is that what you want, Caitlin, to stop me from becoming like you so I don't *become* like you?"

"That doesn't make sense-"

"It makes perfect sense!" Bill was practically shouting now, and Zach moved into position to intercept him should he make the bad decision to get physical. "You've been alive too long. You're heartbroken a dozen times over. I get that. You wake up every morning because you have a driving purpose. Guard the crown, find the crown, use the Goddamn crown to save the world. You know what's wrong with that picture? The crown doesn't love you back."

Seamus stepped closer and held out his arm, "Brother, this isn't the time or place-"

"To be betrayed?" Bill snapped. "You got that right."

"You would have died if Kevin hadn't taken the iridium," Caitlin said quietly.

Bill carried on as if she hadn't spoken. "What are you going to do now? Now that the crown is safe, and the world is safe, and you have a bunch of new recruits to help you stave off the next crisis? Maybe..." his voice dropped, "...you could let yourself *feel* something."

He stalked to the door, throwing over his shoulder, "We're heading back to the coast. Have these people ready to debark as soon as we arrive."

After he was gone, Caitlin sat staring at the carpet while everyone waited in respectful silence for the awkward moment to pass. She let out a faint sigh, opened the triskele box and said to Kevin, "Hand it over."

He reluctantly dropped the nugget in.

Lizbeth rushed back in carrying two bottles of water. "What'd I miss?"

Chapter Fifty-one

East of England

During the entire trip back to the coast, Lizbeth stayed with Caitlin, Zach and Kevin in the lounge. Despite Caitlin's exhaustion and the head wound that had to hurt, she spoke individually or in small groups with the men and women who'd come out of hiding to offer their services. They lined up in the corridor for the privilege. Caitlin's rigid posture and serene countenance made her seem like a queen receiving her subjects. They certainly treated her like royalty. Caitlin calmly accepted their effusive gratitude and pointed out repeatedly that she couldn't have done it without help.

After the dismal failure at Simon's house, Lizbeth could attest to that. She was still in shock that their efforts had paid off this time, and it especially floored her that Kevin and his iridium nugget had been the catalyst. She kept sneaking looks his way. Since relinquishing the nugget, the redness in his eyes had faded, but he still had dark half-circles under them. He hadn't contributed to any of the conversations unless he was asked a direct question, and even then, his response was short and dull.

Zach was the one who chimed in now and then, usually with a comment designed to make everyone laugh. Kevin finally excused himself to go rest in his cabin.

News from the ship's bridge periodically filtered down to the lounge. The world's leading scientists, who'd been scrambling to explain the devastation, were now equally puzzled that it stopped so abruptly. They could come up with no plausible scenario that linked the different phenomena: the earthquakes, volcanoes and auroras, the magnetic field switch, and the violent subspace storm that had incinerated so many satellites in the atmosphere. Under pressure to produce a theory, some chalked the events up to "chaotic coincidence" – bad things sometimes *do* happen simultaneously. Lizbeth didn't blame them. If she hadn't been right in the thick of it, her wildest imaginings wouldn't have conjured up the real reason.

The ship arrived off the coast of England late at night, but Bill insisted everyone disembark. Groups of sleepy people, including Seamus, were loaded into dinghies and dropped on the beach nearest the pier. Caitlin protested, but Bill informed her that if there was any chance the authorities didn't know he'd commandeered the ship, he was going to prevent them from finding out.

"Besides," he told her, "if they do know, or if they find out before we can get everyone off the ship, whoever is on board will be quarantined along with me and the crew. You want to spend however long it takes them to figure out what killed those scientists living on this tin can with me?"

He said, "I thought not," before Caitlin even answered. Lizbeth felt sorry for him. He was being a jerk, but she saw through it as a cover for the raw emotions right under the surface. Caitlin had not only rejected him but done it in a humiliating way. Felicity said that Caitlin preferred to fight her battles alone to protect the people she loved. It looked like sometimes going it alone *hurt* the people she loved.

Lizbeth looked at Zach. He'd dozed off with his head bent backward on top of the couch, Adam's apple protruding. She thought about his grandfather, who'd committed suicide after Zach's grandmother grew old and died.

"Caitlin?"

Both Bill and Caitlin turned.

"Since I'm a – a shapeshifter now, does that mean I'm going to outlive everyone I know?"

Caitlin looked at Bill.

"We can be killed, deliberately or by accident, but we don't grow old. We are rarely blessed with children, and the blessing is in the rarity. Our precious ones are babies one day, friends the next, and before we know it, they're gone – just like that. Every time you lose someone, your heart shrinks a little more until it's as small and hard as a pebble in your chest and you wonder how it could possibly keep beating."

Lizbeth marveled that anyone could deliver such passionate words in such a dispassionate tone.

Bill touched Caitlin's cheek. "Even the smallest heart needs love."

"But isn't always capable of returning it."

191

"I don't believe that."

Caitlin closed her eyes and said softly, "Please."

He took her hand and pulled her to her feet.

Lizbeth looked away, but heard him say, "Please what? Please leave you to wallow in your loneliness? Is that what you really want?"

"I want...to stop having to start over," Caitlin's voice was choked with tears. "I want it to last."

"It will last as long as it lasts. All I can promise you is that while it lasts, it will be amazing."

Caitlin uttered a small laugh; the kind of laugh Lizbeth knew came out against a person's will. Then she sniffed and said, "That's some promise."

Lizbeth thought it was safe to look over but caught them just as Bill lifted the much-smaller Caitlin up into a tight embrace. She looked away quickly, but not before noticing Caitlin's ardent response.

Lizbeth hid a smile even though there was no one to see.

Chapter Fifty-two

The Isle of Wight

After everyone but Caitlin, Kevin, Zach and Lizbeth left the ship, Bill had the captain of the scientific drilling vessel set course for the Isle of Wight. Before Kevin had gone to his cabin, Bill was justifiably furious with Caitlin and not inclined to be generous, so he wondered how she'd convinced him to take yet another risk for them.

It was still mostly dark when Bill brought them to shore in one of the dinghies. In the dim glow from the approaching sunrise, Kevin unwillingly witnessed Caitlin slip into Bill's arms in a passionate embrace.

Love, Kevin thought, *will make a man take chances*.

"I'll come to you," Caitlin said, giving Bill a tremulous smile. "Fare well."

Her car wasn't waiting for them in the parking lot this time. She chose a nondescript green sedan, waited while Lizbeth picked the lock, and told them, "Don't leave any fingerprints." She parked it about a half-mile away from Felicity's house and they walked the rest of the way.

In the muted light of early morning, no one would guess Felicity's hulking stone house was a veritable kaleidoscope on the inside. Kevin took note of the strange car parked in the drive as he walked with Caitlin, Zach and Lizbeth to the front door. Caw flew to a lamp post and perched atop it, calling out a raucous challenge to the local birds.

Before Caitlin could lift the brass door knocker, Kevin threw an arm out to block her.

"Something's wrong," he whispered.

"Do you think you could be more specific with these warnings?" Zach asked.

Kevin shushed him, but it was too late. The door opened and he was suddenly face-to-face with the barrel of a pistol.

"Put your hands in the air, all of you!"

Kevin obeyed, stepping back as the gunman advanced on them. Two police officers, one male, one female, ordered them down on the ground. Kevin kneeled on the gravel and looked at Caitlin. She set the triskele box down near the bushes and stepped away from it before lying down. In his head, he heard her clearly, "*Do nothing!*"

He tried to respond, tried to telepathically tell her, "*Change! Shapeshift into someone else while they can't see your face!*" but he wasn't sure if he'd done it right because she either didn't hear him or chose not to.

The male officer stood over her and asked, "Caitlin O'Connor?"

"Yes."

He knelt and cuffed her before hauling her up. "You're under arrest for escape and kidnapping."

"Kidnapping?" Lizbeth and Zach exclaimed together.

Felicity appeared in the doorway. She shook her head at Caitlin as if to say, "I had no choice."

Kevin saw Caitlin give her a sad, understanding sort of smile.

"Wolfdogge?" Felicity asked.

"I'm sorry, Grandmother."

Felicity nodded.

The officer marched Caitlin to his unmarked vehicle and tucked her inside.

The female officer went over to Lizbeth and asked, "Are you Miss Moreau? I'm Officer Bennett."

Kevin expected her to begin cuffing them all. Instead, the front door opened wider and an attractive black woman rushed out, hands clasped in front of her mouth. In a distinctive New Orlean's accent, she cried, "Lizbeth! Thank God you're safe."

From her prone position in the gravel a few feet away from Kevin, Lizbeth's eyes went wide. "*Mom?*"

The male officer, hand on his weapon as he eyed Zach and Kevin, helped Lizbeth up. "Is this your daughter, Mrs. Moreau?"

With a sob, Lizbeth's mother swept her into a fierce hug.

"For the record, Moreau is her maiden name," Felicity said.

Mrs. Moreau turned her head and snapped, "And if it weren't for you and your crazy family, I wouldn't have had to use it, or to hide out gutting fish for a living!"

"What?" Lizbeth asked weakly.

Her mother stepped back, hands on Lizbeth's shoulders. "What nonsense did Caitlin fill your head with?"

"It's not nonsense," Lizbeth began, but Mrs. Moreau's delicate features, so like and yet unlike Lizbeth's, twisted with rage. She pointed at Caitlin in the back of the police car.

"You stay away from my daughter!"

"Don't worry, ma'am," Officer Bennett said, patting her on the back. "She won't escape a second time."

The officers allowed Zach and Kevin to get up and began questioning Lizbeth about her supposed abduction. Kevin flashed back to the young police officer who'd detained them in London and reacted so strongly to her ID. He *had* recognized her face, but not, as they'd all supposed, because the police thought they were Caitlin's terrorist associates. The police officer realized who Lizbeth was because her mother had reported her missing, claiming Caitlin had abducted her. Kevin realized something else: Len knew Caitlin had been arrested on terrorist charges because he and Simon were the ones who turned her in in the first place. They needed to get her out of the way while they figured out what to do with the crown. Simon had been aboard *The Gossamer,* the ship whose mission Griffey secretly funded, so he had to know who and what Griffey was. Len and Simon would have anonymously called the Chief Inspector because he was the one person they knew had the power, and the desire, to control Caitlin. Their mistake was in underestimating the time it would take for Caitlin to escape and figure out their involvement.

Lizbeth categorically denied being abducted, saying, "I ran away. Caitlin is my grandmother and I wanted to get to know her. She didn't do anything wrong."

"And these boys?"

"They had nothing to do with any of it," Lizbeth said, looking down.

Officer Bennett took Mrs. Moreau aside, but Kevin heard her tell Lizbeth's mother that as long as Lizbeth claimed to have run away, they couldn't file kidnapping charges. "But Ms. O'Connor will certainly be charged for escaping jail, and we'll be questioning her about a recent triple homicide and our missing Chief Inspector, who was the original arresting officer."

Before the officers got into their cruiser, they assured Mrs. Moreau they'd send a car to take her and Lizbeth to the ferry landing.

And then Caitlin was gone. Kevin, Zach and Lizbeth watched the car until it disappeared around a bend in the road. From his perch on the lamp post, Caw let out a plaintive cry that echoed throughout the neighborhood.

"I know you're angry, Annabelle," Felicity said, "but at least come inside to wait. Let the kids say their goodbyes."

"I'd rather eat gator scat. Lizbeth – let's go."

Lizbeth backed away when her mother reached for her, staring into her face with an uncomprehending look. "How could you do this to me?"

Mrs. Moreau tried again to grab Lizbeth's arm. "We'll discuss who did what to whom on the trip back home."

"No! I'm not going back to Alaska. I hate it there!"

"You'll do as I say, young lady! You're my responsibility until you're eighteen, and until that day, I'll do everything in my power to keep your grandmother – either of them – from corrupting you."

Lizbeth's eyes narrowed and her face hardened. "Corrupting me like this?"

Kevin knew Lizbeth had been traumatized the first time she'd shapeshifted, but this time it looked as if she'd mastered the process. As her arms became claws and wings grew from her shoulders, her mother backed away, tripping over her own feet and landing on her backside in the gravel. Lizbeth held the griffin visage, looking rather ridiculous dressed in jeans and Werka's oversized sweatshirt, for maybe ten seconds before shifting back. She directed a satisfied look toward her mother.

Mrs. Moreau scrambled to her feet. Kevin expected her to blubber in shock, but she surprised him. "I see you take after your father. Fair enough. I didn't want you to learn about any of that. I wanted you to have a normal life. Your birthday is less than four months from now. You can choose what you want to do after that. Right now, you're coming home with me. Say goodbye to your friends."

She crossed her arms and walked away down the drive. Kevin heard the crunch of tires on the gravel. Mrs. Moreau stopped next to a car and spoke to the driver through the passenger window.

The sun finally made its appearance, beaming weak rays of light through a thin layer of hazy clouds. The tears in Lizbeth's eyes shimmered but didn't fall. She stretched her arms out, one toward him and one toward Zach. Kevin moved in for a three-way hug, and they held each other for a long moment.

"We'll see each other again soon," Zach said, kissing her on top of the head. "You can be sure of that."

"I can't believe it's ending this way," she said.

"How did you expect it to end?" Kevin asked.

Lizbeth produced a weak laugh. "Parades and accolades? No one even knows what we did. My reward is to go back to frigid Alaska, back to work at wonderful Clowntastic Pizza."

"You work there?" Zach asked in a teasing voice. "I loved that place when I was a kid. Sing the song!"

"No!" Her laugh was stronger this time as she pushed him away and took a half-hearted swipe at him.

"Oh, you'll sing it for me someday, Missy."

Lizbeth's mother called out for her to hurry. Lizbeth went to give Felicity a quick hug. Felicity patted her on the back. "You'll be fine, dearie. And you're always welcome here, remember that."

Lizbeth pulled away, fully crying now. Kevin felt an answering sting in his eyes, but he'd be damned if he was going to bawl in front of Zach.

"Don't forget this," Felicity said. She retrieved the triskele box and handed it to her.

Lizbeth looked down at it with a dejected sigh. "Tell her I'll keep it safe."

Felicity chuckled. "You can probably tell her yourself soon enough. This is Caitlin we're talkin' about."

Lizbeth's footsteps were heavy as she walked to the car where her mother waited. She gave them all a half-wave as her face crumpled. Looking up at the sky through her tears, she said, "'Bye Caw."

For the second time that morning, Kevin watched a car carry someone he loved away from him.

Chapter Fifty-three

Fairbanks, Alaska

There was always one kid in every party terrified of Clownee the Clown. As soon as Lizbeth appeared, peeking out through the sheer fabric eyes of the bulky, smelly headpiece, one little girl let loose with a high-pitched, unending series of screams. Her mother rushed over to sweep the girl into her arms, smiling an apology at the other moms before exiting the big, drafty party room. The wailing of the child accompanied her like an ambulance siren fading into the distance.

The party hostess flipped a switch and music blared from hidden speakers. Trying to stick with the beat, Lizbeth performed the Clownee Dance, shuffling her enormous cartoony shoes and waving her huge cartoony hands. Some of the children danced and sang along, but a few clung to her, clutching at her costume and hampering her every move. The song ended and she smiled, pleased that this time she hadn't dislodged any of the clingers or knocked any of them down. It was hard not to, with the severely limited vision afforded her by the headpiece.

At least it was Monday. The weekends were the worst, with party upon party booked throughout the day. Lizbeth only had to make four appearances today, and this was the final one. She mimed her goodbyes to the children and beat as hasty a retreat as she could manage.

After removing the costume, she said goodbye to her coworkers and boarded the bus for home.

Home was no longer Granma's cabin, which had been destroyed in one of the wildfires sparked by the eruption of the reactivated Buzzard Creek volcano to the south. Now Lizbeth, her mother and Granma shared a cramped apartment with another displaced family in town. In this chapter of the world's history it was not a good time to be poor, but Lizbeth knew there were many millions of people in far worse shape than they were. Her mother had been laid off from her job at the fish market since entire fishing fleets had been lost during the Cataclysm, and marine life in general along the volcanically active Aleutian Islands had suffered. Between them, Lizbeth and Granma made enough to keep them fed and housed, if not comfortably. They'd gotten help after Katrina, but this time government money for disaster victims just wasn't available, given how widespread the devastation was.

Stupid Cataclysm.

To Lizbeth, it was a miracle that places like Clowntastic Pizza were still in business, but she supposed even in troubled times, people had to amuse themselves. Even though Granma's customers were just as needy of spiritual intervention as ever, she was making a fraction of what she'd brought in before the Cataclysm, mostly because she refused to take payment from those who were hardest hit. Annabelle took babysitting and housecleaning jobs where she could find them.

The apartment was empty when Lizbeth arrived home, a rare occurrence. There were no flowers or balloons or cards in her room, not that she expected her mother to waste precious money on such things, or to make the effort, for that matter, given that she was so opposed to Lizbeth gaining the age of majority. With no one at home, there wasn't anyone hogging the old computer Granma had gotten in barter from a client. Lizbeth hated waiting for her allotted half hour every evening.

Stupid Cataclysm.

She sat at the communal work desk, pressed the start button on the PC and listened to the alarming grinding noises the hard drive made while booting up. The dial-up Internet connection, all they could afford, slowly brought up her email provider. She smiled when she saw an email from Zach. The subject line read, "Zach Sings," and the only thing in the body of the message was a link. She clicked on it and waited an eternity for his YouTube page to load. There he was, black hair sticking out in all directions and eyes disappearing with the force of his lopsided grin. When the video started and he began to sing an off-key version of "Happy Birthday to You – You Live in the Zoo," she clapped her hands and laughed. She watched the whole spectacle, even though her connection was so slow the video had to pause and load every ten seconds or so.

At the end, Zach said, "You're a big girl now. When you're ready to come visit, just say the word and I'll raid my savings account to send tickets. I miss you."

Lizbeth sighed happily when the video ended and sent Zach a quick reply. Legally, she was free of her mother as of today, but morally, she couldn't leave. Right now Annabelle needed her paycheck. Yes, her mother had gone to great lengths to hide Lizbeth from Caitlin after her father died. Lizbeth never even knew her real last name was O'Connor. But Annabelle had done it to protect her, and once Lizbeth gave the matter some hard thought, she couldn't blame her. From almost the moment she met Caitlin, she'd been in danger. Once Lizbeth had a chance to explain the truth behind the Cataclysm, her mother had softened slightly. If Lizbeth knew where Caitlin was, Annabelle might even let them develop some kind of relationship, assuming Caitlin wanted one.

Lizbeth had been back in Alaska for weeks before news reached her that Caitlin had once again escaped jail. How hard could it be to get away, really, when she could become anyone or any animal? It tickled Lizbeth to imagine Caitlin ducking around the corner in the jail yard and shapeshifting into a cute puppy dog. Then all she'd have to do is wag her tail and charm the inmates and guards alike. They'd scratch their heads trying to figure out how she got in – and then open the gate and let her trot right *out*. Or maybe they'd call the pound and Caitlin would have exchanged one kind of prison for another, but Lizbeth was sure however she did it, it had been a success.

The doorbell rang and she answered it, surprised to see a delivery guy behind a big bouquet of flowers.

"Oh, my gosh. Who are these from?" She snatched the card from its plastic holder and tore open the tiny envelope. It read, "Dear Lizbeth, I hope you have a happy birthday. Sincerely, Kevin."

She laughed. Kevin's style was such a departure from Zach's. She took the bouquet from the delivery guy, who just stood there, looking like he was waiting for a tip. She didn't have any cash on hand, but she was still wearing her Clowntastic Pizza uniform, so she reached into her pocket and withdrew a handful of game tokens.

"This is all I got," she said.

The delivery guy looked affronted, so she said, "Come on, everyone likes pizza."

He held up a box with a popular ice cream cake label and responded in Caitlin's voice, "I'd rather share a slice of birthday cake with my granddaughter."

Chapter Fifty-four

San Francisco, California

Holed up in his bedroom, Zach tried to ignore the grating scream of the band saw and the steady hammering at the back of the house. It had taken four months for his parents to get to the top of the construction company's waiting list. They'd lived around the damage to their house since then; the gaps in joints at the roof that let in copious amounts of rain, the boarded-up windows, the broken bricks and tiles. It was lucky for his parents that they'd actually purchased earthquake insurance; so many hadn't. Lucky, too, that the insurance company hadn't buckled under the weight of incoming claims; so many had.

San Francisco hadn't fared well in the Cataclysm, but at least it was still on the map, unlike many villages, towns and even a few cities throughout the world. As Bay Area city planners had feared for years, the earthquakes caused havoc on the network of underground gas lines. Dozens had ignited, from the coast to the inland valleys, exploding through entire neighborhoods. Water pipeline breakage had crippled firefighter efforts, and history repeated itself as if no lessons whatsoever had been learned since 1906.

Unreinforced houses, apartment buildings, schools and retail establishments built on sandy soil suffered the greatest damage as the movement of the crust shifted the unstable earth like water. Zach's relatively new neighborhood, with its higher building code standards and solid bedrock under the foundations, survived.

School had been cancelled and hadn't yet resumed. Zach spent the last four months splitting his time between volunteering for the local Red Cross and the police department. The National Guard had been stretched to the limit, and in order to prevent the governor from declaring martial law in the region, local law enforcement had taken on volunteers and trained them to perform more than the usual administrative and community service duties.

The email tone on his laptop sounded just as he was getting ready for his shift. Lizbeth must have been in a hurry, probably running out of time on the lousy computer she shared with her roommates, because she sent a bare minimum reply, "You're such a sweetie. Thanks!"

She didn't even acknowledge his suggestion that she come visit, although he had to admit he'd couched it in vague terms in case she rejected him. They'd been in contact for some time now. He'd gone to great lengths to find her email address, and just in case it looked suspicious, he'd also found Kevin's. He almost hoped some other catastrophe would threaten the world, so they'd have a reason to get the team back together. Well, a mild catastrophe that didn't kill anyone, anyway.

He shut down his laptop and got dressed in what passed for his uniform, black jeans and a black long-sleeved shirt. Even if the department could afford it, outfitting its volunteers was problematic since the clothing industry had suffered such a big hit – losing so many of its third-world factories in the Cataclysm.

At the station, Sergeant Barkley briefed the squad on a situation brewing in what was left of the crime-ridden neighborhood of Hunter's Point.

"Members of the Westmob gang are squatting in a church on Beech Street. The congregation is supposedly gathering today to confront them. Wong, go with Washington and Novak. I want your opinion on how volatile this thing might get."

Zach nodded.

Any assignment was a challenge just navigating the broken streets and piles of rubble in squad cars built for high speed chases on smooth highways. Aside from shattered windows and a crooked steeple atop the wooden structure, the church seemed undamaged, which was probably why it was a target to the gang. Homelessness had skyrocketed, and some poor neighborhoods had become war zones.

A crowd of about thirty people, primarily African American, had gathered on the lawn of the church. Most of the windows were boarded up, but one gaped open, revealing only darkness inside. Washington and Novak approached, with Zach in the rear. Zach didn't focus on the conversation Washington initiated with the church leaders; his mind was elsewhere.

A raven sitting on a nearby telephone pole flew down and landed on the sill of the broken window. After a moment, the barrel of a gun appeared, and Zach tensed up, but the thug who wielded it merely brushed Caw aside. The bird flew off, calling out to Zach,
"Caw! Caw! Caw! Caw!"

"How many are inside?" Novak asked Pastor Williams, a tall man with a heavily lined face and distinguished grey streaks at his temples.

"We think fifteen or twenty."

Washington looked at Zach, who shook his head and held up four fingers.

Novak continued to question the pastor. "Are they armed?"

"They already stuck a rifle out that window there."

Washington called in for back-up as Novak tried to convince Pastor Williams that the danger was real and that he'd best calm the milling congregation down.

Zach stood back and watched with a strangely satisfied feeling. When and if his college ever reopened, he was definitely going to switch majors from Digital Art to Criminal Justice.

Chapter Fifty-five

The North Sea

Repairs to the scientific drilling vessel, which had begun immediately following the lifting of the quarantine, were complete. The Health Protection Agency had isolated what they claimed was a bizarre toxin responsible for killing the six scientists and was highly interested in finding out more about it. They tried to put together the original scientific team but found only a few who were willing to take the risk. Dr Weinstein would have come, since school was out indefinitely after the Cataclysm and he was effectively out of a job, but his health prevented it. Bill Masters had stayed on as director of the project. His desire to become a shapeshifter was so all-consuming, he'd climbed into bed with the government. Kevin didn't know how much he'd told them but hoped the prospect of sounding like a fool stopped him from divulging all he knew.

Kevin stood on deck, alone with his thoughts and his nausea. He found himself wishing the gossamer sphere had struck land instead of sea when it entered the earth's atmosphere so long ago. If it had, the hub of the grid would be underground instead of under water, and he'd be in a deep tunnel shaft somewhere, surrounded by comforting dirt and rock instead of suffering another day on the incessantly rolling ocean.

Bill and the government's scientists might someday locate a sample of the biometal, but with luck they would never figure out what Kevin had—the secret to how a normal person could survive the initiation, and how it had all begun so long ago. Caitlin had convinced Seamus to remove the lore from his website, without telling him why: the story of queen Wyn, Tadg the Small and Aedn gave it all away.

"Without the crown, I was unable to conduct experiments to confirm it," Caitlin said when Kevin asked her about it. "But you are correct. The original three knew, and the lore hints quite broadly that consumption of an animal tainted with the biometal imparts immunity prior to the biometal passing through the barrier of the skin. I have only been able to speculate how that process works on a biological level and am somewhat reluctant to find out."

"You could give Bill what he wants. You could be happy together."

"Unlike the original druids, my grandmother included, I have never been tempted to play God," she'd replied. "Much as I long to—have a companion—Bill is unstable. Blinded, as it were, by his love for me and his desire to become like us. I fear I cannot trust him, which is why I have an assignment for you."

The ship had nearly reached the coordinates to place it directly over the center of Silverpit Crater. He still didn't know how he was going to stop them from drilling, but that was the assignment Caitlin had given him. He thought she had way too much confidence in him, but he had no choice but to try.

"We must leave no loose ends," she'd said.

Once she'd escaped again from jail, she'd hunted Werka down in a small Polish village. Her goal had been to determine what role Werka played within the Guild. When Caitlin posed as Werka's priest and questioned her about it, it turned out Werka had no knowledge of the crown. Simon had thrown her out right after she told him she'd sent Kevin and the others out to look at the old church on the farm property. Simon was furious, but Werka had no idea why.

"Hey, Mort."

Kevin turned. Bill Masters came up beside him, hair plastered back in the stiff breeze.

"How's it going, Bill?"

"Great. How's the lab look?"

Kevin figured this was as good a time as any. There was no one else on deck to see, and this conversation sounded like it was going to get technical. The real Mort, who was home in bed sleeping off the sedative his "mom" had slipped him when she visited unexpectedly, would have answered Bill casually. Kevin had no idea what to say to sound authentic. He relaxed and shapeshifted into his true form.

Bill looked surprised for a moment, then rolled his eyes.

"What are you doing here?"

"Caitlin sent me."

"Maybe she should have come herself."

"She had urgent business in Alaska," Kevin said.

Bill snorted. "Really? For the last four months?"

"Jail will slow you up that way."

"Not her."

"It was a little harder for her to escape this time, since they had cameras on her twenty-four-seven, but you're going to go ahead and think what you want anyway, aren't you?"

"Look, punk-"

"No, you look. Yeah, real deep into your soul. As much as you've convinced yourself your reasons have merit, you know as well as I do that Caitlin is not the reason you want to do this."

"I love her," Bill said. "And she loves me. I want to spare her having to watch me grow old and die."

"I know." Kevin nodded earnestly. "But you need to listen to me. The sphere may be quiet now, but I have it on good authority it won't tolerate being drilled into a second time. You're risking the lives of everyone on this ship."

"It's out of my hands. The HPA is running things now. I couldn't stop them if I wanted to."

"You have to, or we'll all die."

Bill looked at him grimly. "I don't have you people's knack of reading minds. I don't know if you're telling the truth or if Caitlin told you to lie. She's good at lying, did you notice?"

"She's had good reason. Regardless, I'm here to offer you what you want. If you stop the drill, I'll give you this." Kevin held out his hand. On his palm, the nugget glittered dully in the overcast day. Bill stared at it, his face the picture of fascinated fear.

"Go ahead," Kevin said. "Take it."

Bill took a half-step back. "If the HPA get a sample, their doctors can study it, figure out how it works. They can test people to make sure it won't kill them, maybe fix it so everyone can touch it without getting sick."

"Now you sound like Griffey. You think that's really how it will happen? The government's just going to *let* everyone become shapeshifters?" Kevin laughed. "I thought I was naïve."

"Alright, good point, but we can't stop them forever. Disabling the ship now is only postponing the inevitable."

Kevin shrugged. "Give the sphere a few more months and they'll never find it."

Bill's eyebrows lifted. After a momentary hesitation, he held out his hand. "Deal."

Kevin's heart began to beat faster. Caitlin hadn't given him any instruction other than to stop the drilling, but he was pretty sure she didn't want him to kill her lover. On the other hand, if he didn't give Bill the nugget, the whole ship was doomed. He started to hand it over but stopped.

"I got sick hanging on to this thing, and I'm half shapeshifter."

206

"So?"

"So, that's why the initiates only touched the crown. Prolonged exposure, until you're immune, can hurt you."

"Just give me the damned thing."

Kevin put the nugget back into his pocket. "Disable the drill first. Permanently."

Bill looked out over the choppy sea. Kevin felt like a voyeur; he knew Bill was thinking of Caitlin – he was practically projecting his longing.

"Alright," he said. "Give me an hour. It'll be done before we reach the crater."

Kevin waited by the rail, fighting to keep his lunch down. The gunmetal grey water flowing past the ship reminded him of the sphere. Sometimes his conscious mind strayed into memories of the contact and wouldn't let go. He'd relived it so many times, wallowing in the familiar strangeness.

It hadn't taken much research for him to find the Arp 274 triple galaxy on the Internet, since the Hubble Telescope had recently photographed it. As soon as he saw the three forms swirling 400 million light years away, he recognized them. He didn't know much else, like from where in those vast galaxies the sphere originated. The only thing he was sure of was that the entity had been completely surprised that Kevin had the ability to enter its thoughts, if only for an instant. Surprised and very, very threatened.

Kevin didn't know how Bill did it, but he, at least, kept his word. Soon after they arrived at Silverpit Crater, the crew began to scramble like ants through the bowels of the ship, trying to determine why the drill was malfunctioning. No one was on deck to see Kevin tuck the nugget under his tongue and change again.

His blubber protected him from the cold shock of the sea. He surfaced, exhaled through his blowhole and rolled on his side, looking at the ship through the elastic lenses over his eyes.

When Bill realized he was gone, he would be angry, justifiably so, but Kevin the dolphin didn't care.

The end.

www.ingramcontent.com/pod-product-compliance
Lightning Source LLC
Chambersburg PA
CBHW061220170626
46809CB00007B/2536